Even passed out cold with a bullet in him, sick as a dog, and at her mercy, Logan Wade was still Amber Prescott's biggest problem. . . .

"Amber, you'll have to sponge him down." He gestured at her younger brother. "This Logan Wade isn't built any different than Benny. You've been tending to Benny since he was a babe."

" 'Cept he's bigger, I'd say," Benny said, whooping with laughter at the sight of Amber's shocked face. "Amber's got herself a stark naked gunfighter to tend to. Whatcha gonna see while you're spongin' him?" he hooted.

"That's enough out of you, Benny. I'll be fine," Amber said, wishing she believed it. Then suddenly she was alone in the cabin with Logan Wade. She walked slowly to the cot and stared down at him. Even in his weakened unconscious state, covered only by a sheet, there was an aura of power about him, of virility, of masculinity, like nothing Amber had ever encountered before. And she had to sponge the entire rugged, naked length of him! No matter what Pa had said, she had the distinct feeling that changing Benny's diapers had not prepared her for what was beneath that sheet.

She drew the sheet a few inches below Logan's waist, then yanked it back up again. Her heart was pounding, her cheeks were flushed, and she took a steadying breath. This would never do. Feet. Feet were a good place to start, she decided, stomping to the end of the bed. She flipped back the sheet and moistened them with a cloth. As she brushed the sheet to mid-thigh, he moaned. She watched him anxiously.

"After all this, I swear to heaven, Logan Wade, if you die, I'll never speak to you again as long as I live."

JOAN ELLIOTT PICKART

AMBER, SING SOFTLY

PINNACLE BOOKS
WINDSOR PUBLISHING CORP.

PINNACLE BOOKS are published by

Windsor Publishing Corp.
850 Third Ave
New York, NY 10022

The P logo Reg U.S. Pat & TM off. Pinnacle is a trademark of Windsor Publishing Corp.

First Printing: August, 1994

Printed in the United States of America

For my agent, Robin Kaigh, who believed in Amber from the moment they met, and for my editor, Denise Little, who nurtured that belief.

Prologue

Arizona, 1875

The wind had blown viciously for six days and nights, howling like a wounded beast. The hot air was thick with dust, creating an eerie, pale red glow as the desert sunset's colors were muted by the grainy particles.

Horses were restless, edgy from the keening wail of the wind. Young children were fretful, clinging to their mothers, and rubbing at eyes streaming from the biting dirt that showed no mercy.

The tepees in the small camp stood sturdily upright under the onslaught, having been made of buffalo hides and cowhides, and crafted by knowing hands.

The Indians were Apache, and their numbers were few. All that remained in scattered camps were the women, children, and the very old.

Hidden in the outlying areas were the handful of young braves determined not to give up their freedom and move to the white man's reservations, where the majority of their people had already gone.

As dusk inched its way through the dust-filled air, a tall, strong man of thirty years, strode with purpose through the camp that held no more than forty people.

The unnatural luminescence of the approaching night cast its hue over his glistening, burnished skin, making him appear as a golden god. His shoulder-length, straight black hair gleamed, the beads of sweat caught in the thick strands seeming like sparkling diamonds. Clearly defined muscles bunched and rippled beneath his taut skin from the powerful, yet fluent movements of his body.

He was clad only in a breechcloth in deference to the sultry heat, and a strip of buckskin tied around his forehead kept his hair from swinging into his obsidian eyes.

Glances slid his way from those he passed, but no one greeted him, nor spoke. He was held in high regard in the camp, and the set to his wide shoulders and square jaw invited no intrusion on his private thoughts.

His name was Chato.

His destination was a tepee at the end of the clearing, one set slightly apart from the others to indicate the importance of the person within. He stopped, respecting the closed flap of the tepee, and rapped his knuckles on the support pole within his reach.

"Who wishes to speak with me?" a quiet voice said from inside.

"Your grandson. I am Chato."

"Come."

Chato swept back the flap and entered the oppressively hot enclosure, bending low to accommodate his height. A small fire burned in a ground-hearth surrounded by rocks, adding to the nearly suffocating temperature. A cast-iron pot sat among the embers, water simmering with herbs carefully gathered to make the medicine that would bring comfort to the one within who suffered from old age and illness.

"Chato, you have returned," the white-haired woman lying on the pallet said. "Tell me of your news, my grandson."

He moved closer and sat on the ground beside her. He would make no mention, he knew, of the almost unbearable heat in the tepee, the heavy, unpleasant odor of the brewing herbs. To do so would be showing disrespect, and the old woman before him was too dear to his heart for him ever to contemplate committing such an insulting act.

She was Naana, his grandmother, who had raised him and his sister since they were hardly more than babes freed of their carrying boards.

To him, Naana was his mother in his heart and mind, because he was unable to remember his parents. They had been killed in a raid on their village by a band of outcast Indians who

had roamed then, their evil ways falling on
whatever, or whomever, they came upon.

"Chato," Naana said, her voice weak, "did
you find, once again, the brother of your
soul?"

"I found him, as I have always done." He
covered one of her fragile, dry hands with one
of his strong, large ones, knowing she would
accept the touch of affection in the privacy of
the tepee. "Naana, my grandmother, it is over.
The brother of my soul has finished his quest,
the mission he set out to do, not knowing he
had gone in my place."

"You keep words from me, my grandson.
Your eyes tell me that all is not being said that
I must hear."

Chato's hand tightened slightly on Naana's.

"It is truly over, Grandmother. The grandson
of your soul, the brother of mine, is . . .
dead."

"No." She shook her head. "No, I would
have known if he had died. In all these years
that have passed, I knew he was alive. I sent
you out time and again to see if he continued
to do for us what you could not because of the
white man's intrusion into our world."

"I saw him fall, as did the last of those he
sought. He could not have lived from the
wound that poured forth his life's blood. Comanches were near, and true to the Apache
ways, I chose to live to fight another day, rather

than face the band of Comanches who num-
bered more than I could defeat alone."

"Chato, I am old, but my mind, what I
sense, does not dim. He lives."

Chato sighed. "I knew in my heart that you
would speak such as this. I will eat, rest, see
my wife, Lozen, then I will go back, two days'
journey, and bring his body to you, Grandmother."

"It is good. He must be buried with all the
Apache honors due a courageous warrior. He
is one of us, though he knows this only now
in the spirit place. Yet . . . Chato, I will not
believe he is dead until his body is brought to
me. My heart whispers that he lives."

"So be it. I will bring his body to you,
Naana. Then you will sleep, regain your
strength."

"No. I wait for the grandson of my soul so
I may say farewell to him. Then, I will answer
the call of the spirits, and go to them."

"You must not speak words such as those.
You are loved. You are needed here, Grandmother."

"I am ready to meet with the spirits, Chato.
I am weary. It is time for my eternal rest, my
peace. Bring him to me first."

"I will do this for you."

"Yes, my beloved grandson, I know in my
heart that you will. You will bring me Logan
Wade."

One

Texas

He was going to die.

Logan Wade lay on his back in the lush grass by the stream and closed his eyes, gritting his teeth against the white-hot pain that consumed him. His pale-blue shirt felt heavy, but he couldn't tell if the material was soaked more with blood than with sweat. He could feel the perspiration running like a river down his face and through his thick hair.

How long had it been since the bullet had slammed into his shoulder? Two days? Three? He didn't know. All he knew was that he was going to die.

And he didn't care—didn't give a damn.

The weight of the gun strapped down on his hip was oppressive, but Logan lacked the strength to undo the buckle and free himself of the burden. A moan escaped from his lips as the burning pain rocketed through him once again. It was a part of him now, the pain, as though it had always been there, tormenting him.

Somewhere in the deep recesses of his mind, Logan registered the fact that he should be angry that he was going to die at only thirty-two years old. Yeah, he should be angry, or maybe frightened, at least feeling some kind of emotion. But he really didn't care.

No, dying didn't matter, it was the helplessness he was experiencing that was nurturing a seed of angry frustration within him. He'd always been a big, powerful man, who kept his body under his command and in the best condition possible. His strength, combined with a sixth sense that alerted him to unseen dangers, had held him in good stead, kept him alive on more than one occasion.

It would have been better if he'd died the instant the destructive bullet had exploded in his body, rather than to be hardly more than a defenseless babe where he lay in the grass. But few men, he thought hazily, had the choice of the way they were to die.

At least he'd had a voice in the way he had lived. He'd accomplished what he had set out to do. Five years. It had taken five long, lonely years, but he had done it. It was over. It was finished.

And so was he.

He lifted his lashes, barely able to focus his eyes, due to weakness and pain, and stared at the sun skittering through the leaves of the trees overhead. He could smell the water, his dry throat begging for a sip of the cooling liquid, but his body lacked the power to move the few feet to the edge of the stream.

His horse was chomping on the grass, and Logan managed a weak smile. Thunder was a damn good horse, had been his best friend during the past five years. He'd free the animal of the heavy saddle if he could, but it was impossible. There was simply nothing Logan could do now, but die.

Logan's senses seemed suddenly sharper as he heard the chatter of birds, the croak of a frog, smelled the fresh scent of grass, and the sweat and blood of his own battered body.

Texas sounds. Texas smells. He was going to die in Texas. He'd die with his boots on, which the old cowboys thought was so almighty important, but Logan Wade really didn't care one way or another.

Damn, it was hot.

But hell was hotter.

There might have been a time when he'd been eligible for heaven, Logan mused foggily, but not anymore. Not after the existence he'd led for the past five years. Wasn't everything supposed to be passing before his eyes, his entire life replaying in his mental vision? He was too tired, anyway. Just so damn tired.

Logan shuddered as a chill accompanied a spasm of tearing pain. He groaned and swore, then everything went black.

Mercifully quiet, and black.

* * *

Amber Prescott untied the apron and drew it away from the faded gray dress, mopping her brow with the yellowed cotton before draping it across the back of a hand-hewn chair.

Her gaze swept over the cabin, missing no detail of her morning's worth of chores, and the fine film of dust that was already collecting on the once clean furniture and rough wood floor. She had no choice, she knew, but to leave the door and the shutters on the windows open in hopes of capturing an errant breeze.

Amber blew a puff of air up over her face, then tucked several wayward curls back into the bun at the nape of her neck. Her hair seemed to possess a mind of its own in the hot weather, and she wrinkled her nose in disgust. She detested her thick hair that fell nearly to her waist when brushed free. It was heavy, unmanageable, and in her opinion, was the color of old, dried corn. And the curls. She hated the curls that sprung in all directions when the weather was humid.

She'd seen an Indian woman once, she mused, who had sleek, shiny black hair that had flowed down her back like a raven waterfall. It was the most glorious hair Amber had ever seen. The woman's skin had been the dusky shade of a fawn's, not the pale tone of Amber's that turned no more than the color of a peach in the summer. And the Indian woman had definitely not had a sprinkling of freckles across her nose like Amber did. Freckles were embarrassing. She should have been born an Indian. That's all there was to it.

"Maybe in my next life," she said, laughing merrily. But in an instant her smile faded.

From the stories she'd heard from time to time, the Indians hadn't fared well when the droves of settlers had pushed west. The majority of the Indian tribes were on reservations now, with a few isolated camps still in existence. Some of the old chiefs had refused to budge from the land and way of life they'd always known. Since they were considered harmless, the government officials had allowed them to stay, to die where they had been born.

There had been tales, too, of young braves who had vowed to reclaim what had been theirs, Amber recalled, and she'd recently heard of homesteads being burned to the ground, the settlers killed or taken captive.

Why couldn't everyone live together in peace? she pondered. The Indians, white men, immigrants from other countries, all would have something unique to offer in a blending of cultures. And heaven knew there was plenty of room for everyone wishing to make a life for themselves west of the Mississippi.

Amber sighed. She was a grown woman, she thought, at just shy of being nineteen, but at times she felt like a child who knew nothing of a world she'd never seen. She had so many

questions about so many things, a curiosity and
burning desire to learn, understand, and so
much more. She was content and happy there
on the homestead, but recently she'd experienced fleeting feelings of something being
missing, something of importance that had no
name, nor clear identity.

"Enough daydreaming," she said aloud, then
picked up a tin pail off the table and headed
out the door.

Outside, Amber tilted her face upward and
shut her eyes, savoring the heat of the sun
against her skin. She didn't mind the high temperatures when she could be out of doors, free.
Starting off toward the fields, she burst into
song, her voice oddly husky, sounding as
though it came from one much older.

She halted her serenade as she neared the
fields, as her song had been a bawdy one she'd
learned on the wagon train during the journey
from Pennsylvania over four years before.

It had been a journey of hope, of dreams
for a new life in Texas that would bring them
prosperity and happiness. And it had been a
journey of death. The fever had swept through
the wagon train, taking the lives of more than
half of the travelers. Among those who died
had been Amber's mother, Mary Prescott.

Nathan Prescott had wanted to turn his
wagon around and take his daughter and son
back home. Amber had pleaded with her father to go on to Texas, to accomplish the goal

her mother had believed in. Confused and exhausted by his grief, Nathan had agreed to move forward.

Also among the survivors of the fever was Moses, an enormous black man who had worked tirelessly during the epidemic tending to the sick. Those who had once feared him because of his size and color came to trust the big man with the gentle voice.

Moses had been traveling with an elderly Southern gentleman who had succumbed to the fever, and the survivors voted unanimously to give Moses the man's wagon and possessions.

During the remainder of the trip, Amber taught Moses how to read and write. Moses showed Amber's brother, Benny, then only six years old, how to whittle, how to fish, how to soothe a spooked horse. When Nathan had asked Moses to join them as they tackled their homestead, Moses had agreed with a nod of his head and tears in his eyes.

And so they were a family, she mused. They were Amber, Benny, Nathan Prescott, and Moses. They'd worked until they were too tired to eat, sunup to dusk, to build their barn, cabin, then later the smokehouse. They'd plowed the fields and planted the seeds carried in sacred packets from Pennsylvania. They continually prayed for rain, then cursed the dark clouds when they poured forth too much, and they'd come to love their new world. Texas.

It was a wild land, Amber knew, untamed.

Too hot. Too cold. Too dusty. And she never wanted to leave. Well, yes, of late she'd wondered about things beyond her scope of knowledge, had been disturbed by the unnamed ingredient that seemed to be missing from her limited sphere. But even if she were to become wealthy . . . although she had no idea how that would come about . . . and could travel to wherever she wished, she'd always return to Texas.

She would marry a Texan, she had decreed, raise fat, happy babies, grow old, die, and be buried in Texas soil. She was home. And she was staying. The land held a promise for those who could survive its temperament. One either loved or hated it, with no room in the middle for ambivalence. Texas.

"You would have loved it here, Mama," Amber said, glancing up at the clear blue sky that was dotted by white fluffy clouds.

A hawk flew in solitary flight, and Amber shaded her eyes with her hand to watch it dip, then soar, as though it owned the heavens. It disappeared behind a mound of clouds, and she had the urge to call to it, to ask it, if just this once, the hawk would carry her with him on its flight so she might see some of the mysteries hidden from her view.

Shaking her head at her own foolishness, she resumed her trek to the fields where Nathan, Benny, and Moses were weeding the corn rows. The stalks were nearly six feet tall, and neither

Nathan, nor Benny, were visible to Amber's view.

"Moses! Yoo-hoo, Moses," she called.

"I hear you, missy," he yelled.

"I'm going down by the stream to pick raspberries. We'll have hot pies for dessert tonight."

"Sounds mighty fine."

"Are you hiding my Pa and Benny in that corn?"

"I'm here, girl," Nathan said, although Amber still couldn't see him. "You be careful by the stream."

"Get lots of berries, Amber," Benny said, his voice muffled by the tall stalks.

"Enough to give you a bellyache, Benny Prescott," Amber said, then started off again, humming the tune of her bawdy song.

"Don't let me hear you singin' the words to that song, girl," Nathan shouted.

Amber sniffed indignantly and stuck her nose in the air. She did not, however, burst into song.

The freshwater stream that cut through the Prescott land was a blessing. Although an ox had to be hitched to the wagon to tote the heavy water barrels back to the cabin, the stream had eliminated the immediate need to dig a well, a job that was long, backbreaking labor, and required special equipment.

The stream also served as an oasis in the seemingly endless stretch of flat, dry land.

Lush grass rimmed the edge of the water, and tall trees provided shade. It was here that Amber came to bathe in the summer, having discovered a hole in the stream that allowed her to submerge her five-foot-six-inch body all the way to her chin. But her mission today was not a bath, but berries. Ripe, juicy raspberries that she would bake into delicious pies.

Amber's system for picking berries was quite simple, she'd once explained to her father. She put one raspberry in her mouth for every three in her pail.

At the cove, she worked her way forward from the edge, taking her time, enjoying the cool solitude of the trees. Later, she would take off her shoes and wiggle her toes in the sparkling water.

Humming her naughty song again, Amber emerged from the trees, knowing the best berries were closer to the bank of the stream. Her shoes sank into the carpet of grass, and she anticipated the moment when her feet would be bare.

And then she saw him.

The blood-soaked man lying in the grass.

The pail slipped from her hand and rolled away, the raspberries dotting the green grass like precious gems. Amber's hands flew to her cheeks, and a gasp escaped from her lips.

"Dear heaven above," she whispered, moving cautiously forward on trembling legs.

The man moaned, and Amber dropped to

her knees beside him. Her eyes swept over his glistening, black hair, the blood-soaked shirt, then flickered along his muscular legs clad in dusty dark pants. The gun on his hip caused her eyes to widen, then she directed her attention to his handsome tanned face that appeared even darker beneath several days' growth of beard.

"Mister?" she said, hearing the shaky quality of her voice. "Hello? Mister?"

Long, dark lashes fluttered against tanned cheeks, then lifted to reveal cloudy blue eyes.

"I'm going to get help for you," Amber said. "Just don't move."

"I'll be damned," he said, his words slurred. "I went . . . to heaven . . . after all. Hello, Angel."

"No, no, I'm Amber. Amber Prescott. Can you tell me your name?"

"Do we . . . use names . . . in heaven?"

"What? Oh, yes, of course, we do."

"Logan . . . Wade," he said, then groaned as the pain assaulted him. "This can't . . . be heaven. Pain. Damn pain. Must . . . be hell."

"I'll be right back with help," she said, scrambling to her feet. "Don't go away. Oh, what a stupid thing to say," she said, then ran through the trees.

Logan gave in to the blackness that crept over him once again.

Amber came dashing from the cove, her skirt hiked to her knees, heart pounding beneath her breast. Logan Wade. Logan Wade, her mind thundered. He was bleeding to death in her cove, on her grass, by her stream, and she had to save him. He thought he had died, gone to heaven, and she was an angel. Hello, Angel, Logan Wade had said. But then the pain had come, he'd been sure he was in hell, and . . .

"Pa! Moses!" she yelled, as she came closer to the fields. "Pa!"

They emerged from the corn stalks at a dead run toward her, Benny trying to keep up. Nathan Prescott reached Amber first, and gripped her by the upper arms.

"What is it, girl?" he said. His face was flushed, his gray hair streaming with sweat. "What's wrong?"

"A man," she said, gasping for breath. "Logan Wade. He's hurt, by the stream. He's bleeding bad, Pa. We've got to hurry."

"Come on, Moses," Nathan said. "Amber, stay here with Benny."

"No," she said, shaking her head. "I want to help. I told him I'd be back. Please, Pa. He's a big man, and it might take all of us to carry him."

Nathan frowned, then nodded. "All right then. Let's go."

Amber grabbed Benny's hand and nearly hauled the ten-year-old off his feet as she ran after Nathan and Moses. Her lungs ached with a cold pain, and her heartbeat echoed in her ears. They were all moving in slow motion, she thought frantically. They weren't shortening the distance between them and Logan Wade.

"He's right by the stream straight ahead," Amber called finally.

"You're breaking my hand, Amber," Benny said.

"I'm sorry," she said, freeing her brother from her tight grasp.

By the stream, Moses dropped to one knee beside Logan, as Nathan hunkered down. Amber stood at Logan's feet with a wide-eyed Benny beside her.

"That's sure a lot of blood," the little boy said. "I'd say he's dead for certain."

"Hush," Amber said. "Don't say, don't even think, such a thing. Pa?"

Nathan undid two buttons on Logan's shirt and peered beneath the soaked material.

"Bullet," he said. "Still in there as far as I can tell. What do you think, Moses? A gunfighter?"

"I'd say so," Moses said, nodding. "He's wearin' his gun low and tied down with a rawhide strap. Well, we're goin' to have to get that bullet out of there if he's to have any chance at all, Mr. Prescott."

"Pa wants you to call him Nathan," Amber said absently, repeating the ongoing reminder to Moses.

A gunfighter? her mind echoed. Logan Wade was a gunfighter? How could they label a man simply by the way he wore his gun?

She'd heard stories about gunfighters, of how mean they were, ruthless, how they killed, then walked calmly away without a backward glance. What did men such as those know about angels in heaven? No. Logan Wade was not a gunfighter.

"I best go hitch up the wagon," Nathan said. "We'll move him to the cabin."

"No need for the wagon," Moses said. He slid one massive arm beneath Logan's shoulders, another under his knees, then rose slowly to his feet, the injured man in his arms.

"Land's sake," Amber said.

"Moses is the strongest man in Texas," Benny said, pride evident in his voice.

"Amber," Nathan said, "run on ahead and clear off the table, then set some water to boil. Benny, see if you can get his horse without spookin' it. Take it to the barn, brush it down, then feed it."

"I want to see you dig the bullet out of the gunfighter," Benny said.

"His name is Logan Wade," Amber said, "and he's not a . . ."

"Move, boy," Nathan said. "You, too, Amber. You sure you can tote him, Moses?"

"Yes, sir, Mr. Prescott," he said, starting to walk away. "I'm doin' just fine. He can't weigh more than two hundred pounds."

"Land's sake," Amber muttered again, then scooted around Moses, and started running toward the cabin.

Her legs felt like wooden sticks and her lungs were nearly bursting when she dashed into the cabin. Perspiration pooled between her breasts, and honey-colored curls lay in disarray around her face. She stoked the fire, set another log in place, then hung a cast-iron pot filled with water on the hook above the flames. She pulled the chairs away from the table, then removed the small vase of wildflowers from the center and placed it on the mantle.

Moses entered and with a grunt, lowered Logan onto the wooden table. Logan's feet hung over the end, and Amber mentally calculated his height at six-foot-three. He moaned, mumbled, but didn't open his eyes. Moses unbuckled and removed Logan's gunbelt, then set it on a chair. Nathan came into the cabin and tossed Logan's black Stetson on top of the gun.

"Get your sewing shears, Amber," Nathan said. "We need to cut his shirt away."

"Fever," Moses said, placing his hand on Logan's forehead. "This boy is in poor shape."

Amber took the shears from the sewing basket in the side cupboard and handed them to Nathan. She clutched her hands tightly together, and watched as Nathan began to cut away the sweat-and-blood-soaked shirt. Her breath caught in her throat as Logan's chest came into view.

She'd never seen a man's chest, she realized. Well, Pa and Moses sometimes took off their shirts in the field, then came to the back of the cabin bare-chested to wash up, but they weren't men . . . exactly. They were, after all, Pa and Moses.

But Logan Wade was a man. A man with a tanned, muscled chest covered in moist dark curls that tapered to a thin strip disappearing below the buckle on his pants. His arms appeared strong, blue veins visible on the corded biceps and forearms.

Her gaze traveled the entire length of him, seeing the bunching muscles of his thighs, then lingering a moment, a heart-stopping moment, where his sexuality was clearly defined beneath the buttons of his pants. Her cheeks flushed with heat, and she quickly switched her gaze to the ugly, raw wound on Logan's left shoulder.

"Get rags, girl," Nathan said, snapping Amber back to attention, "and a pan of that warm water. Moses, best go to the barn and hone a knife sharp as you can get it."

"Yes, sir," Moses said, then lumbered out the door.

Amber did as instructed, then watched intently as Nathan cleansed Logan's wound and the remainder of his chest with the soft, warm rags. Logan moaned once, but remained still. "Have plenty more rags ready," Nathan said. "We'll need 'em to mop the blood, plus make a bandage, if he lives that long."

"Oh, Pa," Amber said, "Surely Logan isn't going to die, is he?"

"Don't know. He's young, appears healthy as an ox, but he's lost a lot of blood, and there's no tellin' how deep that bullet is in there. Might die from the shock when we have to go in after it. The fever is a bad sign, means infection has already set in, though I've seen fevers break once the bullet was out. We'll do the best we can for him."

"Yes, I know you will," she said, staring at Logan's glistening face. "His eyes are blue, Pa. Blue as the sky. He thought I was an angel from heaven."

"I doubt this boy's gettin' a ticket to heaven," Nathan said.

"You don't know he's a gunfighter, Pa."

"The way he wears his gun says he is. Well, we won't judge him now. He's a man in need of our tendin', and that's all that matters. Prescotts don't turn away anyone we're able to help."

"Here's the knife," Moses said, reentering the cabin. He walked to the fire and stuck the gleaming blade in the flames.

"Horse is tended to, Pa," Benny said, running in the door.

Moses cooled the knife in the bucket of water on the floor, steam rising with a hiss as the blade cut through the liquid. He dried the knife, then handed it to Nathan.

"Well, let's get this done," Nathan said, sighing. "Can't risk him thrashin' when I'm goin' after that bullet. Amber, light the lamp and

bring it close so I can clearly see what I'm
doin'. Moses, you hold his arms. Lay across his
belly if you have to. Benny, you crawl up there
and straddle his legs."

Everyone moved to follow Nathan's instruc-
tions. Amber's hand was trembling as she stood
close to Logan's head with the lamp held to
cast full light on the wound. The heat in the
cabin was oppressive from the fire and the
closeness of the group. She drew her arm
across her forehead, then chewed on the inside
of her cheek as Nathan probed Logan's skin
with his fingers.

"Ready?" Nathan said, and received nods
from Amber, Benny, and Moses.

At the first intrusion of the knife in Logan's
flesh, he jerked upward, causing Moses to press
harder on his arms and torso. Benny planted
his hands on Logan's thighs and tightened his
knees against Logan's.

Nathan started again.

"Sonabitch!" Logan said, pulling against his
restraints. He tossed his head, a pulse beating
wildly in his neck.

"Hold him!" Nathan said, probing even
deeper with the knife.

"He's strong as a bull," Moses gasped.

Suddenly Logan's eyes shot open and he
looked wildly around. "Sweet Jesus," he said,
his voice raspy, "what are you people doing to
me? Get the hell off me."

"Logan," Amber said, placing her hand on

his cheek, "we're trying to help you. We've got to get the bullet out."

He looked at her, his eyes cloudy with pain, fever, and confusion. "You're the angel. You're Amber and . . . Damn it to hell," he roared, as Nathan worked on.

"Yes, I'm Amber," she said quickly. "I said I'd get help for you and I did."

"Your help is killing me!"

"Almost there now," Nathan said. "It's in deep, real deep."

Logan's moan caught in his throat, and he closed his eyes. With his last ounce of strength he fought against the ones causing him such excruciating pain. His muscles strained as he willed himself to fight them off.

"Oh-h-h!" Benny yelled, as Logan bucked him off his legs. Benny landed on the floor with a thud.

"Don't fight us," Amber said. "Logan, don't die. Please. You want to live, don't you?"

Moses held on for dear life.

"Ah, hell," Logan said, and then passed out into black oblivion.

"Praise the Lord," Moses said, his black skin slick with sweat as he stood up. "I was 'bout out of energy to hold him. Lord almighty, that boy is strong. He must be somethin' to deal with when he's fit."

"My butt hurts," Benny said, gingerly rubbing the subject matter.

"Hold the lamp higher," Nathan said, sweat

running into his eyes. "I'm almost . . . Got it!" he said, producing the bloody bullet. "Moses, press rags on here. Quick now. He can't afford to lose much more blood. Amber, you get an alum poultice made up. Girl?"

"What? Oh, yes, Pa, I hear you," she said, moving on shaking legs to the hearth. She wouldn't be sick, she silently vowed. She wouldn't. But there was so much blood, and the memory of that knife digging deep into Logan's flesh . . . No! She couldn't fail him now. She had to make the poultice.

She blew out the lamp and set it on the mantle. After retrieving the alum from the cupboard she shook some into a frying pan and held it over the fire until the alum darkened. Selecting the thinnest rag, she spooned the alum onto it and hurried back to the table. Nathan placed the pad on the wound, then reached for more rags.

Moses lifted and turned Logan's inert body while Nathan bound him, drawing his left arm across his chest and wrapping him tightly so he was unable to move his arm. Logan was covered from his shoulder to nearly his waist, and the stark white of the clean rags contrasted sharply with his bronzed skin.

"Whew!" Nathan said finally, sinking into a chair. "I feel like I just broke a wild stallion."

"That's a fact," Moses said, laughing deep in his chest. "Well, we can't leave him passed out on the table. I'll bring my cot in from the barn."

"What'll you sleep on?" Nathan said.

"Blanket in fresh hay is fine for me. His fever broke. That's a good sign, but he'll need spongin' down if it spikes again. Should strip those dusty pants off him, too. I'll get the cot," Moses said, then headed out the door.

"Pull his boots off, Benny," Nathan said, "while I catch my breath. Amber, you'll have to sponge him, if need be."

"Me?" she said, more in the form of a squeak.

"Got no choice. We can't afford to lose an afternoon's work in the fields. Those weeds are goin' to choke that corn out if we don't keep at 'em. You been tendin' to Benny since he was a babe. This Logan Wade isn't built any different than your brother."

" 'Cept bigger, I'd say," Benny said, whooping with laughter. "Amber's got herself a stark naked gunfighter to tend to."

"You hush your mouth," Amber said, her cheeks flushed with embarrassment. "Just take off his boots like Pa told you to do."

Moses reappeared with the cot and set it against the side wall. Amber busied herself spreading clean sheets over it, then hurried back to the hearth to scrape the alum from the frying pan.

"I'll strip his pants off," Moses said. Amber stared into the frying pan. "There," Moses said, a few minutes later. "He's snug as a bug, and sick as a dog. Fever's liable to come back on him, Mr. Prescott."

"Amber will sponge him down if it does," Nathan said. "We best get back to the fields. I'll be sendin' Benny up from time to time to check on things, girl. Just do the best you can. It's out of our hands now. It's up to Logan and the good Lord. Sponge him down 'bout every half hour if the fever comes. Beyond that, it's wait and see."

"Whatcha goin' to see while you're spongin' him, Amber?" Benny hooted.

Nathan chuckled. "That's enough out of you, Benny," he said. "Maybe you'd like a story or two 'bout the tendin' to your messy butt Amber did when you were a babe."

"No, sir," Benny said, then ran out the door.

"Something goes bad, missy," Moses said, "you fire the rifle and we'll come runnin'."

"I'll be fine," Amber said, wishing she believed it. "Do you think Logan's going to die, Moses?"

"Don't know, missy, just don't know," he said, shaking his head. He left the cabin.

"You all right, girl?" Nathan asked, frowning.

"Certainly," she said, forcing a smile. "Like you said, I tended to Benny for years. Still see him swimming naked in the stream. If I have to, I can sponge Logan Wade without a second thought." Oh, dear heaven above, she was such a liar.

"Well, I wouldn't be leavin' you alone with him if I thought you were in harm's way, but that boy is dead to the world. We'll be in by suppertime. Benny will be back to check on things."

"Fine," she said, clasping her hands behind her back to hide their trembling.

Then suddenly she was alone in the cabin with Logan Wade. She walked slowly to the cot and stared down at him. The sheet was pulled to his waist, his upper body was encased in the bandage. His breathing was labored, and his face and thick, black hair glistened with perspiration. Yet even in his weakened, unconscious state, there was an aura of power about him, of virility, of masculinity, like nothing Amber had ever encountered before. Among all the men she'd seen in her life, there had been none like Logan.

And if his fever spiked, she'd have to sponge the entire rugged, naked length of him!

Well, she wouldn't worry about that now. The fever had broken, and he'd survived the shock of her pa digging for the bullet. Logan Wade was *not* going to die. Maybe the others weren't all that certain he was going to live, but *she* was. She knew, just somehow knew, he *wasn't* going to die.

She placed one hand gently on Logan's forehead, feeling the lingering heat beneath the cold, clammy sweat.

The fever wasn't totally gone, and the best

thing to do, she decided, would be to sponge him now, rather than wait for what might be a fever of crisis.

"So do it," she said, spinning around and marching to the hearth.

She filled a pan with hot water, then ladled cooler water from the bucket until it was tepid. After setting the pan on the floor, she pulled a chair next to the cot, and sat down.

She wrung out the rag and wiped Logan's face, neck, then redipped the cloth and drew it down his right arm. His hands were large, the fingers tapered and blunt on the ends. A smattering of dark hair sprinkled across his knuckles. The palms were rough and callused and, Amber mused, would definitely be felt against a woman's soft skin.

She pulled herself up short and frowned. What a terrible thought to have had. Imagine thinking about Logan's hands on a woman's body. Had he had many women? Those saloon girls she'd heard tales about on the wagon train, when no one knew she was listening in the shadows?

She leaned closer and stared at his lips. Nice lips; full, perfectly shaped. What would he look like when he smiled? she wondered. Yes, very nice lips. Kissable lips. How would they feel pressed to hers? She'd never been kissed, but Lord knew she'd heard enough about it. It was supposed to be wonderful. Lips smashing onto lips had always seemed like a rather silly thing to do. Until now. Until sitting there staring at the lips of Logan Wade.

He moaned. Amber nearly jumped off the chair.

"Mind your manners, Amber Prescott," she muttered, wringing out the cloth.

The time had come, she knew. She couldn't postpone it any longer. She had to sponge the rest of Logan's body. So, she'd whip back the sheet and . . . and die. No matter what Pa had said, she had the distinct feeling that tending to Benny as a babe had not prepared her for what was beneath that sheet.

She drew the sheet a few inches below Logan's waist, then yanked it up again. Her heart was pounding, her cheeks were flushed, as she took a steadying breath.

This would never do. Feet. Feet were a good place to start, she decided, stomping to the end of the bed. She flipped back the sheet and moistened his feet with the cloth. After several dunkings of the rag, she'd gotten all the way to his knees.

She was doing fine, she told herself. So far, anyway.

As she brushed the sheet to mid-thigh, Logan moaned again, and she moved to bend over his face, peering at him anxiously.

"Damn," he mumbled, tossing his head on the pillow. "Must . . . be hell. Hot . . . hot. Pain. Damn."

"Logan, please, be still," she said, placing her hand on his warm forehead. "Please."

He stopped his ramblings, then turned his head to the side, not moving again.

"Good," Amber said, straightening and planting her hands on her hips. "I'm glad to see that you do as you're told. I know in my heart and mind that you're to live, and I swear to heaven, Logan Wade, if you die, I'll never speak to you again."

Two

Chato rode like the wind, his strong horse moving beneath him as though man and beast were meshed into one powerful entity. Sweat poured from Chato's body, then cooled instantly, leaving a residue of dust on his taut, burnished skin.

His senses were constantly alert to all and everything around him, missing no detail. Danger could be anywhere, in the form of white men, renegade Indians, beasts of nature. He'd lived on the edge of danger for so long that it was a way of life to him, a dark, ominous cloud that always hovered near.

And he was tired.

He was a man of thirty years who wished only to live in peace with his beloved Lozen, to pray to the gods of his people for a child of his seed to grow within his wife. She had wept in his arms again last night as she told him that the womanly flow from her body taunted her with the message that there was still no babe within her. He had soothed her as he always did, his own heart aching for the child they saw in their minds, in their dreams.

It would come to be, Chato thought fiercely. There would be a babe. He would take Lozen to the reservation, join the others of their tribe, and live in harmony with the white man.

He was Chato, a brave warrior, but the time for fighting had passed. It was finished. He was not a defeated Apache, but one who possessed the wisdom to know that change had come to the land and the people. It was better, he knew, to look to the future and its promises, than to mourn for a past that was littered with the memories of an era that was over for all time.

But first, his mind whispered, he must fulfill his vow to Naana. His grandmother deserved to have her final wish granted before she went to the place of the spirits for her eternal sleep.

He would not rest until he'd accomplished his goal.

He would bring to Naana the body of Logan Wade.

Chato leaned over the thick neck of his horse, urging him on, closing the distance separating him from the brother of his soul.

The Prescott cabin was larger than those usually constructed during the first years of trying to tame the wild new land of a homestead. It was due, in part, to the availability of the tall trees in the cove, and aided by the fact that Moses seemed to possess the strength and stamina of three men.

The Prescotts and Moses had lived in the covered wagons while the barn, then the log and sod cabin had grown from a dream into a home. Following the code of the west, the barn was constructed first, to provide a safe haven for the animals.

Nathan had wanted Moses to live in the cabin, but he had refused, stating that he preferred to partition off a small area at one end of the barn.

The cabin consisted of a large room that held the wooden table that Logan Wade had been operated on, a side cupboard that had belonged to Amber's mother, a work surface along one wall, and a massive open fireplace topped by a mantel.

In front of the fireplace was a rag rug Amber had made from cloth scraps, and her mother's rocking chair, that had been a wedding present from Nathan to his young bride many years before.

It was the addition of the bedrooms that made the cabin unique compared to those of their distant neighbors. Most families settled for blankets strung over ropes to provide privacy. But Amber was to have a bedroom, Nathan had decreed, as she was officially the woman of the house, and deserved a place she could call her own. He had given her the dou-

ble bed with the brass headboard where he had
slept with his wife, saying he preferred a narrow cot over the memories the bed held.

To Amber, her bedroom was a palace of
splendor with its beautiful bed that nearly
filled the room, and the many-drawered dresser
that had been her mother's. She also treasured
the hand-carved hope chest that had once belonged to her grandmother. Nathan and Benny
slept in the second room, which was small but
served their needs.

During the past four years, the Prescotts had
slowly made additions to their cabin and land.
Every few months they journeyed to Waverly, a
town two days away, to barter, sell, and buy.
Two of the oxen had been traded for six head
of breeding cattle and a milk cow, the other
two oxen kept for labor on the homestead.

One of the covered wagons had been dis-
mantled, thus providing the wooden floor of
the cabin, another enviable luxury. The wood
eliminated the need to dampen a mud-packed
floor each day to keep down the dust.

During the last trip to Waverly, Nathan and
Moses had surprised Amber by trading the last
of the Southern gentleman's fancy clothes and
walking sticks for a small Dutch oven which
stood proudly outside the cabin. It was in her
new oven that Amber made bread and delicious pies. In the future, Nathan had promised, a wood-burning stove would be bought to
aid Amber in her cooking chores.

Compared to the cramped cabin on the dying farmland in Pennsylvania, the new Prescott home was lavish. Amber kept it spotless, and tended to the needs of her all-male family with loving pride. She did it for herself, for them, and for her mother, whom Amber had dearly loved.

The days passed one into the next with hard work and consistency. They all toiled dawn to dusk with little variety except for the changing of the seasons. They rose to face the new day knowing what to expect from the hours ahead. There was a comfortable sameness and peace on the land.

Until Logan Wade.

Amber frowned as she stared down at the large man who lay unmoving on the cot. There was a gray pallor beneath his tan, and his breathing was shallow and irregular. She hadn't completed her task of sponging his *entire* body when he'd begun his ramblings, and she now decided to start over at the top with the hope of keeping his simmering fever in check.

Amber emptied her pan of water out the back door, then mixed the hot and cold to the tepid temperature she sought. Sitting in the chair, she wiped Logan's glistening face, her gaze lingering once again on his lips.

Glancing quickly at the door, then back to Logan's mouth, she tentatively lifted one slender finger and slowly drew it over Logan's lips.

Her breath caught as she felt the softness beneath her fingertip. Though hot and dry from the fever, Logan's lips reminded her of a pussy willow she had once found by the stream.

"Oh, my," she whispered, jerking her hand away.

She'd never dreamed a man's lips would be so soft. Soft as her own, in fact. But when lips met, she wondered, where did noses go? She'd never seen her father kiss her mother, or anyone kiss anyone else, for that matter. She'd only heard the giggling girls in Pennsylvania go on and on about the ecstasy, the excitement, of sharing a kiss with a special beau.

And there she sat, Amber mused, a grown woman, who'd never been kissed. A grown woman, who for the life of her didn't know how it was possible to kiss someone without noses getting in the way.

Well, she'd daydreamed enough, she decided. She had work to do. She would beat Logan's fever, sponge him until her arms fell off if need be. But it just wasn't necessary to sponge *that* part of him. She'd go up to his thighs and down a bit along his belly, but the unknown beneath that sheet was remaining just that, unknown.

Amber completed her top-half labors, then drew back the sheet to expose Logan's muscle corded legs with the smattering of dark hair. She hummed softly as she worked, a gentle lullaby her mother had sung when nursing Benny while rocking in her pretty chair.

Pain.

Burning pain like nothing he had ever known before. And with it was a strange heat that consumed him from the inside out, not like the blazing sun when it beat down upon him.

He had died. Hadn't he? Died and gone to the fires of hell. Foggy pictures inched in around the pain. A woman. An angel. Amber.

Then a mountain of a black man, and a man with gray hair who had tormented him with a knife. He'd fought them off, but would they be back? He had to move on, hide, escape the men and the pain. Maybe he hadn't died after all. Damn, it was hot. And, ah, damn, the pain was killing him. He had to get away.

Logan struggled against the darkness in his mind, concentrating on lifting his lashes so he could see. Blinding light struck against his eyes, but he resisted the urge to seek the solace of the darkness.

A blurry figure came into view, then steadied. A soft sound reached his ears; music, a woman humming. Amber. He recognized her now, knew the soothing sound came from her.

The pain was closing in on him again, he knew, but he mustn't give in to it. The man with the knife might be back to torture him. He had to get the hell out of there.

"No!" Logan said, jerking his leg to throw off Amber's hand, then gritting his teeth against the pain that rocketed through him.

"Logan, don't," Amber said. She pulled the sheet over his feet, then moved to sit in the chair next to him. "You've got to lie still. If you start bleeding again, you'll die for sure. Are you thirsty? Would you like some water?"

He stared at her blankly, and she wasn't sure he even knew she was there.

"You're thirsty," she said, deciding that he was. She walked to the side cupboard and dipped a metal cup into the bucket of cool water. Back at the cot, she slid her hand under Logan's head, lifted it, and brought the cup to his lips. "Try to take a sip."

Water. Sweet, cool water, Logan thought, taking a deep swallow. He'd smelled water when . . . Grass. A stream. He'd been shot and now . . . Where was he? This woman was Amber, that he knew. Maybe she'd help him escape before the man with the knife came back.

"Good, very good," Amber said, lowering his head, then sitting back down.

"Amber," Logan said, his voice sounding strange to his own ears, "help . . . me to . . ."

"I *am* helping you, Logan, the very best I can. You've got to stay very quiet."

"No. Man . . . knife . . . have to . . . go."

Amber frowned. "No one with a knife is after you. You were shot and . . . Knife? Logan, that man was my father. He was taking the bullet out of your shoulder. Don't you remember? I found you by the stream, said I'd bring help, and you thought I was an angel from heaven. My father didn't mean to hurt you with the knife, but he had to get the bullet out. You're safe here. No one is going to harm you."

Logan closed his eyes and struggled to sift through what Amber had said. The pain thudded against his mind and body with a steady cadence, confusing him, making it impossible to think clearly.

"Oh, Logan," Amber said, leaning toward him, "just rest for now. I'll be right here if you need me, I promise."

"Hell," he mumbled, then gave way to the black tunnel of oblivion.

Amber sank back in the chair and drew a weary breath. How could such a small bullet cause such grief? she mused. Who had shot Logan? And why? Was he a gunfighter? No, he was *not* a ruthless, cold-blooded gunfighter.

"Amber Prescott," she said, getting to her feet. "You've got work to do."

The cabin that had been spotlessly clean before Amber had set out to pick raspberries, was a disaster. Blood-soaked rags littered the table and floor, several pans of water were strewn in various locations, Logan's shredded shirt lay in a heap on the floor, along with his pants.

Amber set about cleaning the debris, scrubbing the tabletop until her arms ached from the effort. She burned Logan's shirt and the soiled rags in the hearth, then set a pot of stew to simmer for dinner.

The heat in the cabin was oppressive, and her mind wandered to a vision of the cool stream. She sponged Logan's feverish body, then collapsed into the rocking chair, closing her eyes. A moment later, Benny ran in the door.

"I'm here to check on things," he said, obviously feeling very important. "How's the gunfighter?"

"Benjamin Prescott," Amber said, lifting her head and glaring at him, "you will not refer to Mr. Wade as a gunfighter again. Do you hear me?"

Benny shrugged, then walked to where Logan lay on the cot. "He don't look so good."

"I know," she said quietly, "but I'm doing the best I can."

"You sound sad, Amber," Benny said, coming back to the rocker. "Won't be your fault if he dies. You told me it wasn't nobody's fault when Mama died. You're not goin' to cry if the gunfighter dies, are you?"

"No, of course, not," she said, smiling at him, "but I don't think he's going to die. He's big and strong." Her glance slid to the bullet where it sat on the mantel. "Just wouldn't seem right that a little thing like that could do in such a big, strong man."

"Think I'll be big like that someday, Amber?" Benny said, leaning on the arm of the rocker.

She ruffled his straight brown hair and smiled at him, seeing the face of their mother in his delicate features. Amber didn't seem to take after either her father or mother in appearance, but Benny was a carbon copy of Mary Prescott. He was small for his age and slightly built.

"Oh, yes," she said, "you'll be a strong, strapping man like Logan Wade when you grow up. Maybe you'll even get as big as Moses."

Benny laughed. "No, I won't. Moses is the biggest man in Texas. I'll be like Logan, though, I bet. Maybe I'll wear a gun like his."

"No, you will not. A rifle in the boot of your saddle for protection and hunting is all you'll need. You'll have no call to wear a holster and gun like Logan's."

"Why does he wear it, you think? I still betcha he's a . . ."

"Benny, I'm sure there's just cause for Logan to be wearing that gun. All we need to be concerned about now is seeing that he gets well. You best get back to the fields and help Pa. Tell him I'm doing just fine here."

"Did you sponge Logan?"

"Of course. Several times."

"Bet it wasn't like tendin' to me as a babe," Benny said, laughing merrily.

"Go to the fields, Benjamin," Amber said

firmly. "I'm too hot and tired to be putting up with your chatter and nonsense."

Benny scooted out the door and a silence fell over the cabin, broken only by the quiet creaking as Amber rocked back and forth in the chair.

Would she cry if Logan died? her mind echoed. Yes, she would cry if Logan Wade died. It didn't make sense, she supposed, but she knew she would seek out a private place and cry. But he wasn't going to die. He would fight the infection, the fever, the weakness from loss of blood, and she would help him do it.

Logan moaned, bringing Amber from her reverie. She was instantly on her feet and hurrying to his side. He mumbled something she couldn't understand, but she was unable to rouse him enough to get him to sip more water.

Amber sponged him again, her hands moving with familiarity now over his hot, taut skin. She recognized each corded muscle that came into her view, knew the feel of the springy moist hair on his chest, inhaled the aromas of the alum poultice, sweat, and something she thought was just male, pure and simple. She still didn't move the sheet to discover the mystery of his manhood, but the rest of his body was as known to her as her own.

And his was so very, very different from hers. Where she was soft and gently curved, Logan was rugged and sharp. Her pale hands on his burnished skin stood out in startling contrast. There was such incredible power emanating from Logan, making Amber feel fragile and small in comparison. His large hands could probably span her waist, and she'd come to no more than his shoulder when he stood.

A woman would feel safe in Logan's arms, Amber thought suddenly. Safe and protected against all harm. And there, in that haven, she'd lift her head and he'd kiss her. Those lips, those soft lips would . . .

"Land's sake," she said, plopping down on the chair next to Logan's cot.

She glanced at him quickly, ridden with guilt, half expecting to find him staring at her as he read her mind. Such fanciful thoughts. Such naughty thoughts. A strange tingling sensation started in the pit of her stomach and traveled throughout her, bringing a warm glow to her cheeks. It was the heat, she told herself, and the excitement of the day. She needed some fresh air.

Outside of the cabin, Amber pressed her hands to her cheeks and leaned back against the rough surface of the exterior logs. The sun was beginning its travel westward across the sky, and cooling shadows cloaked the area by the cabin. There was a stillness in the air, a humid, sultry silence marked only by the buzzing of a bee.

Amber ran her hands over her hips to dry her moist palms, then repeated the motion, suddenly acutely aware of her feminine curves beneath the cotton material. Her breasts seemed to strain against the restricting fabric, aching with a foreign heaviness. Her heart thrummed and her pulse skittered, as she replayed in her mind the fantasy scene of Logan Wade taking her into his arms and kissing her.

She saw herself lift up her arms to circle his neck, then mold to his rugged length to receive his lips moving toward hers. He held her tightly to his chest as he lowered his head slowly, slowly to . . .

"Bump my nose," she said, frowning.

The spell was broken, and Amber blinked once as though awakening from a dream. She gasped in horror as she saw that her hands had slid up to the sides of her breasts, and she jerked them away, fussing with her hair with trembling fingers.

What in heaven's name was the matter with her? she wondered frantically. She had never entertained such wanton daydreams before. Never. And she had never been so aware of every inch of her own body. Even her skin seemed to tingle.

She drew a trembling breath, which filled her senses with the aromas of the land. Held captive in the humid air was the smell of dust, of animals, fresh hay, and wild honeysuckle. The scents of her own body reached her; a hint of lye from her sweat-soaked dress, and a lin-

gering whiff of lavender from her precious bar
of store-bought soap.

Sounds reached her, all familiar, but so
sharp and clear it was as though everything
were at her feet. She heard the milk cow bellow, the cattle snort, heard the muffled voices
of Benny, Nathan, and Moses. Birds chirped,
the buzzing bee was joined by others.

Amber's eyes swept over the sky, seeing the
sun beginning to melt like a dab of butter on
a hot skillet. Streaks of purple, orange, and
yellow fingered across the heavens, transforming it into a spectacle of incredible beauty.

Sights, sounds, smells. Everything was magni-
fied, causing Amber to lean harder against the
cabin until the rough wood pressed painfully
into her back. Her eyes skittered back and forth
as a feeling of expectancy, excitement, mingled
with fear, assaulted her. The echo of her heartbeat rushed in her ears. She wanted to run, yet
she wished to stay. She felt alive as never before,
yet afraid of the heightened awareness of herself and all that was around her.

Dear heaven above, what was happening to
her?

"Amber," a voice rumbled. "Amber."

She stiffened, eyes wide, as if coming out of
a semitrance. She placed her hand on her
heart to hush its wild beating as she stood
statue still.

"Amber."

"Logan," she gasped, then spun around and

ran into the cabin. She stopped at the edge of
his cot and looked down at him anxiously.
"Logan?"

Logan lifted his dark lashes and gazed up at
her with feverish eyes. He opened his mouth
to speak, then hesitated, as though the effort
were too great.

"Water," he said finally.

"Yes," she said, nodding. She hurried to fill
a cup, then returned to the cot, dropping to
her knees on the floor. "Drink, Logan," she
whispered, lifting his head and bringing the
cup to his lips.

Logan swallowed deeply, then again, and
again. With a weary sigh he closed his eyes,
and Amber lowered his head gently to the pillow. She pressed her palm to his forehead, feeling the hot, moist skin.

"You are *not* going to die," she said, her eyes
filling with quick tears. "Fight this, Logan. You
can't give up. I'm doing all I can, but you've
got to help me. Oh, Logan, please."

Amber leaned forward and rested her head
on the edge of the cot, the last of her energy
seeming to drain from her body. Seconds, then
minutes ticked by, but she didn't move. Then
slowly, the aroma of the simmering stew
reached her, and she jerked her head up.

Supper. She had to get supper on for Benny,
Pa, and Moses. She hadn't even set the table
or . . .

Scrambling to her feet, she rushed to fill a

pan with tepid water and carried it into her bedroom, setting it on the dresser. She closed the door, then unbuttoned her dress and stepped out of it, revealing her plain cotton chemise. Taking her lavender soap from the small chipped plate, she lathered a soft rag and washed her face, arms, then across her full breasts where they pushed above the thin material. Amber glanced up at her reflection in the mirror and her hand stilled.

Her eyes were bright, appeared larger than usual, were sparkling with something she couldn't define. The weariness of her body was nowhere in evidence on her flushed face. Her hair was in wild disarray, the honey-colored curls trailing down her neck and around her cheeks.

"Who are you?" she said to her image, half expecting it to answer her. "Oh, Amber, stop it," she said, with a snort of disgust.

She quickly finished her washing, then reached in the drawer for a fresh dress, buttoning the pale green cotton. With the pearl-handled brush that had belonged to her mother, she swept her hair into place and secured it with pins. Taking a deep, steadying breath, she picked up the pan of water and returned to the outer room.

As Amber pulled the pewter plates from the cupboard she heard Benny, Nathan, and Moses approach the back of the cabin and begin to wash up. She set the table, ladled the stew into a large bowl, then sliced bread. She had just set a pot of coffee on the grate over the fire, when the trio entered through the rear door.

"Smells mighty good," Nathan said. "How are you, girl? And how's the patient?"

"I'm fine, Pa," she said. "I bring Logan's fever down when I sponge him, but then it spikes again."

Moses walked to the cot and placed his huge hand on Logan's forehead. "He's burning up, all right. He come around at all, missy?"

"A couple of times," she said. "I got him to take a little water, but not much. I've been sponging him from head to toe."

Benny snickered. Amber glared at him.

"Well," Moses said, "we'll change the bandage after dinner, then I'll force more liquids in him if I have to sit on his chest."

"We best eat while it's hot," Nathan said. He took Logan's Stetson and gun off the chair and placed them under the cot. "There saddlebags on that horse of his, Benny?" he said, sitting down at the table.

"Yes, Pa."

"Bring 'em in after supper, but don't be snoopin' in Logan's things. Just put them under the cot. There a rifle in the boot?"

"Yes, sir. A real beauty."

"Bring that, too. You're to tend his horse. Now, let's eat."

* * *

Logan, don't die. Please!

You want to live, don't you?

The words beat against Logan's brain, bringing him from his dark tunnel, badgering him, forcing him to think. Yeah, all right, damn it, he wanted to live. There, he'd admitted it. He hadn't cared if he died, but now . . . Yeah, he wanted to live. Why, he didn't know, but he just did. Fine. Now would that voice leave him alone? Who was that nagging at him? Amber. Pretty, pretty Amber with the gentle hands. Amber, who hummed nice tunes. Why should she care if he lived or died? Nobody cared. But she sounded so sad when she'd pleaded with him to fight to live.

Logan moaned. His shoulder was on fire, burning, like a branding iron pressed to his flesh. He couldn't move his arm!

"Damn it," he said, opening his eyes.

Amber jerked in her chair at the table.

Nathan chuckled. "That boy does have a mouth on him." He pushed himself to his feet and walked to the cot. "Well, now, nice of you to join us."

"What in the hell did you do to my arm?" Logan said, then gritted his teeth against the pain that shimmered through him.

"It's there," Nathan said, placing his hand on Logan's forehead. "We got you bound up like a turkey for market so you don't start bleedin' again. Fever seems gone."

"It is?" Amber said, getting to her feet.

"Yep," Nathan said, nodding. "Water down some of that broth off the stew, and I'll spoon it in him. Then we'll change the bandage."

"Go away," Logan said, raising his head off the pillow.

"Easy boy," Nathan said, pulling over a chair and sitting down next to the cot. "You're not out of the woods yet. You start thrashin' around and you'll rip that wound open for sure. I'm Nathan Prescott, that there is my son Benny. My daughter Amber's been tendin' to you all day. She found you shot by the stream. That big man is Moses, and if you get out of hand here, he'll set you to rights. You understandin' me, boy?"

Logan scowled, then his gaze swept beyond Nathan to the people in the room who were gawking at him. He put a name to each, his gaze lingering an extra moment on Amber, who stood ramrod stiff, staring at him. Moses got slowly to his feet and walked to the cot.

Good Lord, Logan thought, that wasn't a man, it was a giant who could snap him in two.

"Well?" Nathan said.

"Yeah," Logan said, giving Moses a stormy glare before looking at Nathan again, "I hear you."

"Get the broth, Amber," Nathan said.

"Yes, Pa," she said, moving to the hearth.

With her back to the room, she squeezed her eyes closed and pressed her fingertips to her lips. Logan was going to live, her heart sang, just as she'd known he would. His fever was gone, he was understanding what was being said to him. He . . .

"Amber?" Nathan said.

"Oh, coming, Pa," she said. She ladled the gravy from the stew into a bowl and diluted it with warm water. Picking up a spoon and napkin, she walked to the cot. "Here, Pa," she said. Then slowly, slowly, she shifted her gaze to Logan to find him looking directly up at her. His eyes were slightly clearer, a brighter blue, though still a bit cloudy from the pain. "Hello, Logan," she said softly.

"Amber," he said, his voice low as he continued to look at her.

Amber. That was all he said, just her name spoken in a husky timbre. She was held immobile under his gaze, the sound of his voice stroking her like dark velvet, causing her pulse to race, and a tingling sensation to feather up her spine.

Nathan snapped the napkin open, startling both Amber and Logan. She spun around and began to clear the table. Logan frowned at Nathan, who draped the napkin across Logan's chest.

"Open up," Nathan said.

"Just like feedin' a babe," Benny said, peering over his father's shoulder.

"Go away, kid," Logan said, more in the form of a growl.

Benny scooted to the far end of the table, his eyes wide with fright. "I'm doing my chores," he said, then ran out the door.

"Don't you be scarin' our Benny none, Wade," Moses said.

Logan opened his mouth to retort, but before he could speak, Nathan shoveled in a spoonful of broth. As soon as Logan swallowed, the spoon was there again, then again, until the bowl was empty.

"Good," Nathan said, nodding. "Now let's get that bandage changed. Amber, bring the sewing shears and fresh rags."

Amber did as she was instructed, then stood behind her father as Nathan began to cut away the bindings. She riveted her eyes on Logan's shoulder, but she could feel him looking at her, feel the heat of his gaze that seemed to seek the path to her soul.

The wound was red and swollen, draining a yellowish fluid that gave evidence to the lingering infection. The surrounding flesh on Logan's shoulder had turned into a deep purple bruise.

"Don't look good," Moses said.

"We'll need another alum poultice, Amber," Nathan said. He got to his feet and filled a pan with warm water. "Set your teeth, boy," he said, sitting back down. "I've got to clean this up."

At the first touch of the wet rag, Logan's whole body jerked and he sucked in his breath.

"Sweet Jesus," he mumbled, beads of sweat popping out on his forehead and upper lip.

"Keep still," Nathan said, "or Moses will have to hold you down."

"Like hell he will," Logan said, glaring at the big black man. "He leans on me, he'll break every bone in my body." Moses hooted with laughter.

"Then you best keep still," Nathan said calmly.

"Yeah," Logan said, then willed himself not to move as Nathan continued to cleanse the raw wound. Logan clenched his jaw until it ached, and tightened his fists until the knuckles were white, but he didn't move. Sweat poured off his body, his bronzed skin glistening in the dim light in the cabin. "Ah, hell," he finally said, then passed out.

"Here's the poultice, Pa," Amber said. "Logan?"

"He's out," Nathan said. "He's tough, got a lot of grit. Let's get him bound up here, Moses."

"He's going to live, Pa," Amber said. "He's getting better, I can tell."

"Darlin' girl," Nathan said, chuckling, "I'd say this here Logan Wade is just too plain ornery to die."

Three

Chato lay on his belly on a rise above a homestead. The cabin below burned with bright, orange flames that leaped upward as though trying to ignite the night-darkened, starless sky.

His jaw tightened as he saw the bodies of the farmer and his wife on the ground at the rear of the burning cabin, arrows piercing their lifeless forms.

They had, he surmised, been trying to flee to safety, but had been cut down by the half-dozen Comanches who still circled the cabin on their horses.

The Indians' wild yells and whoops of battle victory, filled Chato with fury. Where, he wondered, was there any pride to be gained in killing homesteaders, who wished only to live in peace, tolling endlessly to provide for themselves in this harsh land?

These renegade Comanches, Chato knew, and the other small bands of Indians from various tribes who looted, killed, and burned, would bring the soldiers once again to seek revenge. Death would march on, Indians and white men would die for no purpose.

He watched as one Comanche raised a fist to the sky, then swung his pony away from the circle. The others followed, their victory cries fading as they disappeared into the darkness.

The only sound left in the night was the crackling of the diminishing flames as they ate their fill of what had once been a haven, a home.

Chato sighed. He was weary in body from his hard day's ride, and now was weary in soul from what he'd witnessed below. He had wished only to eat, then sleep, rejuvenate himself for the full day's journey still separating him from his destination.

But rest must wait, he knew, for he would bury the homesteaders. He would place the man and woman together in a grave, hoping that the god they worshiped would seek and find their spirits. The couple had, without making the choice, followed Apache tradition by the fact that their possessions had been burned so that what they owned could travel with them to the spirit place.

With a shake of his head, and a deep frown on his face, Chato got to his feet and reached for the reins of his horse. He walked slowly down the rise, his heart heavy, his mind filled with sorrow.

Would there never be peace in this land? he mused. Would there never come a time when

all men could live in harmony, work side by
side, treat each other with the respect due
those of every race that the gods saw fit to
create? Was Chato, the Apache brave, grandson
of Naana, nothing more than a foolish
dreamer?

He stopped by the bodies of the homesteaders,
and stared at them, seeing the fear on
their lifeless faces in the glow of the ebbing
fire.

The young woman had one arm wrapped
around a small bundle she'd tucked close to
her body as she'd fallen to her death. He
would bury her treasure with her, whatever it
was, he decided, as it obviously held great importance
to her. He'd free the animals that
were in the barn, then leave this scene of useless
death.

A new sound reached Chato's ears, and he
stiffened, alert to danger. His muscles tensed
as the bundle the woman clutched moved, the
noise growing louder. He hunkered down, balancing
on the balls of his moccasin-clad feet,
and shifted the cloth-wrapped package from
beneath the woman. He spread open the top
of the thin material, his eyes widening in surprise.

There, in his large hands, was a baby.

No more than weeks old, the tiny creature
lifted fists as though in anger, wrinkled its
face, and wailed in distress.

Chato stood, his gaze riveted on the babe

who continued to cry as though voicing its anguish over what had transpired that night. He jiggled the child and spoke to it in a voice low and quiet. The babe blinked, then stilled, staring at him with dark eyes as if measuring his worth.

He cradled the infant in the crook of his arm and drew back the remaining cloth. It was a girl-child, he saw, unharmed and healthy.

A babe for Lozen.

He would retrace his path, return to the camp to bring the babe to his wife. Then he would start out once again to fulfill his promise to Naana.

"You are Jude from this moment on," he said to the baby. "You are the daughter of Chato and Lozen. So be it."

He lifted the baby in both hands high above his head to show her to the gods of his people. Jude. She was an Apache now, and the gods would smile down upon her.

"Jude," Chato yelled, his voice echoing into the night.

Amber lay in bed staring up into the darkness. She was exhausted. She wanted to blank her mind and sleep, but she was coiled, tense, unable to relax.

She shifted in the bed, trying for a more comfortable position, then frowned as her nightgown became tangled around her legs.

Sitting up, she straightened the material, then flopped back onto the pillow with a sigh, her heavy blond braids thudding against her breasts.

Strange, wondrous and, yes, she admitted, frightening changes had taken place within her since finding Logan Wade by the stream. It was as though she had stepped forward into a place where she had never been before; a place of discovery, of womanhood.

What kind of woman was she to become? she wondered. From what hidden, brazen section of her inner being had risen the vision of Logan holding and kissing her? Was there an Amber Prescott within her who would bring shame to the Prescott name with her wanton, shameful ways? Merciful heaven, no. She was good, pure, decent, had been touched by no man.

Actually, she decided, rolling onto her stomach, it was all Logan Wade's fault. *He* was the one who had called her an angel. *He* was the one who lay naked beneath that sheet, and who required her to touch him like she'd touched no man before. And *he* was the one with the pussy-willow lips, and the eyes that seemed to pin her in place hardly able to move, or breathe.

How childish she was, she chided herself in the next instant, for blaming a barely conscious man for the ramblings of her mind, the new stirrings within her own body.

"Oh, Logan," she whispered, as she drifted at last into sleep, "what are you doing to me? What's happening . . . to me . . . Logan?"

Logan jerked awake, waited for the pain from the sudden movement to subside, then listened for any sound in the dark room.

What had awakened him? he wondered. It had been as though someone had shaken him from his deep sleep, calling his name with an urgent plea.

He turned his head, his eyes growing accustomed to the darkness, and saw the closed doors on the far side of the cabin. Amber was in the front bedroom. He didn't know that for a fact, just sensed it, knew that was where she lay sleeping.

Amber, he mused. Amber, the angel from heaven, who sang so pretty, so softly. Amber, with the gentle hands, the beautiful face, the voluptuous body. She was a grown woman, but there was an aura of innocence surrounding her. Yet, her lips were made to be kissed, beckoned to a man to . . .

"Ah, hell," Logan muttered, shifting on the cot as his manhood began to react to his thoughts of Amber. Why was he wasting his time thinking about Amber Prescott? He had enough problems without the physical discomfort of wanting a woman he couldn't have.

Well, at least he knew all his body parts were

working, he thought dryly. His mind was clear, too, so the fever must be about gone. The pain in his shoulder was still a bitch, but there was nothing he could do about it, but lie there at the mercy of the Prescotts and their huge mountain Moses.

The summer moon slid from behind a cloud and sent a silvery luminescence over the room. Logan glanced around, really seeing all of the cabin for the first time, his gaze lingering on the rifle hanging above the mantle.

It was a nice cabin, he decided. Better than most he'd seen there in northern Texas. And the Prescotts were kind, decent people. Some folks wouldn't have helped a blood-soaked, dying man, who'd obviously been shot. A man who wore a gun on his hip. But they'd taken him in and saved his life. A life he didn't think he'd wanted saved.

You want to live, don't you?

Amber's words echoed in his mind again, and he could hear the tears in her voice as she'd spoken them.

"Yeah," he said quietly, "I want to live, Amber."

His mind skittered over the past five years, waiting for the hate that had sent him on his mission of revenge to surface, but it never came. Within him, instead, was a void, an emptiness. The anger was gone, but there was no inner peace in its stead, only a nothingness, that brought a chill rippling through his body.

Without the hate, a part of him was gone. To be replaced by what? What was he to do with the rest of his life? Where would he go? He'd had a purpose, a driving, burning need for so long that he felt stripped bare without it.

He was bare, all right, he thought. He was naked as a buck in a homesteader's cabin. The questions would probably start now that he could think straight. Nathan Prescott would want to know the nature of the man under his roof, eating his food, being tended to by his young and beautiful daughter. Why had there been a gun slung low on his hip, Nathan would ask, instead of just the usual rifle in the boot of his saddle? Who had shot him, and why?

Yeah, the questions would come, and Logan was not inclined to answer them.

Damn, he was tired, he realized. He had to get some sleep. He still didn't know what had jolted him awake in the first place. Amber was probably sleeping like the dead. Poor woman had had a helluva day because of him.

Logan's eyes shifted again to the closed door of the front bedroom. She was in there, he just knew it. She probably wore one of those high-necked, long-sleeved gowns that covered her from head to toe. A virgin's gown. Her breasts were full, would fit into his hands like . . . Her lips were as soft as a petal of a flower and . . .

"Damn," Logan said, as heat shot across his

loins. What kind of bastard was he to lie there thinking randy, lusty thoughts about Amber Prescott? He was in her father's home, been saved by her father's hand.

But when Logan had looked at Amber, really looked straight into those big brown eyes, he'd felt as though he were drowning. A knot had tightened in his gut that hadn't been just lust, but something else he couldn't define.

This was crazy, he told himself. When he saw Amber at dawn's light, he'd see her for what she really was; a pretty, young, homesteader's daughter, who'd tended to him when he was down and out. She was lovely, but not enough to cause him to lose sleep over her with the blood pounding heavily through his veins.

"Enough," he said, shifting on the cot. Lord, he was thirsty. His throat felt like desert sand.

He lifted his head to gauge the distance between the cot and the bucket of cool water by the hearth. His gaze fell on the chair near the foot of the cot where a tin cup sat. Was there water in that cup? Had Nathan set it there in case Logan got thirsty in the night, but not too close that he might bump it over?

With a muffled groan, he sat up, gripping his shoulder as the pain rocketed through him. He inched his long legs to the floor, dragging the sheet with him. Dizziness assaulted him, and he closed his eyes until it passed. He wanted, needed, that water. Gritting his teeth, he stretched out his right arm and caught the

edge of the chair with his fingertips. If he
could just move it closer, he could get the cup.

"Hell," he said, as the dizziness closed over
him again. The floor seemed to tip toward
him, and he jerked, his whole hand connecting
with the chair and sending it toppling backwards to crash onto the floor. The tin cup of
water flipped into the air, spilling its precious
contents, before rolling toward the hearth. "Ah,
damn," Logan said, then bent his head where
he sat, too dizzy to move.

Amber scrambled from the bed and stood
statue still, her heart pounding. She'd been
deeply asleep, was still not totally awake, but
she'd heard a noise, she was sure of it. Had
Pa heard it, too? Would he wake to check on
what had caused it?

"Logan," she whispered, now fully alert.
"What if it was Logan?"

Without further thought, Amber pulled
open the door, rushed to the outer room and
over to the cot, her mind racing. Logan was
sitting up. He shouldn't be doing that. He
could tear open his wound, start it bleeding
again.

"Logan," she said, placing her hand on his
bare shoulder. She vaguely registered the fact
that the sheet was drawn across his lower body.

"Yeah," he said, slowly lifting his head and
opening his eyes. "Sorry I woke you."

"What were you trying to do?"

"Water," he said, waving his arm in the general direction of the toppled chair. "Didn't quite make it, though."

"I'll get you some water," she said, hurrying to the bucket.

The second bedroom door opened. "Amber?" Nathan said, peering out.

"Yes, Pa, it's me. Logan needs some water. He knocked over the chair, so I'm getting him some."

"All right. Then go back to bed. You need a good night's sleep after the day you put in."

"Yes, Pa," she said, ladling water into a cup.

Logan watched as Amber bent over the bucket. She'd come out of the front bedroom, he realized, just like he'd known she would. And she had on her virgin nightgown. Braids. Her hair was in long braids. He didn't know she had that much hair twisted into that bun. What would it look like brushed free, flowing down her back?

Amber turned and walked toward him, and Logan sucked in his breath. The moon had suddenly shifted again, and Amber's body was outlined beneath the thin fabric of her nighty. He could see the fullness of her breasts, the slope of her hips, her long slender legs that swept up to end at the secret place of her femininity. His heart thundered, and his manhood stirred under the sheet.

"Here's your water," she said, standing directly in front of him.

Logan snatched the cup from her hand, sending mental messages to Amber to not drop her gaze below his waist until he had himself back in control. Something he probably wouldn't be capable of doing if she didn't get the hell out of there. He drained the cup and shoved it back into her hand.

"Thanks," he said gruffly.

"More?"

"No."

"Is there anything else you want, Logan?"

Sweet Jesus, he silently moaned, what a question. She hadn't meant anything provocative by it, but a man could lose his mind thinking about the answers he'd like to give.

"No," he said, his voice gritty.

Amber sat down on the bed next to him and placed her hand on his right arm. Logan jerked in surprise.

"Your skin is cool," she said. "I think your fever is completely gone. I just hope it doesn't come back on you."

"It won't," he said. "Good night. Thanks for the water. I was really thirsty. Didn't mean to wake you, though, but I did, so I'm sorry. Well, good night." Dear heaven and saints, this woman had to get off that bed, his mind yelled. If Nathan came out there, saw Amber sitting next to him, *and* saw the bulge beneath that sheet, Logan Wade was a dead man. "Good night, Amber," he said again.

She frowned. "Are you all right? You didn't ramble on this much when you were filled with fever." She placed her hand on his forehead. Logan flinched. "You feel cool, but . . ."

"It's the pain," he said quickly. "Makes a man edgy, not himself."

"Oh," she said, nodding. "That makes sense. I wish I could do something about the pain. Would you like me to talk to you for a while to take your mind off it?"

"No! No, that's not necessary. I'm going back to sleep now, and you should do the same. Lord, you smell good," he said. Dear God, had he said that? Had he opened his mouth and said that? What in the hell was the matter with him?

"It's my lavender soap. I got it in Waverly the last time we went in. It's such a pretty bar of soap, I almost hate to use it, but I can't resist."

"You deserve a pretty bar of soap, Amber," he said, his voice low.

"I do?" she said, looking directly into his eyes.

"You do," he said, meeting her gaze.

Time lost meaning. They didn't move, they simply looked at each other, then Amber ran her tongue over her bottom lip. Logan groaned, and tore his gaze from hers.

"Is the pain worse?" she asked.

"Not exactly," he said, laying his arm across his thighs. "Go to bed."

"I will. Logan, could I ask you a question without you thinking poorly of me?"

"I could never think poorly of you, Amber," he said, turning to look at her again.

"Well, I'd ask my ma, but I don't have her anymore, and I don't think Pa would understand why I want to know."

"What's the question?" he said, frowning slightly.

"Well, when a man and woman kiss, how do they keep from bumping noses?"

Logan opened his mouth to speak, clamped it shut again, and shook his head. "What?" he finally said.

"Don't noses get in the way?"

"Noses. Noses? Amber, how old are you?"

"Three months shy of nineteen."

"And you've never been kissed?"

"No," she said, sighing, "I haven't. I realize I'm a grown woman, should have a husband and babes by now, but after my mama died I took her place tending to Pa, Benny, and Moses, too, of course. I'll marry, I suppose, when the time is right, and I already understand about wifely duties and all, because I've seen the animals mating when they're in heat."

"It's . . ." Logan cleared his throat roughly, ". . . not quite like that between a man and a woman, Amber."

"No? Oh. Well, I'll think that through another time. It's kissing that has me confused."

"The noses," he said, rolling his eyes to the heavens.

"Yes."

"It's not that complicated. You just sort of tilt your head a bit so that . . . I really don't think I should be the one explaining this to you, Amber. It's not my place."

"Tilt my head how?"

"Damn. All right, look," he said, lifting his hand to gently cup her chin. "Like this."

"Then what?"

"Then, if I were the man who was going to kiss you, which I'm not, I'd move my head close to you like this, then tilt it a tad in the other direction and . . . then . . ."

"Yes?" she whispered.

Amber's sweet breath flitted across Logan's lips that were close, so close, to hers. His fingers tightened on her chin as they stared into each other's eyes, hardly breathing, neither moving.

"Then," he said, his voice raspy, "I'd kiss you . . . without bumping . . . your nose."

"Are you sure you'd miss my nose?" she asked, a thread of breathlessness evident in her voice.

"Trust me."

"I do, Logan. I honestly do."

He was lost. Gone.

A shudder ripped through Logan, and while

his mind roared at him not to do it, he brushed his lips over Amber's, feeling the dewy softness, tasting the hint of sweet nectar, and wanting more, much much more.

When she didn't pull away, he slid his tongue over her bottom lip with gentle insistence in his quest to gain entry to the honeyed darkness within. Amber parted her lips slightly, and he slipped his tongue inside her mouth as his lips covered hers. His hand moved to the back of her neck as the pressure of their mouths increased. Her lashes drifted closed.

Amber felt as though she were floating away from herself as tingling sensations swirled throughout her. The feel of Logan's lips on hers, the rhythmic motion of his tongue dueling with hers was ecstasy. A liquid heat started in the core of her femininity and spread like a rampant brush fire. The sound of her heartbeat echoed in her ears.

And the kiss went on and on.

Logan lifted his head a fraction to draw a ragged breath, then plummeted his tongue deep into Amber's mouth once again. His shoulder throbbed with a steady, painful cadence, but he didn't care. Nothing mattered but kissing this exquisite woman who was responding to him in total abandon.

Lord, how he wanted her!

He wanted to see her naked in the silvery glow of the moonlight, kiss, touch, caress every inch of her silken body. He wanted to fill his hands with her breasts, then move his mouth to their ripeness to suckle like a babe. And then, he would bury himself deep within her honeyed warmth and teach her the dance of lovers. He would be her first, and he would be gentle, patient, lead her safely to that place of oblivion and bring her back, holding her in his arms.

Logan's manhood throbbed with the want and need of Amber Prescott. He was full, hot, heavy and aching for her. He heard a quiet purr of passion escape from her throat, which heightened his own raging desire.

Dear Lord, his mind thundered, he had to stop.

This was an innocent virgin in his arms, who trusted him to do her no harm. Her father and brother were a room away. A father, who had saved Logan's life and brought him into his home. This was no saloon whore he was kissing, wanting, lusting after. Damn it, it was Amber. Beautiful, sweet Amber, who looked like an angel and sang so softly, who deserved better than to have the likes of him kissing and touching her. He had to stop. Now. Before it was too late.

"Amber," he said, tearing his mouth from hers. "No more."

She drew a deep, shuddering breath and stared at him with a smoky brown gaze. "Logan? Oh, Logan, I have never felt so . . . so alive, and strange, and wonderful. And to think I was worried about noses. Thank you for kissing me, Logan."

"Don't say that," he said, running his hand down his glistening face.

"Why not?"

"Damn it, Amber," he said, "I feel guilty enough without you thanking me like I did you a big favor. If you knew what I was thinking, you'd get that rifle from over the mantle and shoot me."

"Don't be silly," she said, trailing her fingertip over his lips. "Your lips remind me of pussy willows. They're so soft, so . . ."

"Go to bed," he said, his jaw clenched. "You have no idea what you're doing to me, and I'm not about to explain *that* to you, too. I shouldn't have kissed you, and it isn't going to happen again."

"It isn't?" she said, an instant frown on her face.

"No."

"I'm sure I'd get better at it once I had more practice."

"Amber, you get any better at kissing, I'll lose my mind. You were wonderful."

"Oh, how nice," she said, smiling at him warmly. "I'm sure you were, too, except I don't have anything to compare it to. I just know I feel very special and, well, different somehow. There was a heat inside me when you kissed me, Logan. Does that make sense?"

"Believe me, it makes sense," he said, sighing and nodding his head.

"Did you feel it, too?"

"Yeah."

"Logan, are you sure you don't think poorly of me because I . . ."

"Amber," he interrupted, placing his hand on her cheek, "I'm very honored to have been the first man to kiss you. But listen to me for a minute. I'm not a boy, I'm thirty-two years old. I'm not accustomed to kissing a beautiful woman and stopping with just that. And you *are* a beautiful woman, Amber Prescott. So, you see, we can't do this again, because I'd go further than I have any right to, and that mustn't happen. What I'd take from you belongs to the man you'll marry. Do you understand?"

"I guess so."

"Good. Will you go to bed now?"

"Yes," she said, getting to her feet. "Do you want me to help you lie back down?"

"No, I'll manage. Really. I can do it."

"All right. Good night, Logan," she said softly, then walked across the room and entered her bedroom, closing the door behind her.

"Good night, Amber," he said, to the silence.

He eased himself back onto the pillow, gripping his shoulder until the pain lessened. Fatigue washed over him with a numbing intensity, and he made no effort to fight the somnolence that claimed him.

One last thought flitted through Logan's

mind before he slept. He had never, *never,* desired a woman the way he did Amber Prescott. And because of that, he had to leave there as quickly as possible.

Amber curled up in a ball in bed, her fingertips pressed to her lips. She could still taste Logan Wade, smell him, feel his rough beard against her soft skin. The memory of their kiss was etched indelibly in her mind, the heated sensations still swirled within her. The wondrous trembling made her shudder with desire.

Oh, what ecstasy it had been to be kissed by Logan. She had never dreamed it would be like that. How childish it now seemed to have fretted about the bumping of noses. She was filled with a sweet ache like nothing she had ever experienced before. Her breasts were heavy as though needing a soothing touch.

But Logan was never going to kiss her again.

She'd understood what he'd been saying to her, she supposed. He didn't just kiss women, he mated with them like the animals in heat. There had to be a more polite way to phrase that, but no one had ever discussed it with her. A woman mated only with her husband, so Logan wouldn't kiss her again.

Amber registered a sense of loss that caused a sob to catch in her throat. She'd had a fleeting glimpse of a new and glorious place, and it was being whisked away before she could explore it further.

She wanted Logan to kiss her again. And again, and again. Oh, dear, was that wanton of her? No, Logan said he didn't think poorly of her for kissing him, but she wasn't planning on telling Nathan Prescott that she'd kissed Logan Wade. It was so very, very sad that Logan's lips would never again touch hers.

With a wobbly sigh, Amber closed her eyes and drifted off into a restless slumber.

The next sensation that Logan registered was the feel of a dry, callused hand on his forehead. His eyes shot open, and he found himself staring up at Nathan Prescott.

"Mornin'," Nathan said, his voice hushed. "Amber and Benny are still asleep. I got up early to tend to you. Imagine you need to relieve yourself. Brought the chamber pot."

"Thanks," Logan said gruffly.

Nathan assisted Logan, and no words were exchanged. Nathan took the chamber pot out the back door, then returned to stoke the fire in the hearth, and set a pot of coffee on the grate. He gathered fresh rags and the sewing shears, then pulled a chair next to the cot.

"Fever's gone," Nathan said, cutting away the bindings. "Infection must be 'bout cured. Yeah, looks better. No need to tie your arm down now that you're not out of your head.

You ought to have the good sense to keep still.
I'll just bandage over the wound. I figure all
you need is rest and food to get your strength
back. I'll get my shaving gear and scrape off
that growth on your face."

"Thanks," Logan said, as Nathan went back
into the bedroom. Ah, hell, he felt guilty as
sin itself. He'd kissed that man's innocent
daughter. Kissed her, and pictured her naked
beneath him as he buried himself in her feminine darkness. If Nathan knew, he'd slit his
throat while he was shaving him.

Nathan returned with a towel, a shaving mug
and brush, and a straight razor. He sat back
down, then shaved Logan with swift expertise,
while Logan lay tense, coiled like a wire, waiting for the razor to slice through his jugular
vein.

"That oughta help make you feel human,"
Nathan said, when he completed his task. He
set the supplies on the floor, crossed his arms
over his chest, and frowned. "Logan," he said,
"you're a long way from being able to leave
here, and you're welcome to stay till you're
back on your feet. There's only one thing I
want to know."

"Yes?"

"You didn't shoot yourself, so there's others
involved. Is my family in danger because you're
here?"

"No, there's no one after me."

"That's all I need to know," Nathan said, nodding.

"You said yourself, Mr. Prescott, I didn't shoot myself. You also saw the gun I wear. Don't you wonder what kind of man I am? I'm here, under your roof."

"You plannin' on doin' us harm, boy?"

"No. No, of course not."

"Well, if you're no danger to us, and there's nobody lookin' for you, I'd say that covers it. I'm not askin' to know your personal business, Logan. I'm just lookin' to protect my family. Oh, and call me Nathan. Your horse is in the barn, your belongings are under the cot. I hear Amber movin' around in her room. She'll be puttin' a fine breakfast on the table right soon. Hungry?"

"Yeah, sure, but . . ."

"Well, she'll fix plenty. She cooks as good as her mama did."

"Mr. . . . Nathan, I owe you a helluva lot. You saved my life and . . . Look, I'll be getting out of your way as soon as I can sit in a saddle."

"Don't rush it, or you'll end up dead in the desert with the buzzards pickin' at your carcass."

"I've got a little money in my saddlebags. Not much, but you're welcome to it," Logan said.

"Not necessary."

"Damn it, quit being so nice to me!"

Nathan chuckled. "Don't you deserve it?"

"Hell, no," Logan said, running his hand down his face.

"Don't fret 'bout it. I'm goin' to go milk me a cow. Be back in shortly," Nathan said, getting to his feet. He glanced up as the bedroom door opened. "Mornin', Amber."

"'Lo, Pa," she said, not looking at him as she smoothed the skirt of her faded pink dress.

"Coffee's set," Nathan said, heading for the door. "Logan there is ready for one of your fine breakfasts. Moses and I will be in directly. Benny's due up any time."

Nathan left the cabin and a heavy silence fell over the room. Amber slowly lifted her head to find Logan looking directly at her.

"Hello, Amber," he said quietly.

"Logan. I see you had a shave."

"Yeah, your pa did it. Feels a lot better. So does this smaller bandage. Amber, about last night. I . . ."

"It's not necessary to discuss it, is it? I mean, is there a rule or something that says we have to talk about it?"

"No," he said, smiling at her, "there's no rule like that."

"Oh, Logan," she said, her voice hushed, "that's the first time I've seen you smile. You really do have a marvelous smile."

He frowned. "We're not discussing my smile, or lack of it. I just don't want you feeling ashamed about what happened last night. I accept full responsibility. You can put it right out of your mind."

"Oh, I couldn't possibly do that," she said, walking to the fireplace. "Since you have no intention of ever kissing me again, I'll have to cherish last night as a precious memory. I will never forget the feel and taste of your lips on mine, Logan. Never."

"Ah, hell," he muttered, closing his eyes. He was in deep trouble. Very deep trouble. Because there was no doubt in his mind that he'd never forget the feel and taste of Amber Prescott, either!

Four

One of the slogans in the West was, "Eat it up, wear it out, make it do." The Prescotts heeded that code. Nothing on the homestead was wasted.

There had been, at one time, three other families within five miles of the Prescotts' land, but the number had dwindled to one. Two of the homesteads stood empty, the new land having defeated those who had come by covered wagon to find their dream. Their hopes shattered by failed crops, weather, and the loneliness of their existence, they headed back from where they had come, the shining light in their eyes for prosperous tomorrows dimmed.

But the Prescotts had stayed and so had their neighbors five miles to the north, the Hunter family. Patricia and Dustin Hunter were in their middle twenties, and had five sons. Nathan often joked that the Hunter boys were peas in a pod, each sporting the bright orange hair and multitude of freckles, as their mother did—all built short and round like their father.

The Hunters struggled to make do on their

homestead, waiting for the day when the boys would be able to further help their father tend the land. The oldest boys were nine-year-old twins, the youngest just taking his first steps. But the Hunters toiled endlessly, facing each day with optimism and hope for better times.

The Prescotts and Hunters traded surplus food to add a variety to their meals, and Amber had watched with loving pride whenever Nathan tucked an extra slab of smoked meat into the Hunters' basket. Patricia raised chickens and provided the Prescotts with eggs and poultry in exchange for corn and meat.

While she was preparing breakfast, Amber's thoughts drifted to Patricia Hunter, who was a friendly, outgoing woman. Her hips had spread with carrying each unborn baby, and she often laughed about not being able to get through the cabin door if she didn't stop having Dustin's babes. She always appeared tired, could pass for ten years older than she was, but there was a continual smile on her face.

If there was one thing Patricia knew, Amber decided, as she set the table, it was about the mating that took place between a man and a woman. After all, Patricia had given herself to Dustin at least five or six times, and had the boys to prove it. What it had required to create twins, Amber didn't know.

Maybe, just maybe, Amber mused, she could muster up the courage to ask Patricia some womanly questions the next time the Hunters came over. Logan's veiled statement that the joining of a man and woman was not like what Amber had witnessed between the animals in heat, was piquing her curiosity beyond endurance.

With a decisive nod, Amber broke eggs into the skillet and fried them over the open flame in the hearth. She began to sing a lighthearted ditty about an elf in the woods, who changed the colors of the leaves with his magic wand. Her husky voice floated through the air, filling the cabin to overflowing with its resonance.

Logan lay on the cot, his good arm under his head as he watched Amber perform her chores. Her soft voice seemed to stroke him like dark velvet, the sultry timbre causing his pulse to quicken. His blue eyes swept over her from head to toe, missing no detail of her enticing figure. A figure he had seen silhouetted to perfection in the silvery luminescence of the moon.

Amber's honey-colored hair was twisted into a tight bun at the nape of her neck, but Logan now knew that her hair was long, very long. He wanted to draw his fingers through those braids, feel the silken strands, watch the cascade fall over her full breasts.

Logan shifted on the cot, his eyes never leaving Amber, as he envisioned her breasts; bare, heavy in his hands, sweet honey in his mouth. His gaze roamed on to the slope of her hips, and his memory gave him the shape of her slender legs he'd seen shadowed beneath her nightgown.

He was drawn again to Amber's lovely face; the large dark eyes, the dusting of freckles across her nose, the flush of the sun's touch on her cheeks. And her lips. Sweet Jesus, those lips. Never had a kiss stirred such instant, heated passion within him. Hers had been the kiss of an innocent, who possessed the instincts of a woman who would not be afraid, nor embarrassed, to give herself to her man in total abandon.

And Logan Wade wanted her.

His manhood stirred and Logan frowned, angry that he was to once again suffer that discomfort in addition to the throbbing pain in his shoulder.

Damn that Amber Prescott and her childish nonsense regarding where noses went when people kissed. It was her fault, all of it. She'd come waltzing out there last night in her thin nightgown, plunked herself down next to him on the cot, then asked her stupid question about noses. He was a man not a saint, and she'd been temptation itself. She'd kindled a fire within him, an aching, burning need, he had no way to extinguish. He wanted her, couldn't have her, and was suddenly mad as hell.

"Damn it," he said.

"Pardon me?" Amber said, turning to look at him.

"My pants," he said, scowling at her. His pants? his mind echoed. "Where in the hell are my pants? I'm sick to death of lying around naked as a buck. I want, I demand, my pants."

Amber placed the plate of eggs on the table, and planted her hands on her hips. "Your pants, Mr. Wade," she said tightly, "are so caked with dirt they could stand in the corner on their own. You may have them once they're washed, which I don't intend to do today."

"Well, hell," he grumbled. "Where's my saddlebags? I have another pair in there. Oh, yeah, Nathan said my things were under the cot."

"So, get them," Amber said, slicing bread with more force than was necessary.

"Fine. I'll just crawl under there with my bare butt waving in the breeze," he said, starting to move back the sheet.

"Halt," Amber said, raising her hand. "Don't you put one foot on the floor. The very idea." She stomped across the room, reached under the cot, then swung the heavy saddlebags up to land with a thud across Logan's knees.

"Ow! Damn it," he roared. "I don't need broken kneecaps to go along with my other problems."

"Your problem, sir," she said, spinning on her heel and returning to the table, "is the state of your disposition. And I would appreciate it if you'd quit swearing every two minutes."

"I'll swear, damn it, whenever I feel like it, Miss Prescott."

"Amber?" Benny said, coming out of the bedroom. "What's all the hollerin' 'bout?"

"Our guest," Amber said, giving Logan a stormy glare, "is not in a sunshine mood."

"You shouldn't rile him, Amber," Benny said in a hushed voice, his eyes wide. "He's liable to shoot you."

"Don't tempt me, kid," Logan said, struggling to sit up as he gripped his shoulder.

"How dare you frighten my brother," Amber said. "Do you kick dogs, too?"

"I'm warning you, Amber," Logan said, waggling a long finger at her, "I've had enough of your . . ."

"Well, well," Nathan said, coming in the door with Moses, "isn't this a happy group? They can probably hear you all the way to Waverly."

"Logan's goin' to shoot Amber, Pa," Benny said, wringing his hands.

"I am not!" Logan yelled.

Nathan chuckled. "What we need here is some food. Breakfast ready, girl?"

"Yes," she said. "Eggs, the rest of the stew, and bread. Sit down and get out of my way. I can't serve this up with everyone milling around."

"Mercy," Moses said, sinking into a chair,

"I'd take on an ornery heifer 'fore I'd cross you this mornin', missy."

"Amen to that," Logan said, nodding his head.

Amber opened her mouth to retort, but Nathan spoke first, a wide grin on his face. "I'll fix Logan's plate. I'll prop your pillow against the wall, and you can eat right there in bed, Logan."

"I should hope so," Amber said, then sniffed indignantly. "The man is naked as a buck, as he's so fond of informing me."

Benny giggled. Amber glared at him.

The conversation during the meal consisted of Nathan and Moses outlining their chores for the day, the emphasis being on continuing to remove the choking weeds from the rows and rows of corn. Amber kept her eyes on her plate, absolutely refusing to look in Logan's direction.

Rude, rude, rude, that's what Logan was, she silently fumed. Imagine throwing a tantrum over a pair of pants. Goodness, he was more handsome than ever, now that he was shaven. Oh, who cared? Handsome or not, he was still rude. But that smile. It had just spread across his face, revealing straight white teeth and crinkly little lines by his beautiful blue eyes. That smile had caused her heart to flutter, and a strange sensation had feathered down her spine. That smile, however, did not erase the fact that Logan Wade was rude.

"Good meal, girl," Nathan said, pushing back his chair and getting up. "Moses, when we come in at noon, bring a chair from the barn. Logan can try sitting up to the table to eat."

"I can hardly wait," Amber said, under her breath.

"I heard that," Logan said.

Nathan chuckled and shook his head.

"Pa," Amber said, "after I clean up here I'm going down to the stream to pick raspberries. I hope I can find my pail."

"Fine," Nathan said. "Just be careful in the cove."

"Oh, I will," she said. "You never know what kind of critter might turn up."

Logan snorted in disgust.

"I'm gettin' out of here," Moses said, heading for the door. "The sparks in this room could start a mighty big brush fire."

"Come on, Benny," Nathan said, laughing. "We'll leave these two to solve their differences."

As Moses disappeared, and Benny ran after him, an expression of concern settled onto Logan's face.

"Nathan," he said, "wait. Amber shouldn't be going to that cove. There's young, renegade Comanches on the loose. They're dangerous because they're not afraid to die for what they believe is just cause for trying to drive the white man off of their land."

"We've had no trouble this far north," Nathan said. "Not even when the Indian raids were at their worst. We heard tell of homesteads being burned, folks killed, or taken captive, but nobody in these parts has been bothered."

"I still don't think that Amber should . . ." Logan started, then stopped. "I'm sorry. I'm overstepping my bounds. It's none of my business."

Nathan looked at Logan for a long moment, nodded, smiled, then left the cabin.

Amber began to clean up the clutter from the meal, totally ignoring Mr. Logan Wade. She heard him moving on the bed and surmised he was rummaging through his saddlebags for his ever-so-important pants, but she didn't look at him.

She scrubbed the dishes in a metal pan to within an inch of their lives, then clanged them into place in the cupboard. The table was wiped up, the floor swept, the chairs pushed neatly in.

She made a trip to the smokehouse and returned with a beef roast, which she set to simmer in a pot over the low fire in the hearth.

Logan was still being rude, Amber decided, staring into the glowing flames. He could speak to her, should apologize for his foul mood and the tangent about his pants. He'd eaten every scrap of his huge breakfast and hadn't uttered one word as to how delicious it was. She'd had quite enough of his insulting silence.

She spun around, dark eyes flashing, then her mouth dropped open. Logan was sound asleep. He was slouched back against the pillow, his neck appearing to be at an uncomfortable angle, a pair of dark pants having fallen to the floor. He had apparently run out of energy, and succumbed to his fatigue.

"Oh, Logan," Amber said, a gentle quality to her voice.

She walked to the edge of the cot and picked up the heavy saddlebags, seeing that the leather buckle was strapped firmly closed. She shoved the double-sided pack under the cot, then folded Logan's pants across the foot.

"Logan," she said, resting her hand on his cheek, "wake up just long enough to shift into a more comfortable position. Logan?"

"Hmmm," he said, slowly lifting his dark lashes. "Hello, angel," he murmured, his voice low and husky with sleep. "Are you going to sing softly for me, Amber?"

She smiled. "Of course, I will, whenever you like. Now, move down a bit before you get a stiff neck."

Logan did as he was instructed, groaning from the effort as he clutched his shoulder.

"Is the pain worse?" she asked, sitting on the edge of the cot.

"No, just not any better. There's no reason that it should be. I'm just not used to being so helpless. I'm sorry I snapped at you earlier. I was taking my problems out on you, and I apologize. And I'm sorry I scared Benny, and I've never kicked a dog in my life. And, Amber? I'm a breath away from kissing you, so you'd better move off this cot, and go pick your raspberries."

Amber's eyes widened. "You're going to kiss me again? But I don't understand, Logan. You said you'd never kiss me again, because you'd want to go on to mating, because that's what you're used to doing with women."

"I don't mate like one of your damn farm animals in heat, Amber," he said, none too quietly.

"Well, what would you call it?" she said, matching his volume.

"Amber," he said, his voice gentling, "when did you lose your mother?"

"Over four years ago on the wagon train coming here from Pennsylvania."

"Didn't she ever explain things to you? You know, man and woman things?"

"No," she said, sighing. "Ma said there was time enough for me to know when I found the man I wanted to marry. Then she'd sit me down and explain it all to me. I figured out the wifely duties part by watching the animals when . . ."

"Yeah, you told me," he said, frowning. "You've got the general idea, but not exactly. I mean, it is the male who . . . But he doesn't . . . Animals are different. They . . . Damn it, why am I having this conversation with you?"

"You started it. You said you were a breath away from kissing me. I simply reminded you that you said you'd want to mate if . . ."

"No, I didn't say that. It's not barnyard rutting, Amber. It's making love. With a whore in a saloon it's plain old sex, but with someone special it's making love. Got that?"

"Making love," Amber said slowly, testing out the sound of the words. "Making love. My, that does have a nice ring to it, doesn't it?"

"It's a helluva lot better than referring to it as being in heat."

"I thoroughly agree," she said, nodding. "Which do you like better? Plain old sex, or making love?"

"Oh, hell," he said, closing his eyes. "I'm never going to survive this. Go pick your raspberries."

"I thought you were going to kiss me."

"I changed my mind," he said, opening his eyes and scowling at her. "We're talking the subject to death."

"Logan, I think I should tell you that I like kissing you very much, I really do. But as far as mating . . . I mean, making love . . . Well, you said yourself that I should only be doing that with my husband. And since I'm not a whore in a saloon I don't do plain old sex, either. So, if you did decide to kiss me again, that's all you could do. Just kiss me."

"I know," he said quietly. "Believe me, Amber, I do know that. You're a beautiful, desirable woman, but I'd never do anything to hurt you. You're so open and honest, and your father is one of the finest men I've ever met. I won't betray your trust, or his."

"Thank you," she said, smiling warmly as she placed her hand on his cheek.

Logan stared at her for a long moment, warring with himself in his mind. He meant it, he told himself, every word. He'd never hurt this delicate, innocent creature, nor mock Nathan's gift of kindness. Logan could kiss Amber Prescott, taste and feel the sweet nectar of her lips, but go no further. He would watch her open her petals like a spring flower, but only so far. The hidden treasure within was not his to have. So be it. He was a man, capable of restraint and self-control, even if it had been a helluva long time since he'd had to use them. Those saloon whores were hotter than a pistol when he . . . No, by damn, he could do it. He could kiss Amber, then stop. And he sure as hell wanted to kiss her.

Logan lifted his right hand and slid it to the back of Amber's head. "Come here," he said, his voice low. "I do want to kiss you, Amber."

She placed her hands flat on the pillow on either side of his head and leaned toward him as the pressure of his hand at the back of her head increased. Her heart was racing with anticipation, with infinite joy that Logan was going to kiss her. What she had thought was never again to be, was about to happen.

"Oh, Logan," she said, close to his lips.

Logan drew the whisper of Amber's breath into his mouth as she spoke his name, then slid his tongue over her bottom lip to sample her sweetness. She parted her lips and their mouths met, tongues darting against the others. The rhythmic motion was matched by a pulsing heat deep within Amber that rambled throughout her. Her knees began to tremble and she pressed them together as she leaned further into Logan, savoring the feel of his mouth moving urgently beneath hers. Her breasts ached, straining against her dress.

As Amber's breasts brushed over his chest, Logan stiffened from the fiery impact of the feathery touch. His manhood stirred beneath the sheet, became full, heated, as his entire body responded to the passionate kiss. He felt as though he were drowning. Drowning in the taste, the feel, the aroma of Amber Prescott. She filled his senses, but even more, she brought a warmth, like rich brandy, to the chill of his soul and mind. He was alive again, whole; the recipient of good instead of evil. He was the teacher of the innocent, rather than the one to learn the brutal lessons of life.

Amber. Logan's mind hummed her name like a litany, his body ached with the want and need of her. The loneliness of the past five years blurred into oblivion, taking with it the memories of what he had done. He was in a home, a real home, that spoke of caring, and he was kissing a woman who was every decent man's dream.

Decent man?

The words pounded against Logan's brain. His past slammed into his mind with haunting pictures, and the icy chill crept back into his soul. With it came the guilt that the woman he was touching and kissing, delicate, innocent Amber, deserved better than what he was.

"Amber," he said, jerking his mouth from hers, "that's all."

He closed his eyes for a moment, striving for control, then opened them again to see her kiss swollen lips, the flush on her cheeks, the smoky haze in her brown eyes. He placed his hand on her shoulder and gently pushed her upward and away from him.

"Oh, Logan," she said, her voice shaky as she slowly sat up, "I feel so . . . so strange, so . . . You didn't tell me that kisses got better and better, that there would be more new sensations inside me than the first time. It's wonderful, but . . . Should I be frightened?"

"Only of me," he said, his voice gritty. "Don't be afraid of what you're feeling. You're a beautiful, passionate woman, who is discovering who you are, the mysteries of . . . well, of being a passionate woman. That's nothing to be ashamed of. But, Amber? I'm the wrong man to be teaching you these things."

"Why?"

Logan frowned. "You come from a different world than I do."

"Pennsylvania?"

"Ah, no, damn it, that isn't what I mean," he said, pushing himself up to lean against the wall. He gritted his teeth as the pain shot through his shoulder, then looked at her, a deep frown on his face. "I'm talking about your world of decency, goodness, this home, your family. You belong here, have earned the right to be a part of all this. I'm an intruder from another place. That doesn't give me the right to touch, to have, what's here. I'll be moving on as soon as I'm able, and when I go I have to leave everything as I found it when I came."

"As though you'd never been here at all?" Amber said, her voice hushed.

"Yeah," he said gruffly.

"But it's too late, Logan. Do you think I'll ever forget your kisses? Forget how you feel and taste, and the things that happen inside me when . . ."

"Stop it," he said, grabbing her arm. "You *will* forget, because it didn't mean a damn thing. So, yeah, you've been kissed a couple of times, but it's not an earth-shattering event. Don't make more out of this than there is. I saw a pretty woman, and I kissed her. Hell, I do it all the time without a second thought. And I've had the ever-famous plain old sex with so many, I can't remember what they looked like."

Quick tears filled Amber's eyes. "Our kisses meant nothing to you?" she asked, hardly above a whisper. "Nothing? How can that be, Logan? You said you were feeling things inside you just like I was."

"Lust," he said, averting his eyes from hers. "That's all, just a man lusting after a woman. There's nothing fancy or special about a couple of kisses, Amber. You've got no complaints. You satisfied your damn curiosity about where noses go when people kiss. We both enjoyed it, it's over, so forget it. Just forget the whole damn thing."

Tears spilled onto Amber's cheeks as she stumbled to her feet. She brushed them angrily away and turned to face Logan, who was scowling at a spot on the far wall.

"I understand now, Mr. Wade," she said, her voice trembling. "I was available, and you were getting bored just lying around with nothing to do. So, why not kiss silly little Amber? How did you keep from laughing right out loud? How childish of me to think that what we shared held any importance for you. Well, don't give it another thought, as I certainly don't intend to."

Ah, Amber, no, Logan's mind thundered. He was hurting her so badly, but he had no choice. He was hurling a pack of brutal lies at her for her own good. But, damn it, he didn't want her to cry. He'd never meant to make her cry.

"I'm going to go pick my raspberries now," Amber said, walking slowly toward the door. "Know what I think, Logan? I realize you've had plain old sex so many times that you've lost count. But I believe you've never made love, because your heart would be involved as well as your body. I feel sorry for you, Logan, I really do."

Logan's head snapped around and his blue eyes flashed with anger, but before he could speak, Amber disappeared out the cabin door. He whipped back the sheet and reached for his pants where they lay on the foot of the cot. His abrupt motions sent spasms of pain through his shoulder, and he welcomed its existence as he wrestled with the pants, struggling to draw them on with one hand. Sweat beaded his brow, the pain increased, and his mind told him he deserved to suffer with every move he made.

He'd hurt Amber Prescott, he knew it, and despised himself for it. The kiss of moments before had shattered every resolve he had made to kiss her, but go no further. He didn't possess the self-control he'd given himself credit for having. Amber had responded even more freely to his touch than the first time, and he'd drunk of her sweetness like a dying, thirsty man. He couldn't trust himself around Amber, and the realism of that fact felt like a knife twisting in his gut. He was a bastard, no doubt about it.

Swearing in a steady stream, Logan managed to button his pants, then collapsed on the cot, exhausted, drained, riddled with pain. He closed his eyes, only to see in his mental vision, the tears shimmering in Amber's eyes. Tears caused by him.

If only she hadn't cried.

He wanted to go after her, tell her that he'd been lying, that their kisses shared had been like none before. He wanted to bring a smile back to her face, and hear her sing a happy song with her soft, husky voice. He'd kiss away her tears, hold her, tell her how beautiful, special, rare she was, and mean every word of it, because it was true. Her big brown eyes would be warm, her smile for him alone, her laughter his own precious gift.

"Ah, Amber," he said.

He pushed himself up to a sitting position and swung his feet to the floor. He lunged upward, then staggered to the table as dizziness washed over him. His chest was heaving as he sank into a chair and laid his right arm on the table, his forehead resting on his clenched fist.

Amber's words hammered at him, and there was nowhere to go to escape from the truth of what she had said. He had never made love. Not once in his entire life had he experienced

anything more with a woman than a physical
release of sexual tension. He'd never thought
about it, it had never mattered before.

Making love, his mind whispered. What
would it be like to take a woman he really
cared about? Take? No, maybe not. There
would be a giving involved, an assurance of her
pleasure first. His woman would have everything he had to offer. Amber would call his
name in a passion-laden voice, and he'd come
to her, take her to a place she'd never been
and bring her safely back. He'd bury himself
deep within her, and plant his seed to create
a child. He'd . . .

"For God's sake, Wade," he said, lifting his
head. He was crazy. He'd heard about men
who'd gone crazy from raging fevers. Their
brains fried, turning them into lunatics. Picturing Amber as his woman, his special woman,
making love with her, creating a baby within
her wasn't sane. "Yes, it is," he mumbled. Oh,
it was sane, all right. It was like one of those
elusive dreams that he'd given up on long ago,
shadowy thoughts of how different his life
might have been, a moment of self-pity for all
he didn't have, would never have. Well, enough
of that. He wasn't sitting around feeling sorry
for himself.

What had Amber said? *She* felt sorry for *him*?
Who in the hell did she think she was saying
such a thing? Kiss a woman a couple of times,
and she gets all uppity, considers herself a

know-it-all capable of seeing into his soul. Hell. Who had ever heard of feeling sorry for a man because he'd never made love with a special woman? He'd like to tell Amber Prescott what she could do with her almighty pity.

Well, he thought dryly, he wasn't going to get the chance to tell Amber anything, because she'd probably never speak to him again. But that was for the best, it really was. He'd leave as quickly as possible, and she'd forget he'd ever been there. Forget that he'd kissed her. Forget what he looked like, and not even remember his name.

"Fine," Logan said, nodding. That was exactly how it should be. Some young buck would come along and marry her, give her a houseful of pretty babies. She'd hold her babe to her breast and sing softly as she nursed while rocking in that chair by the hearth. Amber's smile, her kiss, her body, would belong to another man. So be it.

And the picture of it all in his mind brought on the darkest depression Logan Wade had ever known.

Five

Texas, in 1875, was a vast, sweeping expanse of land of such magnitude it was beyond the comprehension of many who traveled it. It was also a blend of the old and the new, depending on the proximity to the railroad. The Texas and Pacific Railroad chugged its way from New Orleans through Dallas and Ft. Worth, while the Southern Pacific line connected San Antonio to Houston. The tracks meshed at El Paso and moved westward.

But in the strip of land in northern Texas where the Prescotts had homesteaded, there was no railroad supplying the nearest town of Waverly. Wagons loaded to overflowing arrived in Waverly on sporadic visits, bringing the latest goods purchased in the larger, railroad-fed cities. A trip to Waverly was always considered an exciting event for the Prescotts, as they never knew what surprises awaited them there.

Amber knew the code of the West that dictated that men reached out their hand to help one another. And she knew her father with his wise and gentle ways, who would break in half his last crust of bread before he'd see a man go hungry.

Deep within her, she was not surprised that Nathan had brought the injured Logan Wade into their home, and offered him refuge for as long as he required it. That Nathan and Moses were convinced that Logan was a gunfighter, would make no difference to Nathan while Logan was in need of assistance.

All these things were true, Amber knew, but as she left the cabin hurt and angry from the impact of Logan's chilling words, she irrationally decided that her upset was the fault of her father for leaving her in charge of the care of one such as Logan.

Her heart ached and her steps were leaden as she walked in the direction of the cove. A wobbly sob escaped from her lips, and a single tear slid down her cheek. She couldn't, wouldn't, think about the kisses she had shared with Logan, she vowed, nor the wondrous trembling and yearning deep within her that his kiss and touch had evoked. She was a jumbled mass of confusion and fear, and simply couldn't face herself and what she had done.

It was too cold, too heartless of Logan to have kissed her, then dismissed the enchanting events as meaningless, something as common to him as waking up in the morning.

Their lips had touched, she mentally argued, and their tongues, and her breasts had brushed against his chest. How could that mean nothing to him? To her it was the most glorious experience of her life; a private, treasured, sharing episode between herself and a man who was like none she had ever seen, or met, before.

She had stepped over an invisible line to enter the world where Logan stood. She had been a woman, kissing her man, and rejoicing in the new sensations that had stirred within her. And to Logan it had meant nothing?

"I'll shoot him with his own gun," Amber said, quickening her step.

"Amber girl," Nathan called from the cornfield. "Wait!"

Amber shielded her eyes against the sun with her hand, and saw Nathan hurrying toward her. She planted her fists on her hips, pursed her lips, and tapped her foot impatiently as she watched him approach.

"Whew," Nathan said, stopping in front of her. "That sun is mighty hot already. Goin' to be a scorcher. Well, girl, you look ready to chew nails. Your mama used to say it was better to spit roses."

"I would not have believed," she said, "that Nathan Prescott would have left his only daughter, his dear, sweet, only daughter, to care for, alone . . . alone, I say, the likes of Logan Wade."

Nathan whooped with laughter, then struggled to control it in the next instant as he saw Amber's fury build.

"I'll walk you to the cove," he said. His expression was serious, but his eyes danced with merriment.

"Fine," she said, then spun around and stomped off.

Nathan shook his head and grinned as he slowly followed her. "Kissed ya, did he?" he said.

Amber stopped so quickly she nearly toppled over. Her back was ramrod stiff, her arms straight at her sides, hands clenched into fists. She whirled to face Nathan, her dark eyes flashing.

"What . . . did . . . you . . . say?" she said, eyes narrowing to slits.

Nathan ambled up to her. "I figure Logan kissed ya, that's all. Would take more than his foul mood at breakfast to get you in such a state. Wouldn't surprise me none, if he kissed you. He's a healthy, young, lusty buck. He'd know a beautiful woman when he saw one."

"I'm not a beautiful woman," Amber yelled. "I'm your baby daughter."

Nathan smiled at her gently. "Let's go into the cove, Amber," he said. "It's cooler in there, and I want to talk to you a bit."

"But . . ."

"Come on," he said, circling her shoulders with his arm and leading her toward the thick trees.

Amber's cheeks flushed with embarrassment as she stole a glance at her father from beneath her lashes. He knew. Nathan Prescott knew she'd been kissing Logan Wade. Oh, merciful heaven, this was terrible. What would her pa think of her now? What was he going to say to her? How was she going to explain her wanton ways to him?

Nathan moved on through the trees to the edge of the stream, where he splashed water on his face, then drank his fill from cupped hands. Amber retrieved her pail that had come to rest at the trunk of a tree, and glanced nervously at her father as he pushed himself to his feet.

"Let's rest our backs against that tree," he said.

"Yes, Pa." She settled on the ground next to him and leaned against the prickly bark.

Several long, agonizing minutes passed, and Amber was sure Nathan would hear the rapid thud of her heart.

"Logan Wade," Nathan finally said quietly, causing Amber to jump. "Did he kiss you, girl?"

Amber swallowed heavily. "Yes, Pa," she said, hardly above a whisper.

"Was it the first time you'd been kissed by a man?"

"Yes, Pa."

"Figured it was. How'd you feel 'bout it, Amber?"

"Wonderful," she said dreamily. Nathan chuckled. "No," she added quickly, "not exactly wonderful. I mean, after all, how important can a kiss be? I don't intend to give those two kisses a second thought."

"Two, is it?" Nathan said, grinning at her.

"Do you think poorly of me, Pa?" She stared at her hands that were clutched tightly in her lap.

"No, Amber, I don't think poorly of you. I'd never do that. I've felt mighty bad that you don't have a husband and babes by now. I've needed you here to tend to the woman's work, and you've missed out on a lot of things. It's time you knew that you're a woman, a beautiful one like your ma, and I figured Logan would make it clear to you. I'm bettin' he kissed you, then said he'd take no more than that from you."

"Yes, Pa, he said exactly that."

Nathan nodded. "I know you're wonderin' why I left you alone with Logan." He paused. "I trust him, Amber."

"You said he was a gunfighter."

"Maybe he is, maybe he isn't. All I know is, I sense something about that boy, see things in his eyes, that remind me of . . . well, of myself, many, many years ago."

"What?" Amber said, sitting bolt upward. "You never wore a gun like that or . . ."

"Oh, but I did," Nathan said. "Yep, I slung it low on my hip and tied it down with a rawhide strap. I was fast on the draw, too. 'Course now, I had a reason for that gun, I told myself, because I was a deputy sheriff in the Kansas

territory. I killed men, Amber, when they drew
on me first, but I can't say it bothered me
none to see a man die from my gun."

"Oh, Pa," she said, her eyes wide. "I never
knew you were . . . I mean . . . land's sake, I
don't know what to say."

"Your pa was a gun-totin', lusty buck,"
Nathan said, laughing softly at his memories.

"Pa!"

" 'Tis true. But then, Amber girl, I met your
mama. Oh, Lordy, she was a pretty thing, like
a china doll. I'd tip my hat to her on the street
and she'd smile. That smile of hers warmed
me through better than barroom brandy. She
wasn't much over sixteen years old, and had
laughter dancing in her eyes, and goodness in
her soul. I'd lay in my bed at night thinkin'
of her, imaginin' what it would be like to have
her in my arms."

"Really?" Amber said. Pa? Pa having lusty,
randy thoughts? Mercy.

"Know what I discovered 'bout myself, girl?
I was lonely. Lordy, was I ever lonely. The cold
metal of a gun don't bring no comfort to a
man in the dark hours of the night. And so,
I took to courtin' your ma, not knowin' if she'd
give the time of day to a man who'd killed,
and had a reputation for visitin' the saloon
whores more than most."

"What did Mama say, Pa?" Amber said,
scrambling to her knees.

"She looked up at me just as feisty as you

please and said, 'I already picked you for my own, Nathan Prescott, but I won't be havin' the father of my babes totin' no gun other than the rifle in the boot of his saddle.' "

"She said that? My mama?"

Nathan chuckled. "She surely did," he said smiling gently. "Lordy, I was the happiest man in Kansas. I hung up my gun, and married my darlin' Mary. We went to Pennsylvania to homestead. We had a good life, and I miss her to this day."

"Oh, Pa, I know you do," Amber said, placing her hand on his arm.

"Like I said, girl, I see myself in Logan. I sense the goodness in him, and the loneliness. I can *feel* his loneliness, Amber. If Logan Wade says he'll kiss you but take no more, then I believe him. It's time you were kissed, knew about the womanly feelings in you."

"I felt strange when he kissed me, Pa. Wonderful and strange," she whispered. "It was like nothing I had ever imagined. But then . . . then Logan said hateful things about it meaning nothing, because he goes around kissing women all the time. I felt as though my heart was splintering into a million pieces."

"Logan know you'd never been kissed before?"

"Well, yes, because I was asking him about noses and . . . Yes, he knows."

"Then I'd say his conscience gave him a quick kick in the butt. Amber girl, I'd bet my last dollar that I'm not wrong about Logan. I know we found him with a bullet in him and a gun on his hip, but there's just cause for it, I know there is. Don't take harshly what he said about kissin' you. Give him a chance to sort things through a bit. Understand?"

"I guess so. But, Pa, he's going to be leaving here as soon as he's able. I think about that and I get so sad, I truly do."

"He's a long way from sittin' in a saddle, girl. Don't be lookin' for misery that isn't here. There's no tellin' what the future holds. Now then, you pick your raspberries, and I'll get back to the field. And, Amber? You *are* a beautiful woman. You'll always be my baby daughter, too. I'm mighty proud of you girl, mighty proud."

"Oh, Pa," she said, flinging her arms around his neck, "I love you so much. Thank you for telling me about you and Mama, and for not thinking poorly of me for kissing Logan."

"You're a good girl," he said, patting her back. "Remember that you're a Prescott, and you won't be doin' no wrong at all. But sometimes, Amber, what we've always thought to be wrong, really isn't. That might not make sense to you right now but . . . Well, time will tell. I'll see you at the cabin later."

"Bye, Pa," she said, watching as he left the cove.

She sank back against the tree and closed her eyes, her mind whirling from the story

Nathan had told her of his youth, of the man he had been. How difficult it was to picture him young and wild, she mused, wearing a gun, spending time in rowdy saloons.

And Nathan saw himself in Logan. Logan was lonely? Logan, who bragged about how many women he knew and had mated with? And Logan had said those dreadful things to her because he was feeling guilty about kissing her? Well, she had kissed him, too, so if there was blame to be placed it was partly hers.

Oh, so much was happening to her so quickly, she thought, and she couldn't understand it all. She wanted to turn back time, come to the cove to pick raspberries, and not find an injured man lying by the stream.

No, that wasn't totally true. If Logan hadn't been there, he couldn't have kissed her later. He couldn't have looked at her with his beautiful blue eyes, and made her blood hum in her veins. She would not have had the wondrous glimpse of the woman within herself.

Amber sighed and pushed herself to her feet. She began to pick the lush juicy raspberries, but they all went into the pail, her appetite for the sweet treat nowhere in evidence.

Her mind flitted between the amazing story Nathan had related of his youth, and then to Logan. Questions beat against her brain. Who was Logan? she wondered. Who had shot him, and why? Was he truly good as Nathan had so adamantly stated? Was Logan lonely? And, oh, dear heaven, was it possible that the kisses they had shared *had* meant something to him?

Give Logan a chance to sort things through, Pa had told her, and she would, Amber decided. Yes, she'd do just as Pa had said. She'd never known Nathan Prescott to be wrong about a man, and that meant that she had chosen wisely when allowing Logan to be the first man to kiss her. That was a comforting thought, and Lord knew she could use one to help ease the jumbled maze in her mind.

Slowly, the heavy ache of pain in Amber's heart ebbed, and she began to pop raspberries into her mouth as she continued to fill her pail.

She hummed the tune of her bawdy song, then started back to the cabin. There was a lightness to her step now as she swung the pail at her side, her face tilted upward to feel the heat of the sun on her skin.

A soft smile was on her lips.

She was going home, to Logan.

"Riders comin'," Moses yelled. "Can see the dust. There's riders comin'."

Amber was snapped out of her dreamy state, and she stopped in her tracks. She turned toward the field of corn, and saw the billow of dust in the distance. It was too big, she knew, to be the Hunters arriving in their wagon, too big for one man, who might be in search of fresh water.

Nathan, Benny, and Moses emerged from the

tall stalks of corn, and began to run in her direction where she stood halfway between the cornfield and the cabin.

"Get to the cabin, Amber," Nathan called.

"Why?" she shouted. "What . . ."

"Amber," Logan bellowed, from the doorway of the cabin. "Come on. Hurry up."

"Well, land's sake," she said.

She wrapped one arm around the pail of raspberries, placed her other hand flat on the top of the sweet fruit to keep it in place, and began to run. Her dress flapped against her ankles, slowing her pace. She reduced her speed to a walk as she came near the cabin, her heart pounding and her cheeks flushed from the heat.

"Inside," Logan said.

She came to a dead stop and stared at him. He was leaning against the frame for support in the open doorway. And in his right hand was his gun, the sun glinting off the shiny metal.

"Dear heaven," she whispered.

"Damn it, Amber," he said. "Get in here."

Amber didn't move. Her feet refused to obey the foggy command from her brain as she continued to stare at the gun in Logan's hand.

Nathan, Benny, and Moses came thundering up behind her. Nathan grabbed Amber's arm, and nearly hauled her off her feet as he moved her along with him.

"Pa, what . . ." she said, coming out of her semi-trance.

"Hush, girl," he said. "Can't tell who they are, Logan," he went on, when they stopped in front of the cabin doorway.

"How many rifles do you have?" Logan said.

"Just the one over the mantle. It's loaded, ready to fire. I shoot straighter than Moses."

Logan nodded. "Everyone inside. Close the shutters on the windows. Nathan, get the rifle and stay by one window, Moses can stand by the other. Amber, Benny, keep down and out of the way. Moses, if need be, get my rifle from under the cot."

"Forevermore," Amber said. "Isn't this a lot of fuss considering we don't even know who's coming?"

"That, Amber," Logan said, shifting his weight slightly against the doorframe, "is exactly the problem. Whoever it is, that dust cloud says there's more than a few of them. Now shut up, and get inside like you've been told."

Amber stomped passed him, shooting him a dark glare. "Yes, sir, Mr. Wade. I might say, though, that you won't be doing anyone much good when you pass out cold on your face from standing on your feet too long with your almighty gun in your hand."

"Amber, that's enough," Nathan said. He got the rifle down from above the mantle. "Sit down on the floor with Benny."

"Amber?" Benny said, his voice shaking. "How come we gotta do this? I'm scared, Amber. Who's out there in that dust?"

Amber put one arm around Benny's shoulders and pulled him close to her. "Probably a couple of cowhands herding some cattle toward a homestead, Benny. Sit down here on the floor with me. This is a big to-do over nothing, you'll see." They settled onto the floor.

Moses closed the shutters and stood by one set of windows. Nathan went to the other set. Logan remained in the open doorway.

"You holdin' up okay, Logan?" Nathan said.

"Yeah," he said, sweat glistening on his bare torso. "They're coming around the corn now." He paused. "Army blues."

"The army?" Nathan said, peering out through a crack in the shutters. "Yep, sure enough. 'Bout a dozen of 'em. Never seen 'em this far north."

"Uniforms don't mean a thing," Logan said. "It's not that hard to get your hands on army uniforms. Stay out of sight, and let me do the talking."

"Are you saying they might be outlaws wearing army uniforms?" Amber said.

"Maybe, maybe not," Logan said.

"Amber?" Benny said.

"Shh," she said, tightening her hold on him. "Everything's going to be fine, Benny." Wasn't it? Oh, dear Lord, please let everything be all right. Logan was standing in clear view in the doorway. What if those men really were outlaws and . . . She couldn't bear it if anything happened to Logan. He had that God-awful gun in his hand, he was too weak to be on his feet this long, and . . . Oh, Logan. Logan! "Don't worry, Benny."

The pounding sound of horses drew nearer, and Amber's heart seemed to match the thudding tempo, beat by racing beat. The horses were stilled, several snorting, others whinnying.

Logan shifted again, straightening his stance, the gleaming gun in his hand pointed at the men Amber couldn't see.

"Well, hell's fire and more," a voice said. "Damned if it isn't Logan Wade. Figured you must have become buzzard bait by now, Wade."

Logan lowered the gun to his side. "Hello, Mercer. You're a long way from home."

"That's the truth. We're tired and dry. Can we water our horses?"

Logan nodded.

"All right, men," Mercer said. "Dismount. Water your horses, fill your canteens. Take a rest in the shade, but don't touch what isn't yours, or leave any debris on the ground."

Amber leaned to one side, trying to get a glimpse of the man named Mercer, but could only hear the murmur of voices, creaking of saddles, and the ongoing snorting of horses. A shadow fell over Logan, but she still couldn't see the man whom Logan obviously knew.

"This your homestead, Logan?" Mercer said.

"No. What are you doing up this way?"

"Comanches," Mercer said. "Renegades causing problems for homesteaders. They're burning, killing, just won't settle down and accept the changes. Most of the trouble has been over the border in Arizona, but we're keeping a close watch on the situation. I've seen you look better. Catch a bullet?"

"Yep. So you haven't spotted any Comanches this far north?"

"No. We're patrolling up here, looking for tracks, then we'll move on down south. This is a nice place. Whose is it?"

"Come in," Logan said, stepping back. "Open the shutters, Nathan, Moses. Amber, you and Benny can get up. This man is worthless, but he's regulation army."

Mercer chuckled and stepped inside the cabin, taking off his hat in the process. Amber got to her feet, still holding Benny close to her side. Her gaze slid over the dusty soldier who had entered.

He was, she decided, about Logan's age, was tall with blond hair, and a very handsome face. He had a trim, muscular body, accentuated by the cut of his uniform.

"This is Captain Jim Mercer," Logan said. "Jim, this is Nathan Prescott, Moses, Amber and Benny Prescott. This is their homestead."

Jim Mercer shook hands with Nathan, then Moses, and nodded at Amber. "Ma'am," he said, smiling at her. "Mr. Prescott," he went on, redirecting his attention to Nathan, "we appreciate your letting us rest here a spell and water our horses. My men won't disturb you in any way."

"You're more than welcome to what's here," Nathan said. "We're just surprised that there's army up this way."

Logan wiped a line of sweat from his brow with his thumb. "I think I'll sit down."

"Let's all sit," Nathan said. "Amber, would you fix a pot of coffee?"

"Yes, Pa." She nodded, then glanced down, realizing she was still clutching the pail of raspberries. "I could make raspberry pies for your men, Captain."

"That's very kind of you, ma'am," he said, smiling at her again, "but we won't be here that long. We've got a lot of ground to cover before nightfall."

"Can I go watch the soldiers and stuff?" Benny said. "I never saw a bunch of soldiers."

"Just don't get in their way," Nathan said.

" 'Kay," Benny said, then ran out the door.

The four men sat down at the table, while Amber busied herself making the pot of coffee. Logan and Nathan set the guns in the center of the table.

"Sure wish you were up to par, Logan," Jim Mercer said. "I could use your kind of tracking on this. Can you sit a saddle?"

Amber spun around from the hearth. "No, he certainly can't. He's probably set himself back by being on his feet too long as it is. Land's sake, Captain Mercer, I'd think you could see that he's in no condition to . . ."

"Amber," Logan said gruffly, "you've made your point quite clear."

"Oh." She turned back to the fire.

"Well, well, well," Jim said, grinning at Logan, "that's very interesting. You surely are being tended to mighty fine here, Logan. Ah, yes, there's nothing better than being fussed over by a beautiful woman. I'm amazed that you were slow enough on the draw to stop a bullet, but you sure did pick a good place to recuperate. I swear, Logan, you live under a lucky star."

"Shut up, Mercer," Logan said.

Jim laughed, and Nathan joined him. Moses smiled. Logan glared at each in turn. Amber pulled cups from the cupboard and plunked them onto the table.

Darn right, she was tending to Logan Wade just fine, Amber fumed. Why everyone thought that was something to laugh about, she didn't know. Logan looked like a brewing storm, but the others were having a roaring good time and . . . Beautiful woman? Captain Mercer had said she was a beautiful woman. Logan had said it, and her pa, too. Could it be true? Was she, Amber Prescott, with her wild, old-corn colored hair, and freckles on her nose, truly beautiful? No. Well, maybe . . . just maybe . . . yes.

"Could we talk business here?" Logan said, his frown firmly in place.

"Sure enough," Jim said, controlling his merriment. His smile faded, and a serious expression settled over his features. "Feels good to be out of that saddle. There's tension in the air, Logan, things brewing with the renegades, and we never know where it's going to flare up. I used to envy you, the way you'd turn up, track for the army until you had enough money to suit you, then disappear again to God only knows where. There's times I'm more than ready to shuck this uniform. But . . ." He shrugged. ". . . I'll stick it out for another hitch. Been a soldier since I was sixteen, and it's really the only life I know."

Amber set the coffeepot in the center of the table. Nathan filled the cups. Amber settled into the rocking chair.

"My advice to you folks," Jim Mercer went on, "is to stay alert. You may not have any trouble from the Comanches, but it's best to be prepared. Keep a rifle next to you while you're working your fields. Set up a warning system that tells each of you to head for the cabin."

"Fair enough," Nathan said, nodding.

"If the Comanches come," Jim continued, "make your early shots count before they have a chance to set fire to the cabin. You've got an edge in that Logan's the best man with a gun that I've ever seen. Remember that general who offered to hire your gun, Logan? Lord, he was furious when you said you weren't a gunfighter for hire no matter how many brass buttons he had. Tracking for the army, yes, but you didn't hire out your gun. The old man turned purple."

"Facts are facts," Logan said quietly.

Logan Wade was not a gunfighter, Amber's heart sang. She'd known it all along, and now she was hearing it said in words.

Jim chuckled. "You gotta admit, Wade, that you strap that gun low like a gunfighter, can outdraw anyone I've known. Can't blame the general for coming to the conclusion that he did."

"I set him straight."

"That you did, friend." Jim drained his coffee cup, then got to his feet. "Best be moving on. Sure fine to see you, Logan. Mr. Prescott, thanks for your hospitality. Ma'am," he said, directing his attention to Amber, "don't take any nonsense from this surly brute. He can be as ornery as the day is long. I expect you've got him firmly in hand, though. Beautiful women have a way of being able to do that. Good day to y'all."

"Good-bye, Captain Mercer," Amber said.

The men left the cabin, Nathan taking the rifle with him. Amber was left alone with her thoughts. She replayed in her mind every word Jim Mercer had said about Logan, savoring them, holding them within her like precious treasures.

"Mount up, men," Jim Mercer yelled outside. "Let's ride out."

In a few minutes, the sound of galloping horses reverberated through the air. And then, all was silent. Logan came back into the cabin, and dropped heavily onto a chair at the table.

"At any sign of trouble, fire one shot," he said, his voice weary. "Your pa will do the same. If you're away from the cabin, get back here fast. Take a rifle when you go to the cove. Better yet, don't go to the cove alone at all."

"But . . ."

"Don't argue with me now, Amber." He placed his right arm on the table and rested his forehead on it. "Yell at me later, after I've rested."

Within moments, his deep, even breathing told Amber that Logan was asleep. She sighed, then moved to the side cupboard where she rinsed the raspberries in clear water. She worked as quietly as possible, not wishing to disturb Logan. Gathering the supplies she needed to make the pies, she set about her task, her back to him.

Yet, she could feel his presence even as he slept. She was aware of his strength, the aura of power surrounding him, and could not push far from her mind the memory of his lips on hers. What she had told her father had been true. The mere flicker of the thought of Logan leaving brought a wave of icy misery washing over her. No, she didn't know what the future held, but of one thing she was very certain. Because of Logan Wade, she would never be the same again.

An hour later, Logan stirred, groaned, and opened his eyes, wondering for a moment where he was. He lifted his head and saw Amber. He started to speak to her, then hesitated, reliving in his mind the cruel words he had hurled at her before Jim Mercer had arrived.

Her back was to him, and he wanted to postpone the moment when he might once again see tears shimmering in her eyes. Those tears had cut him to the quick, to his very soul. Amber was not meant to cry; she should smile, laugh, and sing softly. That he had caused her tears, was yet another guilt he would have to bear.

As Logan sat up straighter, the chair moved slightly, and Amber turned at the sudden noise.

"Oh, you're awake," she said, smiling at him. "I was trying to be quiet, but I'm afraid I did bang the pans a bit." Patience, Amber, she told herself. She had to let Logan think things through like Pa had said. "Feeling better?"

"Yeah," he said, frowning. She was smiling? What had she done? Decided he was right? Dismissed their kisses as unimportant, and put the whole thing out of her mind? Like hell she would. He was the first man to kiss her, by God, and she wasn't going to treat him, and what they had shared, so lightly. No, sir.

"I'm making raspberry pies, Logan," Amber said pleasantly. "I hope you like raspberries. These are the biggest, juiciest ones I've seen. Would you like a cup of cool water? It's awfully warm in here."

"Yeah," he said, squinting at her. "Water." Was she putting up a brave front, pretending as though she hadn't been upset? Well, pride he could understand only too well. Lord knew where his sense of pride had taken him; on a road through hell.

"Here," she said, placing a mug in front of him. "Maybe I'll make three pies. I'll have enough berries if I stretch them a bit."

"You don't have to chatter on for my benefit, Amber," Logan said quietly, after draining the mug.

"I was just making conversation," she said, halting in her work to look at him.

"Would you like to talk about it?" he said. "Would that help?"

"Talk about what?"

"Damn it," he said, smacking the table with his palm. "Oh-h," he moaned, clutching his shoulder. "Oh, damn."

"That was a dumb thing to do," she said, frowning at him.

"Amber," he said, gritting his teeth against the pain, "you left here crying before the soldiers came, and now you're as happy as a bee on a marigold. I know I hurt you, so you don't have to pretend that I didn't."

"Well, you see, Logan, tears often have a way of washing away what's troubling a person. It's sort of like rain, clearing away the dust, making things fresh again. I appreciate your concern, but it isn't necessary."

"Meaning?" he said, his voice rising again. "That you've forgotten our kisses like so much dust and dirt?"

"Well," she said slowly, ladling berries into the dough-lined pan.

"Damn you, Amber, those kisses were special. They were special to you because they were your first, and to me because I was the man you chose to find out where the damn noses go. And . . . and because I've never kissed anyone like you before; someone sweet, and innocent, and so damn beautiful. So don't you dare say those kisses weren't important, or I'll shake you until your teeth rattle."

Amber smiled. It was a soft smile, a gentle and serene smile. It was a smile of understanding, infinite wisdom. It was the smile of a woman.

She looked at Logan and saw the total man; the strength in his massive body, his blue eyes that could be piercing cold with a winter chill beneath the surface, then change to fathomless smoky depths laden with heated passion.

She'd heard his voice roaring with anger, trembling with pain, then the soft sound it became when he breathed her name. He was power and pride, arrogance and sensitivity, combined to create a virility that was exciting and threatening.

He was Logan Wade.

And she loved him.

She had emerged, she knew, from the cocoon of her childhood, spread her wings like the most delicate, beautiful butterfly. She was woman. It was as glorious as the most breathtaking sunrise announcing a beginning, a newness like none before.

Her body hummed with the pure joy of the realism of where she had been, and where she now had gone. She had stepped across a threshold that held mysteries she wished to explore further, knew there were discoveries to be made, treasured, held fast in her heart. What had been shadowy unknowns were now bathed in golden sunlight, beckoning to her to come closer yet.

And she was in love with Logan Wade.

Logan watched the play of emotions on Amber's face and squinted at her, searching for a clue as to what she was thinking. He had the strange feeling that while she was standing there before him, she really wasn't there at all, but had drifted away to a place known only to herself. Her expression had been one of wonder, awe, then settled into . . . smug? No, not smug. It was . . . serene, peaceful, and there was a gentle quality to her lovely features.

What in the hell was the matter with her? Logan wondered. Why didn't she say something? He wasn't sure he liked that smile, as it spoke of a wisdom he hadn't seen before. Her dark eyes seemed to be seeking and finding the path to his soul, and an eerie spell had fallen over the cabin, erasing time. Damn it, he'd had enough of this.

"I best get this pie in the Dutch oven," Amber said. She picked up the pan and left the cabin, leaving Logan scowling after her.

He pushed himself to his feet and returned to the cot, stretching out and staring at the ceiling. Amber returned, then took the second pie to the oven. Logan heard her come back in and begin to clean up from her cooking, but he didn't look at her.

Damn it, he thought, what was going on inside Amber Prescott's head?

He felt as if the cabin were closing in around him, making it difficult to breathe. He leveled himself upward, then got to his feet.

"I'm going outside," he said gruffly. "I need some fresh air."

"Oh," Amber said, turning to face him. "Well, would you like me to take a chair out there for you?"

"No."

"The sun is moving over a bit. There's shade on the side of the cabin."

"I'm perfectly capable of recognizing shade when I see it, Amber."

"Yes, of course, you are," she said pleasantly.

"And don't tell me I'm too weak to be moving around this much, because a man knows his own body and what he can do."

"I don't doubt that for a minute. I'm sure you know exactly what you're doing. If you say you're strong enough to take a stroll, then by all means do precisely that."

"Damn it, Amber, what's with you?" he yelled.

"Pardon me?" she said, raising her eyebrows.

"Ah, hell, forget it," he said, walking across the room and out the door.

There was a lovely smile on Amber's face as she watched Logan leave. Then she resumed her chores, humming softly.

Outside, Logan filled his lungs with fresh air. The weather was still humid and hot, but was better than the stale heat in the cabin. He glanced toward the barn and had the urge to see Thunder, to know that the horse was safe.

He gauged the distance to the building, felt the tremor of weakness in his legs, then clenched his jaw and started forward. Halfway there, his body was glistening with sweat, his shoulder throbbing with pain, but he moved on, his bare feet stirring the hot, dusty soil.

Inside the barn, he went to the stall where Thunder stood, and rested his head on the broad back of the horse.

"How you doing, boy?" he said. "They treating you all right? Yeah, you look fat and sassy."

With a weary, painful sigh, Logan sat down and leaned his head against the wooden panel, shutting his eyes. He waited until the pain subsided, then opened his eyes again to look up at the huge horse.

"Fine fix I got us into, right, boy?" he said. "Well, I guess you're not complaining. I'm the one in trouble. Amber been out here? Have you seen her, Thunder? I've never met a woman like her before. Never. I've got to get you and me away from this place. Fast. She's getting under my skin, that Amber Prescott."

Was he really sitting there talking to his horse? he thought, shaking his head. Well, all lonely cowboys did that. Lonely? Him? Yeah, he was, there was no use in denying it. Lonely and tired, and having no idea where he'd go, or what he'd do, when he left the Prescott homestead. His mission was over. He had to start a new life for himself, leave the past buried and move forward. To what? Hell, he didn't know.

A sudden noise caused Logan to stiffen, and his hand flew to his right hip where his gun was supposed to be.

"Howdy, Logan," Nathan said, coming to the opening of the stall. "Goin' to shoot me with a handful of pants?"

"Sorry," he mumbled.

"Surprised to see you this far out."

"Yeah, well, I haven't made it back yet,"

Logan said, chuckling. "I think that was the longest walk of my life."

"Well, I just came to sharpen this hoe. That's a fine animal you've got there."

"He sure is, and I appreciate the way you been tending to him. I seem to spend a lot of time thanking you for things, Nathan."

"No need." He paused. "That Captain Mercer seemed like a decent fella."

"He is. Good friend, excellent soldier."

"He thinks mighty highly of you, Logan."

He shrugged, looked at Thunder again, then back up at the older man. "Nathan, it's about Amber."

"Fine girl, my daughter."

"Yeah, she is, and I . . . Nathan, would you saddle my horse for me, then bring my things from the cabin?"

"Why would I do that, boy? I didn't dig that bullet out of you to send you out in the desert to die."

Logan lunged to his feet, gripping his shoulder. "Damn it, man, I have to leave here. Now."

"Oh?" Nathan said, looking up at him with a calm expression on his face. "Why's that? I find it hard to fathom your bein' afraid some Comanches might mosey by."

"Of course, I'm not. Damn it to hell, I kissed your daughter, your sweet, innocent Amber. Not once, but twice, and there's no guarantee I won't do it again."

Nathan nodded slowly. "I see. Well, I best get this hoe sharpened."

Logan's hand shot out and grabbed Nathan's arm. "Nathan, aren't you listening to me? I can't be trusted around your daughter. I want her, desire her, like no woman I've ever met before."

"Well, then, boy," he said, looking at him steadily, "I suggest you figure out just why that is. And, Logan? The answers aren't in your head, they're in your heart."

Logan dropped his hand and watched as Nathan ambled away, then began to sharpen the hoe on the stone wheel.

The answers were in his heart? Logan's mind echoed. What in the hell was that supposed to mean? The lusty instincts he had for Amber were centered beneath the buttons on his pants. His heart wasn't involved in this damnable mess. Was it? No. Was it?

"Damn it to hell," Logan bellowed.

And Nathan Prescott, his back to Logan, was smiling.

Six

The journey back to camp took Chato twice as long as he'd anticipated. Moments after he set out the next morning, he realized that he would have to hold his horse to a gentle pace to keep from jarring the tiny baby he held protectively in the crook of his arm.

The going was slow, and he stopped often to allow Jude to suckle on a clean, water-soaked cloth. On several occasions he smashed fresh berries in the thin material, and smiled as the infant eagerly sucked the sweet syrup that coated the cloth.

She was a pretty baby, Chato decided, with big dark eyes, and a crop of dark curls on her head. Her skin was fair, nearly translucent, but the sun would change it in time to a golden, healthy hue.

She was chubby, with dimples on her elbows and knees, and there was no doubt in his mind that she had fully developed lungs. When Jude was unhappy, she voiced her complaints at high volume.

He spoke to her in Apache and English, deciding she would learn both languages, just as he, Lozen, and Naana had done. Jude was not a child of his body, his seed, but of his heart and soul, and so would she be to his wife.

In the few hours since he'd declared Jude to be the daughter of Chato and Lozen, he had felt the bond between them grow solid, his love for the babe already strong.

Chato entered the camp in the late afternoon of the second day since finding the infant. The wind had at last quieted, leaving the air hot and still. As he swung to the ground from the back of his horse, a young boy ran to take the reins. Chato smiled at the youth, then strode across the central area of the camp.

"Lozen," he called, as he neared their tepee. The flap was drawn back to capture any errant breeze.

Lozen appeared in the opening, a smile instantly on her face as she saw Chato approach.

She was so beautiful, his Lozen, Chato thought suddenly. Even after all these years, he was always struck anew each time he saw her by her exquisite beauty. She was small-boned, delicate, her eyes large and dark, her hair a raven waterfall when he set it free of the braids. The soft buckskin of her simple dress hugged her slender body that only he touched when they were alone. Her dusky skin was like the dew on the morning grass, her breasts full, and sweet as nectar.

She was Lozen, wife of Chato, and he loved

her with all that the gods had given him in mind and body to declare him to be man.

"Chato, I didn't expect your return so quickly," Lozen said, when he stopped in front of her. "Have you granted Naana's wish so soon?"

"No, not yet. Come inside. Close the flap behind us so we will not be disturbed."

"Is something wrong, Chato?"

"Come."

Inside the tepee Chato sat on the ground and motioned to Lozen to sit opposite him. She did as instructed, looking at him questioningly.

"My wife," he said, "I have brought you, us, a gift that I pray you will cherish as I do."

"There, in that bundle you hold? What is it, Chato?"

"Lozen, when the gods decree it to be time, you will carry the child of my seed within you, and give birth when the proper number of moons have passed. It will happen, Lozen, I am certain of that. The babe from your womb will be our second child, because I have brought you our daughter."

"What?" she whispered.

He swept back the cloth and held the naked baby toward Lozen with both hands.

"This is Jude. She will be the daughter of our hearts and souls."

With trembling hands, Lozen reached for the baby. She gazed at it for a long moment, then cradled it against her breasts. Tears spilled onto her cheeks as she looked up at Chato again.

"Jude. Our daughter. Oh, Chato, thank you. I don't have words to . . . Oh, my husband, I love you so much. We will raise her well. She will be proud to be the daughter of Chato and Lozen."

"It is my prayer that we will raise her in a time of peace. I'm weary from the battles we can't win, burdened by the hate. Once I have kept my promise to Naana, we will go to the reservation, Lozen."

"If that is your wish, Chato."

"I'm a proud Apache warrior, but I also take pride in my wisdom. It is senseless to die for what we cannot change. There are those among the young braves from this camp who call me coward for not fighting the white man to the death. Let them say what they will. I am Chato. I answer only to myself."

"So be it, my husband."

"I will rest now, then I must go, complete my journey and bring the body of Logan Wade to my grandmother. Take Jude to Naana so the old one can see our child. Then come back to me, Logan, to lie with me."

Logan nodded and got to her feet. Chato watched her go, then stripped off his dusty clothes. He stretched out on the large pallet, and waited for his beloved Lozen.

* * *

Logan slept restlessly that night as Nathan's words spoken in the barn crept into his dreams and taunted him with never-ending echoes.

He woke early, pulled on his pants, and managed to ease on a shirt, which he left unbuttoned and hanging free. As he gritted his teeth against the pain in his shoulder while he dressed, he mentally repeated his reply to the nagging voice in his mind.

There were no answers in his heart regarding his feelings for Amber Prescott.

And, he still knew, he had to leave the Prescott homestead as quickly as possible. From what Jim Mercer had said, there was little danger that far north from the Comanches. He could repay part of his personal debt to Nathan by helping to protect the Prescotts and Moses, but Logan's expertise with a gun simply wasn't needed there. He had nothing to offer but his burning lust for a beautiful, innocent young woman.

Logan left the cabin and made his way to the barn, deciding he had no appetite for breakfast. In the barn, he told Moses he wouldn't be in for the morning meal, then leaned his back against a wall.

He stared down at his left arm, which he kept close to his body to avoid further pain in his shoulder, then set his jaw, slowly raised his arm from his chest, and straightened it.

Sweat poured down his face from the grinding pain the motion had caused. A muscle twitched in the strong column of his neck as he repeated the process, bringing his arm back to his chest, then out again. A tremor swept through his body, but he pushed on; back and forth, back and forth. Five times. Ten. Twenty. Forty.

With a groan, he rested his head against the wood wall and closed his eyes. The pain running through his arm and shoulder felt like hot lava.

He opened his eyes again, and continued the exercise, over and over. Time lost meaning, and hours past. Finally, his trembling legs gave way, and he sank to the ground, resting his head against the wall.

He slept.

The next sensation Logan registered was someone placing a warm hand on his right shoulder. His eyes shot open, and he found himself staring up at Moses.

"Noon. Time to eat," Moses said.

"Yeah, all right," Logan said, running his hand down his glistening face.

Moses extended his beefy hand. "I'll help you up. You look like you took on a mad heifer and lost."

"Yeah?" Logan said, smiling slightly. "You haven't seen the heifer yet."

Moses laughed, the booming resonance seeming to bounce off the walls of the barn and fill it to overflowing. In the next instant, he slid his large arm around Logan's waist and lifted him up to stand on his feet.

"Lord," Logan said, "you could have warned me you were going to do that."

"Gotcha where you needed to go," Moses said, white teeth flashing against his black skin.

Logan nodded, then attempted to brush the hay and dust from his pants with little results. He scowled as he saw the rivers of dirt on his chest where the sweat had poured down him.

He was a filthy mess, he realized, and these were his only clean pants, due to the fact that Miss Sassy Mouth Amber had no intention of washing his other pair until she was damn good and ready. Wasn't his fault he'd be coming to her table looking like he'd rolled in the dirt. She'd better not have any choice words to say on the subject of his appearance, or he'd tell her to shut her mouth.

Moses's gaze slid over Logan from head to toe.

"Something bothering you?" Logan said gruffly.

Moses chuckled. "You could use a dunk in the stream. Well, let's get up to the cabin and wash 'fore we go inside. Missy don't take kindly to no one trackin' in filthy dirty. And you, Logan, are filthy dirty."

"Well, hell, what does she think she's doing? Putting on a fancy tea party?"

"We'll wash up," Moses said firmly. "Come on."

"Hell," Logan said, following Moses out into the bright sunlight.

Logan's irritation grew with each plodding step he took. Grown men dancing to the orders of a slip of a girl. Ridiculous. What did she figure this was? The army? Where men lined up for inspection by the commanding officer? Who in the hell did she think she was, deciding that everyone had to be squeaky clean before they could eat at her almighty table? And another thing. Amber better not still be smiling that funny little smile of hers. He didn't like that smile, not one damn bit.

" 'Round back," Moses said, snapping Logan out of his mental tirade.

Logan looked up in surprise to find they were already at the cabin, and nodded in approval at his returning strength. He eased his arm away from his chest to hang at his side, then followed Moses to the rear of the cabin.

"Well," Moses said, stroking his chin, "don't see how to get you clean 'cept to dump a bucket over your head. Be all right, I guess, long as we get a dry bandage on once we do it."

"This is a helluva lot of fuss about a bit of dirt and . . . Aagh!" Logan hollered, as Moses unceremoniously dumped a full bucket of water over Logan's head. "Damn it, man, you're drowning me."

"Land's sake, what's all the noise?" Amber said, appearing at the back door. "Oh, my," she said, laughing, "you look like a wet puppy, Logan."

"A wet . . . Damn it, Amber, I'm not a puppy," he yelled. Moses shoved a towel into his hand.

"No, you're right," she said, still smiling. "You remind me more of an angry bull. Food's on the table. Hurry along now."

"Hell," Logan grated, mopping his face and chest, then wiping his wet shirt.

"Tsk, tsk," Amber said, spinning around and going inside the cabin. "Such language in a steady stream. That Logan Wade would curdle butter." She placed a plate of bread on the table and surveyed the selection of food.

"You best quit pushin' Logan," Nathan said, chuckling as he sat down at the table. "He's got a mighty short fuse at the moment, which is understandable, all things being considered."

"Well, he swears too much," she said. "After all, there's a lady present."

"Where?" Benny said, appearing confused.

"Sit down, Benjamin," she said. Nathan laughed.

Logan and Moses entered the cabin and took their places at the table. The group ate in silence for several minutes, taking the edge off their appetites.

"I'm mighty tired of hoeing weeds," Nathan said finally. "Got to be done, though, before they choke out the corn."

"Most weeds we ever had," Moses said. "Price to pay for those good rains."

"Beans," Logan said.

"I didn't make beans," Amber said.

"No," he said, looking at Nathan. "That's not what I mean. If you plant beans at the base of the corn stalks, you don't have to worry about the weeds. For some reason, bean plants don't choke out corn. Plus, you get a bean crop in the bargain. The two just raise themselves, and you're free to do something else that needs tending to."

Nathan put down his fork and leaned toward Logan. "Are you sure about this, Logan?"

"Yep," Logan said, nodding. "I've seen it done many times. It's too late for this year, but you could do it in the spring. Wait 'til the corn comes up about a foot, then plant the beans at the base of each stalk."

"I'll be damned," Nathan said, sinking back in his chair.

"You're sure smart, Logan," Benny said, awe evident in his voice. Logan winked at him, and Benny beamed.

"Where did you see this done?" Amber said.

"Around," he said, shrugging. "Here in Texas, Kansas, New Mexico, all over."

"You been in California, Logan?" Benny said.

"Yeah, I was there."

"Did you see buckets full of gold?" Benny asked.

"No, I sure didn't. There was no gold anyplace near where I was."

"Do you have family, Logan?" Amber said, trying for a casual tone to her voice. Were there people waiting for him somewhere? A woman who loved him, just as she did?

"No. No family," he said, redirecting his attention to his plate. "No one."

"I wouldn't like being all alone," Benny said. "I guess, well, maybe you'd best stay here with us if you don't got nobody to love you, Logan."

Logan's head snapped up and he looked at Benny as the little boy returned his gaze steadily. A strange tightness gripped Logan's throat and he was unable to speak.

Nathan cleared his throat. "Let's get a dry bandage on that shoulder, Logan, and a fresh shirt," he said, pushing back his chair.

"I'll get some clean rags for the bandage," Amber said.

Oh, sweet Benny, she thought. He'd spoken in innocence as only a child could. Little did Benny know how very loved Logan was right there on that homestead. Logan had appeared stunned by Benny's words, and she had been holding her breath waiting to hear how he'd respond. But he'd said nothing, just stared at Benny like he'd never seen him before. What had Logan been thinking?

Logan left the table, sank onto the edge of the cot, then tugged off his wet shirt. Benny followed and sat down next to him.

"You got yourself a shadow there," Nathan said to Logan, as he pulled away the wet bandage. "Benny, give the man room to breathe."

"He's all right," Logan said. "Guess you decided I'm not going to shoot Amber, huh, Benny?"

"No, you wouldn't do that," Benny said. "Amber says she bets I'll grow up big and strong like you, Logan."

"That right? Well, I wouldn't be surprised. You're a good size already. You're a fine big boy, Benny," Logan said. He shifted his gaze upward to find Amber smiling at him from where she stood by the side cupboard. He looked at her for a long moment, then redirected his attention to Benny. "Yep, a fine, strapping boy."

"Think so?" Benny said, a wide grin on his face.

"Know so," Logan said, nodding.

"Wound looks good," Nathan said. "Probably still pains like the dickens, but it's healin' well. Be patient 'bout it, Logan. You could still tear it open again if you push yourself. Come on, Benny, we have to get back to the corn field."

"I wish we could plant those beans right now," Benny said, scooting off the cot. "I'm sure tired of tendin' to those weeds."

"Keep rememberin' this is the last year we'll do it, thanks to Logan," Nathan said. "See you at suppertime, Amber."

"Bye," she said, watching as Nathan, Benny, and Moses left the cabin.

Logan stretched out on the cot, resting his good arm under his head as he slowly raised and lowered his left arm.

Amber began to clear the table, glancing often at Logan as she worked. She frowned as she saw him grit his teeth against the pain the movement of his arm was causing him, but kept still, knowing he would snap at her if she cautioned him to be careful. Why was he pushing himself like that? she wondered. Why didn't he just be patient like Nathan had said?

"I appreciate your being so kind to Benny," she said. "He knows he's small for his age, and it bothers him. He needs a lot of reassuring that he'll grow up to be big and strong."

"Like me?" Logan said, continuing the exercising of his arm. "Didn't know you considered me so big and strong, Amber."

"Well, you're not exactly short and puny."

"Compared to Moses I am."

"I've never seen another man as huge as Moses. Logan, was that true what you said? You don't have any family?"

"No, I don't."

"What happened to your parents?"

"They died."

"When?"

"A long time ago. I think I'll sleep for a while now. My exciting morning wore me out."

"I'll be quiet then." She paused. "Logan?"

"Now what?"

"What about brothers and sisters?"

"Damn it," he said, raising his head to glare at her, "I said I was tired. I want to sleep, if you don't mind."

"Sorry," she said. "I won't say another word."

"Thank you," he said, lowering his head and closing his eyes.

Four seconds passed.

"Logan?"

"Sweet Jesus!"

"I just wanted to say . . . Well, the way you talked to Benny? You're a very nice man, Logan Wade."

Logan's only comment sounded distinctly like a snort of disgust.

Nice man? his mind repeated. No, he certainly wasn't, and hadn't been in a long, long time. Stay there, Benny had said, since he didn't have anyone to love him. He'd felt as though he'd been punched in the gut when Benny had spoken those words. A strange emotion had gripped him, a warmth had flowed through his veins, and closed off his throat. How long had it been since anyone had cared?

If he opened his eyes, Logan knew, he could see Amber, watch her move as she did her chores, and listen close, so close, so as not to miss it, if she sang softly.

If he called her name, would she come to him? Sit by his side? Lean over him, and press

her sweet lips to his? Her full breasts would
brush over his chest. Her tongue would meet
his. Then . . .

"Damn," Logan muttered, as heat shot across
his loins. He was going to sleep. Now. The
mere thought of Amber Prescott was driving
him crazy.

Logan willed himself to blank his thoughts,
ease the tension in his body, find the solace he
sought in sleep. He dozed. But not before he
heard once again in his mind Amber's question, "What about brothers and sisters?"
Logan's light slumber was plagued by haunting
dreams.

"Amber, Amber," Benny yelled, barreling in
the door, "Mrs. Hunter's comin'."

Logan jerked awake and sat bolt upward.
"Ah, damn," he said, clutching his shoulder.

"Benny, hush, Logan is asleep," Amber said.

"Not anymore," he grumbled.

"I'm sorry, Logan," she said, glancing
quickly at him, before turning back to Benny.
"Patricia is here? Where, Benny? I'll be so glad
to see her. Are Dustin and the boys with her?"

"No, she came alone in the wagon. She
stopped by the field to talk to Pa and Moses."

Amber pulled off her apron and draped it
over the back of a chair. "I'll go meet her,"
she said, running out the door.

"Benny, wait," Logan said. "Who's this Patricia Hunter?"

"Hunters live on the next homestead. They're our neighbors, and we trade things. You know, eggs, and meat, and stuff. They got five boys, and I sure wish they'd come today so we could play. Can I go now, Logan? I want to see Mrs. Hunter 'cause she's really nice."

"What? Oh, sure, go ahead."

"Bye," he said, dashing out the door.

Logan ran his hand through his hair and frowned. Whoever Patricia Hunter was, she'd come to call. If a man had to be nearly drowned before he could eat at Amber's table for a noon meal, what high and mighty rules did she have about greeting company? Well, his pants were fairly clean again due to Moses's dunking. "Yeah, all right," he grumbled, reaching under the cot for the saddlebags. "Don't want to get Miss Snooty all in a snit. I hope to hell there's a clean shirt in here."

Amber ran across the expanse between the cabin and the field, her eyes dancing with excitement. "Patricia," she called. "Hello, hello."

"Amber," Patricia yelled back. "I'm coming." She flicked the reins over the back of the horse, and the wagon started forward again.

Amber stopped, a bright smile on her face as she waited for Patricia to reach her.

"Whoa," Patricia said, halting the horse.

"Climb up here, Amber, and we'll ride to the cabin. It's much too hot to be running around."

Amber scrambled up onto the seat beside her, and the two immediately embraced, hugging each other tightly.

"Oh, Patricia," Amber said, "it's so good to see you. Where are Dustin and the boys?"

"Dustin, bless his heart, said he'd watch the boys, and give me a chance to have a quiet visit with you." She flicked the reins again. "Go, horse. I'm in need of a cool mug of water. I brought some eggs."

"And I have raspberry pie for you. Have you had any news from Waverly? Has anyone passed by your cabin?"

"No, no news from Waverly. Some soldiers stopped. My, that Captain Mercer was a fine-looking man. Dustin didn't pay much heed to the army warning us of Comanche renegades. There aren't any up this far."

"The soldiers were here, too. I've no news from Waverly, but we do have a visitor. Well, not exactly a visitor, but he's here."

"That didn't make sense," Patricia said, frowning. "Who's here?"

"Pull the wagon into the shade by the side of the cabin. His name is Logan Wade. I found him by the stream. He'd been . . . He was hurt, but he's on the mend now."

"Lucky man to be taken in by you Prescotts. You're all so generous. Oh, I'm so thirsty.

That's a mighty hot drive over here. Best get those eggs out of the back before they fry right in the shells."

The two women slid off the seat, then Patricia reached in the back of the wagon for the wicker basket. They entered the cabin, and Amber stopped so abruptly, Patricia bumped into her.

"Logan?" Amber said, her eyes wide.

He was standing by the hearth, a steel gray shirt securely buttoned over his previously bare chest. His hair was neatly combed; heavy over his ears, and low on his neck. And he was smiling.

"Good afternoon, ladies," he said, bowing slightly. "You must be Patricia Hunter, ma'am. I'm Logan Wade, and I must say this is a real pleasure. It's not often a man gets to greet two pretty ladies at one time."

Amber's mouth was open as she stared at him.

"Why, thank you, Mr. Wade," Patricia said. "You're most kind."

"Call me Logan. And every word is the truth. You two are like flowers of beauty in this barren wasteland. Now, I'll just make myself scarce, and leave you to enjoy your womanly talk. Good day," he said, then bowed again before striding out the back door on his long legs.

"Amber, close your mouth," Patricia said, laughing.

"Land's sake," she whispered, "what on earth came over *him?*"

"That," Patricia said, walking to the bucket and filling a mug with water, "has got to be the most handsome man I have ever seen in all my born days. No offense to my Dustin, of course. But, Amber, your Logan is one mighty fine-looking buck."

"He's not mine," Amber said, snapping out of her semi-trance.

"More's the pity," Patricia said, sitting down at the table. "So, what are you going to do about it?"

"About what?" she said, frowning. She sat down opposite Patricia.

"Making Logan yours, silly girl. Men like that don't come along every day of the week, you know. They're just so lusty, so randy, those big strapping fellas. He kiss you yet?"

"Patricia!" Amber said, blushing crimson.

"Oh, good, he did. I bet that Logan knows how to kiss, too. Was it wonderful?"

"Patricia!"

"Well, was it?"

"Beyond my wildest dreams," Amber said wistfully, staring off into space.

"Splendid. I must say, though, for an injured man he looked mighty healthy."

"He's still weak, tires quickly. Pa says Logan's a long way from sitting in a saddle, but I don't know, Patricia. He's getting stronger all the time. That means he'll be leaving soon and . . ." Amber stopped speaking as unexpected tears sprung to her eyes, ". . . and I don't want him to go," she finished, her voice hushed.

"Oh, you sweet, sweet girl," Patricia said, covering Amber's hand with hers. "You've fallen in love with Logan, haven't you?"

"Yes. Oh, yes, Patricia, I have." She sniffled. "I can't bear the thought of him going, but why wouldn't he? There's nothing here for him."

"Nothing? Have you looked in the mirror lately, Amber Prescott? You're a beautiful woman. A woman overdue for a man in her life. There's definitely something here for Logan Wade. You. Does he have family? People waitin' on him to return?"

"No, no one. He's all alone."

"Not anymore, he's not," Patricia said gleefully.

"Logan . . . Logan is the first man I've ever kissed, Patricia," Amber said, clutching her hands tightly together in her lap.

"And?"

"I felt new, strange, and, oh, so wonderful. I was all hot inside, like my blood was running a race through my body, and my breasts felt . . . Oh, dear, this is really very embarrassing."

"No, it's womanly," Patricia said gently. "Logan has changed you from a child into a woman, and that's the way it should be. We know in our hearts when we've found the right

man. I can see it in your face, your eyes, hear
it in your voice. You truly love him."

"Yes, I do. But, Patricia, I know so little
about man and woman things. My mama never
told me, because she didn't think I needed to
know until I found the man I wanted to marry.
I thought, well, maybe you could tell me about
mating because, after all, you've been with
Dustin five or six times to get those boys."

"Five or . . . What?" Patricia said, her eyes
widening.

" 'Course, Logan said I shouldn't call it mating like the animals do it. He said it's plain
old sex with the saloon whores, and making
love when it's someone special."

"You and Logan discussed it?"

"Well, sort of. It all started by me asking
him where noses went when people kissed.
Then, I said I understood about wifely duties
because I'd seen the animals mating. He got a
little riled up about that, and told me about
plain old sex, and making love. Well, no, he
didn't tell me in detail, just said I shouldn't
call it mating, or being in heat."

"Merciful heaven," Patricia said, shaking her
head. "And you think I've been with my
Dustin about five or six times?"

"Well, yes. See, I'm not really sure what's involved in creating twins. I thought maybe it
took a time for each babe when you made
twins. I just don't know," she said, shrugging.

"Amber, darling, listen to your Patricia.

Logan is right. With someone special, it is making love. It's beautiful, Amber, the most beautiful, private, sharing thing a man and woman experience. But you don't come together just to create a babe. My Dustin is a lusty buck, and he reaches for me night after night."

"Really?" Amber whispered.

"Really," she said, nodding. "It's not my wifely duty, it's my womanly joy."

"I had no idea," Amber said, her voice filled with awe.

"Obviously not," Patricia said, suppressing a smile. "I won't even ask about the noses and the kisses. Do you understand what I'm saying about making love?"

"Yes. Yes, I do. No, I don't. Well, I understand now that it's not just to make babes. But Logan said it's not exactly like what I've been seeing between the animals."

"No, it isn't. But it's not my place to explain further. That teaching is up to Logan, just like my Dustin taught me."

"But, Patricia, Logan isn't my husband."

Patricia sighed and got to her feet. She paced for several minutes, deep in thought. Amber watched her anxiously, following the back and forth motion of her friend. Patricia plunked back down in her chair.

"Nathan would probably have my hide for what I'm about to say," Patricia said. "Granted, I came to Dustin on our wedding night an innocent, but that was back in Virginia, in the city, where the rules were set firm and it never entered our minds to break them. Don't you see, Amber, this is a new land. Texas is wild and untamed. We've had to adjust to a harsh way of life, forget where we came from, who we were. It's only those who learn to change that will be strong enough to stay."

"What are you saying, Patricia?"

"Oh, Amber, I'm not suggesting you entirely throw out the beliefs of your mama and Nathan. All I know is that sometimes out here we have to grab onto life and hold tight to the moment. It's not wanton or wrong, it's just different from the way we were raised. Nathan is so kind and wise, I think he'd understand that. 'Course, he is your pa, too, so maybe he wouldn't. Amber, I am *not* telling you to make love with Logan Wade. All I'm saying is listen to your heart, listen to the woman that is newly born within you. Trust yourself, that voice. You'll know if it's right for you, my dear friend, you'll know."

"Oh, Patricia," Amber said, her eyes shimmering with tears, "how can I ever thank you for talking with me like this, for not laughing at my ignorance, for being so very kind to me?"

"I love you like a sister. I would have said these things to my own, with no prickle of guilt. Follow your heart's song, Amber Prescott. You, who sing so beautifully, so softly and serenely, will have no difficulty hearing the song of your heart. Whatever you do, will be right and good. I truly believe that."

"Oh, Patricia," she said, tears spilling over onto her cheeks.

"Don't you dare make me cry," Patricia said, laughing as tears filled her eyes. "What would Dustin say if I came home all puffy-eyed and sniffling. Now! Show me how far you've sewn on that quilt you want to trade in Waverly next trip, then I must be heading back. Dustin's patience wears thin after a time when he has five little boys clamoring after him. He'll be mighty glad to see me when I get home. Mighty glad," she said, winking at Amber.

"Oh, my," Amber said, blushing a pretty pink.

"Come. Show me your quilt," Patricia said. "Enough serious talk for one day. Oh, Amber? Twins are made all at one time. You don't piece them together like that quilt of yours."

"Fancy that," Amber said, frowning slightly.

Then the mingled laughter of the two women danced through the air like tinkling wind chimes. The quilt was examined, Patricia gushed her praise, then eggs were exchanged for raspberry pies, Amber insisting Patricia take two to feed her brood. After a long hug, they parted, Amber standing in the doorway of the cabin to wave until Patricia disappeared from view in the wagon.

Amber drew a deep, steadying breath and

wrapped her hands around her elbows as she
stared up at the bright blue sky that was dotted
with fluffy white clouds.

"Oh, Mama," she whispered, "I do love
Logan so much, so very much. I'm going to
listen to my heart, just like Patricia said. Don't
think poorly of me, Mama, if the song of my
heart tells me I should go to Logan. Please,
Mama?"

Suddenly, as though a gentle hand had been
placed on her shoulder to gain her attention,
Amber turned, her gaze going to the barn.
Logan was leaning against the opening, his
arms crossed loosely over his chest.

Despite the distance between them, Amber
could feel the intensity of his eyes on her, and
her pulse skittered under his scrutiny. He was
too far away for her to read the expression on
his face, but she knew, just knew, he was looking at her. She didn't move. She simply stood
there watching him, seeing the wide set to his
shoulders, the strength in his massive body.

An amalgam of emotions assaulted her. She
wanted to run across the dusty soil, fling herself into Logan's arms, and declare her love
for him. And a part of her wanted to hide,
crawl back into the cocoon within her and be
once again a child. She wanted to turn back
time to the safe place of her youth, yet rush
the clock ahead to discover yet more of the
mysteries that her new found womanhood had
to offer. She was confused and frightened, ex-

hilarated and joyously happy in one jumbled
maze in her mind.

And she was deeply in love with Logan
Wade.

They moved at the same instant, as though
a silken web had been woven around them,
pulling them toward the other. Slowly, slowly
they walked forward; eyes meeting, holding,
heartbeats quickening. A hazy mist crept in
around them, erasing everything but the one
within their view.

They met halfway between the cabin and
barn, but didn't speak. Blue eyes and brown
held the other immobile. The hot sun beat
down upon them, but they didn't feel it.

Then Logan lifted his hands and cradled
Amber's face. His eyes swept over each of her
features in unhurried pleasure, as Amber's
knees trembled.

Then still without having spoken, Logan lowered his head and claimed her mouth with his.

Seven

The kiss was long, and sweet, and sensuous. Hearts beat in a wild tempo, and heated desire surged through their bodies in consuming waves. The kiss was the meeting of lips and tongues, but not of bodies as Logan held himself away from Amber with only his large hands cupping her face, and his mouth moving seductively over hers.

And then too soon, much too soon, the kiss was over. Logan ended the embrace, and stepped back, a deep frown on his face.

"I didn't set out to do that," he said, his voice gritty. "I just suddenly did it."

"And I'm glad," Amber said. Her voice was unsteady as she smiled up at him.

"Have a nice visit with your friend?"

"Oh, yes. I always enjoy being with Patricia. Wouldn't you like to come back to the cabin and rest?"

"Yeah, I suppose so."

They turned and walked side by side, Amber acutely aware of Logan's height, the strength in his powerful body, his aroma, the very essence of him as he stayed close to her side.

"You're certainly moving your arm better," she said, willing her knees to stop trembling.

"It's coming along. I decided I'd better start exercising it, pain or not, before the muscles get too weak. What did you and that Patricia Hunter talk about?"

"Lots of things," she said, entering the cabin with Logan behind her.

"Like what?" he said. He crossed the room and sat down on the cot.

"Things that women talk about," she said, checking the meat simmering over the hearth. "She thought you were very charming. I, for one, hardly recognized you with all that polite folderol."

Logan chuckled. "Like that? I didn't want to embarrass you, you know, with my uncouth ways."

"You'd never embarrass me, Logan," she said quietly, turning to look at him.

Their eyes met and held for a long moment, then Logan shifted and stretched out on the cot, staring up at the ceiling. Amber began to set the table for supper.

He'd kissed her again, Logan's mind raged. He'd been looking at her from where he'd been standing by the barn, and the next thing he'd known, he'd been kissing her. He hardly remembered moving. It was as though she'd called his name, beckoned him to come, and he'd gone to her, unable to stop himself.

He'd heard the warm, lilting sound of womanly laughter drifting from the cabin, and it had brought a smile to his lips. He was glad Amber had a friend, someone she could talk to.

But what did women say to each other when they were alone? he wondered. Men bragged about time spent with women, but did women tell their private doings? Had Amber told that Patricia about the kisses Amber and Logan had shared? What would she have said about those kisses? That they were the most wonderful . . . Hell, she didn't have anything to compare them to because he was the first man who had ever kissed her. What if that Patricia woman had told Amber to find some young buck in Waverly next trip in, kiss the pants off him, then decide if Logan was any good at kissing?

"Amber," he said, swinging his feet to the floor. "Damn," he said, clutching his shoulder.

"Land's sake, Logan," she said, planting her hands on her hips, "you'd think you'd know not to jerk up so fast with that shoulder the way it is."

"It's doing fine," he said, gently massaging the aching wound. "I'd like to talk to you a minute."

"Oh, well, certainly."

"Come sit down."

Amber walked to the cot and sat next to

Logan, folding her hands in her lap, and smiling up at him. He frowned at her, then the frown deepened.

"What did you wish to speak to me about?" she said.

"Did you . . . What I mean is . . . Amber, did you tell Patricia Hunter that I kissed you?"

"Oh," she said, shifting her gaze to her hands. "Well, yes, I did."

"Hell."

She looked up at him again. "Logan, I realize that it was a private thing between us, but I really needed to talk to Patricia, because I don't have my mama. It's time I knew about man and woman things, mating . . . excuse me . . . making love and all. Patricia is like a big sister to me, the closest friend I have, so I asked her some questions. I told her that you'd kissed me, and that . . ."

"That what?" he said, leaning slightly toward her.

"That it was wonderful."

"And? What did she say? Did she tell you that you had to kiss more than one man before you knew what was wonderful?"

"Mercy, no."

"Oh," he said, obviously surprised. "She didn't?"

"No. Should she have?"

"Damn it, no," he said, his voice rising. "You don't start lining up young bucks, and having a contest, for God's sake."

"Now that," she said, laughing, "is a very silly thought."

"I should hope so," he muttered.

"Was that all you wanted to discuss?"

"Yeah. No. You asked her about man and woman things? Making love?"

"Yes."

"And?"

"She said . . . Oh, Logan, she said it so nicely," Amber said wistfully. "She said being with Dustin wasn't her wifely duty, it was her womanly joy."

"Not bad," Logan said, nodding. "I guess your Patricia Hunter is all right after all."

"She told me the most amazing thing."

"Oh, man," he said, rolling his eyes to the heavens, "here it comes."

"Well, you see, I thought Patricia had been with Dustin five or six times, because I wasn't sure what it took to create twins."

"What?"

"I surely had that figured out all wrong," she said, laughing merrily. "Patricia said that Dustin, or a big strapping man like you, would reach for his woman night after night after . . ."

"Lord," Logan said, wiping a line of perspiration from his brow with his thumb. "She actually said that?"

"She did," Amber said decisively.

"Anything else? No, forget it, I don't want

to know. Yes, I do, damn it. What else did she say?"

"Well, she said you were right, that what takes place between a man and woman isn't exactly like the animals I've been seeing. But then she said her Dustin had taught her about making love, and it wasn't her place to tell me more. It would be up to . . . well, up to the man I choose, to teach me what I need to know."

"Sweet Jesus," Logan said, as heat shot across his loins.

"Isn't that right, Logan?"

"Yes, Amber," he said, through clenched teeth, "that's exactly right."

"I'm so glad I talked to Patricia. Things are so much clearer to me now. I think it's marvelous that a man and woman can make love whenever they want to, not just when they decide to create a babe. Don't you?"

"Yeah, marvelous," he said, running his hand down his face.

"Your hand is shaking, Logan," Amber said. "Are you all right?"

"I'm dying," he said, under his breath.

"Pardon me?"

"I'm fine, fine. Well, I'm certainly glad you had your chat with Patricia. It was time you understood things about . . . things. I guess that all that remains is for you to pick the man who . . ." Logan stopped speaking as a knot tightened in his stomach, ". . . who will teach you about making love."

Damn it to hell, he didn't want anyone touching her. No one, but him. The thought of another man's hands on her soft skin, a mouth on her full breasts, and . . . No!

Amber saw the tight set to Logan's jaw, could feel the tension emanating from his massive body, was aware of the cold glint in his blue eyes. He was picturing it in his mind, she realized. He was seeing her with another man, and he didn't like it, not one little bit. Oh, glory be, he cared about her. He truly did.

Would he come to love her, as she loved him? she mused. But how could he love her if he wasn't there? He was pushing himself to exercise his arm, to gain back his strength. Was his mind focused on leaving? She wanted him to stay forever, love her, and make love to her.

Make love to her? Oh, yes. Yes! The song in her heart was clear and strong, its message sung by a litany of angels. She loved Logan Wade with every breath in her body. She had chosen her man, the one she would give herself to. Then she'd hope and pray that he'd love her in return, and stay by her side for all time.

"Amber," Logan said quietly.

"Yes?"

"When you pick that man, be sure he's the right one. Will you promise me that much?"

"I promise."

"You won't rush or anything, will you? Just because you know all these womanly things now, there's no hurry to . . . Well, try it all out."

"Well," she said, sighing deeply to suppress her smile, "I am nearly nineteen years old."

"That's young, very young."

"It is not. You said yourself that most girls my age are married and have babes by now. I really must be giving serious thought to my future."

"Ah, damn, this is all my fault."

"What is?"

Logan picked up Amber's hand and cradled it between his two large hands, staring at her slender fingers nestled in his long, tanned ones.

"If I hadn't kissed you," he said, his voice low, husky, "you might not have questioned all the rest for a long time yet. I had no right to . . . to wake up the womanly feelings in you. You were as innocent as a child when I came here, Amber, and I changed you."

"Yes," she said, nodding, "you did." And now she loved him. "I'm grateful to you for kissing me, changing me." Because she loved him, would always love him. "I'd been waiting for you, Logan, and I didn't even know it." And she wanted him to make love to her. "You're a fine man, Logan Wade."

"You seem to be forgetting you found me by that stream with a bullet in me, and a gun strapped on my hip. That doesn't add up to being a fine man."

"You weren't wearing that gun when you kissed me. And your friend Captain Mercer made it clear that you aren't a gunfighter, won't hire out as one. But even if Jim Mercer hadn't said those things, it really wouldn't matter to me who you were, or what you did, before you came here."

"It should."

"Did it ever occur to you that I'm not the only one who's changed since we've shared our kisses?"

Logan's head snapped up and he looked at her; a deep frown on his face.

"I must get supper on," she said, slowly pulling her hand from his. "Why don't you wash up now? Then Moses won't be tempted to dump a bucket of water on you again."

"What? Oh, yeah, I'll go right now," he said, watching her walk away.

She was smiling that funny little smile again, he realized. That wise, secret smile that made his back hair stand up. What was she suggesting? That a few kisses had changed him? Now *that* was really crazy.

Logan got to his feet and went out the back door. He removed his shirt, washed, then pulled the shirt back on and buttoned it. Wandering to the side of the cabin, he leaned against the rough exterior and gazed out over the sprawling land.

Peace. There was peace on that land despite its harshness, the ongoing labor it required, he thought. It gave something back to a man beyond the yield of crops. It could evoke a fierce sense of pride, and it held an aura of . . . peace, of coming home.

What would it be like, he wondered, to belong, really belong there, to not be a stranger just passing through?

And what would it be like to make love with Amber Prescott?

Lord, how he wanted her.

He had no right to feel this way, he told himself. No more right than he'd had to kiss Amber in the first place. But he *had* kissed her, and was now witnessing the woman within her blossoming due to *his* touch, *his* kiss.

"Damn," he said, as his body reacted to his wandering thoughts.

He shifted his weight, then settled back against the cabin.

He had to leave.

But, ah, damn it, he didn't want to go.

The reality of that fact slammed against Logan's mind, and caused a trickle of sweat to run down his back.

He wanted to stay on the Prescott homestead.

He needed to belong, there, with them.

And he wanted to make love to Amber.

Because of that, he knew, because of the driving, coiling knot of desire twisting his insides, he would have to leave. He might have found his place there, been extra muscle and willing hands to help tend the land, if it weren't for his lusty ways.

The last five years of his life, what he'd done, how he'd lived, had taken its toll. He couldn't stay with decent people, nor be trusted around a beautiful, innocent woman.

"Logan," Benny yelled, causing Logan to jerk in surprise. The boy came running across the dusty ground, and came to an abrupt halt in front of Logan. "Howdy, Logan," he said, beaming up at him.

" 'Lo, Benny," Logan said, smiling. "You best wash up before Moses decides to drown you like he did me."

"He sure did dunk ya," Benny said, laughing. He dashed around to the back of the cabin.

Logan followed and crossed his arms over his chest. "I'm going to be checking those hands mighty close, Benny. I don't want any gritty field dirt falling in my food from your hands."

"They'll be clean, Logan. Don't you worry none," Benny said, sinking his hands in the pan of water. "Logan?"

"Yeah?"

"Can you shoot that gun of yours real good? And draw fast? Really fast?"

"Yeah. Wash your hands."

"I am," he said, splashing his hands vigorously in the water. "See? Could you show me sometime how fast you can draw? We could line up some bottles and . . ."

"No, Benny," Logan interrupted, "I don't think that would be a good idea."

"Why not?"

"It would be different if I were a marshall, or a sheriff, but I'm not. If I were, then I'd be proud to show you how I can handle a gun that's used to keep the law. But . . ."

"It doesn't bother me none that you're a gunfighter," Benny said. " 'Course, you scared me some at first, but not no more."

"I'm not a gunfighter," Logan said, raking his hand through his hair. "Not the way you're thinking, at least. A real gunfighter is for hire—men pay him to kill other men. I've never done anything like that, Benny. Never."

"But you shot men, right? Killed 'em?"

"Yeah," he said, sighing deeply, "I have. But not as a hired gun, Benny. I wouldn't want you thinking that of me. I just did what I had to do. Does any of this make sense to you at all?"

"I don't know," Benny said, frowning.

Logan hunkered down and turned Benny to him by gently gripping his shoulders. "Listen to me, boy. What you're doing here on this land, working with your pa and Moses, is good. You're learning things that will make you a fine farmer, rancher, when you grow up. But even more important, Benny, you'll be a decent man. Don't ever strap a gun on your hip, because once it's there, it's mighty hard to take it off. Settle for a rifle in the boot of your saddle, then sit tall and proud in that saddle, Benny Prescott, because you will have earned the right to do it."

"I understand, Logan," he said. Benny flung his arms around Logan's neck. "Honest, I do."

Logan ignored the searing pain in his shoulder caused by the force of the little boy flinging himself against his chest, and held Benny tightly to him. Then as if sensing her presence, Logan slowly lifted his head to see Amber standing in the back doorway. There was a warm smile on her face, and tears shimmering in her eyes.

"Thank you, Logan," she said, loud enough for only him to hear.

Logan gazed at her for a long moment, then reached up and ruffled Benny's hair. "Wash those hands, cowboy," he said. "I still say I'm not eating your field dirt."

"Yes, sir," Benny said, grinning ear to ear.

Benny returned to his washing, and Logan pushed himself upward, turning as he caught a motion out of the corner of his eye. Nathan and Moses stood by the edge of the cabin.

"What Logan said is true, Benny," Nathan said, walking slowly forward. "A gun strapped on, is a hard one to take off. 'Tis best to never strap it on at all."

"Logan's gun is off him," Benny said. "It's under the cot."

"We took it off to tend to his wound,"

Nathan said. "Whether he puts it back on is up to him alone. Supper ready, Amber?" he said, looking over at her.

"Yes, Pa," she said, her eyes riveted on Logan. Say it, Logan, her mind screamed. Say you'll never again strap on that gun. Oh, dear Lord, Logan, please.

Logan met Amber's gaze. "I washed up, Moses. You missed out on your chance to drown me."

"More's the pity," Moses said, laughing heartily. "I was just gettin' the hang of that."

Logan watched as Amber spun around and disappeared inside the cabin. He knew from the pleading look on her face that she'd wanted to hear that he was never again going to wear that gun.

He wasn't going to strap it on again, ever. He knew it, but couldn't say it, because it really didn't change anything. Leaving a gun under a cot wouldn't transform him into a decent man who could stay among these people. He still couldn't be trusted around Amber, so he'd be going soon.

Very soon now, he'd say goodbye to Amber Prescott.

"Clean enough?" Benny said, holding out his hands to Logan.

Logan turned Benny's hands back and forth. "Yep," he said finally, "I'd say you did fine. You're one of the best hand scrubbers I've come across in the state of Texas, Benny."

The group was laughing as they entered the cabin, then stopped, statue still, as they saw Amber. She was standing by Logan's cot, tears streaming down her face. In the center of the bedding, lay his gun and holster, the late afternoon sun glistening over the shiny metal of the weapon.

"There it is, Logan," she said, her voice trembling as she pointed at the gun. "That gun is the reason you're pushing yourself so hard to get well, isn't it? You can hardly wait to feel the weight of it on your hip, then in your hand."

"Amber, don't," Logan said quietly. "Don't do this."

"Take it!" she yelled. "Pick it up. Go shoot someone. You told Benny to never strap a holster on, but it's too late for you, right? This ugly, monstrous thing is a part of you."

"Stop it," he roared. "You don't understand. You have no idea what you're talking about."

"Then say it. Say you'll never wear that gun again."

Logan opened his mouth, then clamped it shut in the next instant, a muscle jumping in his jaw.

"Damn you, Logan Wade," Amber said, sobbing, then ran out the front door.

"Sweet Jesus," Logan whispered, staring at the ceiling. "What have I done to her?"

"Well," Nathan said calmly, sitting down at the table, "I'd say you've got your hands full there, Logan." He waved Benny and Moses onto their chairs. "Pass over that bread, Benny."

"Me?" Logan said, towering over Nathan. "You're her father. You go talk to her. She's crying her heart out, for God's sake."

"Not 'cause of me," Nathan said. "Want some of this bread, Moses?"

"Damn it, Nathan," Logan bellowed. "I don't know what to do with a crying woman."

"Tell her to blow her nose," Benny said. "Whenever I cry, Pa says, 'Benny, blow your nose.' "

Nathan chuckled. "That's for little-boy tears, son," he said to Benny. "Womenfolk need more than that."

"Oh," Benny said, shrugging.

"If you're so wise," Logan said, "then go to her, Nathan. Lord, I can't stand this. She's out there somewhere crying."

"She's gone to the cove," Moses said. "Missy's in the cove, sure as I'm born."

"Moses," Logan said, "do you realize that poor girl has a heartless father?" Nathan laughed. "Go to her, Moses. Talk to her. Tell her not to cry."

"Can't tell her to stop doin' somethin' I didn't cause her to do in the first place," Moses said. "Take it easy goin' to the cove. Don't want you tearin' that shoulder open on the way. Best get to it, Logan. I don't figure

there's any Comanches up in these parts,
but . . ." He shrugged.

"Damn . . . it . . . to . . . hell!" Logan
strode from the cabin with Nathan's and
Moses's laughter following him out the door.

The colorful first streaks of the summer
sunset that were inching across the sky went
unnoticed by Logan as he walked in the direction of the cove, his jaw set in a tight, hard
line. When his bare toes connected with a large
rock, he cut loose with a loud string of exple-
tives.

Tomorrow, somehow, Logan fumed, he was
pulling on his boots. That's what he wished it
was; tomorrow. Then this hornet's nest he was
about to walk into would be behind him, finished.

He didn't know what in the hell to do with
a crying woman.

Tell Amber to blow her nose. Jesus.

And why was *he* the one elected to go find
Amber, calm her down, deal with her tears?
he asked himself. She had a father. A brother.
Moses. But did they stop stuffing their faces
long enough to tend to Amber? Hell, no.
They'd dumped the whole sorry mess on him.
Just because it was his gun that had set her
off . . . Ah, damn, it *had* been his gun that
had made Amber cry.

But he didn't know what to do with a crying
woman.

"Damn it," he said aloud, "my life was never

this complicated before I fell in love with Amber Prescott."

Logan stopped.

He stopped dead in his tracks, his eyes widening as his thundering heart slammed against his ribs. "Damn it, Wade," he whispered, "what have you gone and done?"

He was in love with Amber? his mind hammered. In love? Loved her? He did? Ah, hell, he did. How in the blue blazes had that happened? What a stupid thing to do. It was going to be tough enough to leave her, but now? Now it would be like a knife twisting in his gut on the day he rode out of there on Thunder. Damn that Amber Prescott, she had no right to do this to him.

Logan set off again, oblivious to the throbbing pain in his shoulder that came with each heavy, thudding step. At the edge of the cove, he slowed, working his way through the thick trees.

Memories assaulted him as he moved forward. Memories of seeing the cove as he'd sat bent in the saddle, too weak, too racked with fever and pain to think clearly. He'd wanted a drink of water. One last drink of water before he died. He hadn't cared that he was going to die, hadn't cared at all. There had been nothing more for him to do, no reason to go on living.

And then she'd come. The angel. Amber. And he hadn't died after all. She'd pleaded with him to fight the fever, begged him to live, forced him to look deep into his soul and realize he really didn't want to die.

Beautiful Amber, with her big, dark eyes, and silken skin, her voice that was so husky when she sang softly. Amber, with lips like sweet nectar, and a lingering aroma of lavender from her pretty bar of store-bought soap.

Her hair was a glorious, honey-colored waterfall, her breasts ripe and full, beckoning to him to fill his hands with their bounty. She was child and woman mingled together into a precious treasure.

She was Amber.

And he loved her.

And now, because of him, she was crying.

Logan stepped onto the thicker grass near the stream. The rainbow colors of the sunset filtered through the leaves on the trees and cast a rosy glow over the area. The bubbling water caught the reflection, transforming it into a jewel-like flow of churning water.

The air was heavy with humidity, intertwined scents, and muffled sounds of nature. The almost eerie quality of the entire expanse brought the irrational thought to Logan's mind that he had been transported to a place beyond reality, not of the here and now.

And then he saw her.

Amber was sitting by the edge of the stream, her shoes and stockings removed, bare feet submerged in the cool water. Her head was bent, shoulders slumped, and the tremor of her body told Logan she was still crying.

He took a deep breath, stared up through the thick leaves for a long moment, then moved slowly forward. He hunkered down beside Amber, and placed his hand gently on her shoulder, saying her name in a near whisper.

"Amber."

She didn't move. Her hands were clutched tightly in her lap, and tears trailed down her cheeks. Her breathing came in short, sobbing gasps, but she didn't move, nor acknowledge his presence.

"Amber, please," he said, a gritty tone to his voice, "don't cry. We'll talk. I'll try to explain about the gun, but I can't even think when you're crying. I'd rather be shot again, than to see those tears, know I caused them. I never meant to make you cry, Amber. I swear to God I didn't."

Amber slowly turned her head, then lifted her lashes to look up at him. A moan tore from Logan's throat as he saw her tear-stained face, the moisture clinging to her lashes like dewdrops, the sadness in the dark pools of her beautiful eyes.

"Oh, God, Amber, I'm so sorry."

"Logan," she said, flinging her arms around his neck. "Oh, Logan."

"I'm here," he said, laying her gently back onto the soft carpet of grass. "I'll hold you. Everything is going to be all right."

He stretched out next to her, cradling her head on his right shoulder, then wrapping his other arm around her waist. Her tears started fresh again, sobs racking her slender body, and he tightened his grip on her. He held her, simply held her as she cried, his lips resting lightly on her moist forehead.

Her pain, her sorrow, was his, he knew, because he loved her. His jaw was clenched so tightly that it ached, as the sound of Amber's sobs struck against his senses with an unrelenting force. He felt helpless, useless, his strength and masculinity powerless against the insidious force of unhappiness that tormented her. He could do nothing but hold her; knowing, hating, the realism that he was the cause of her distress. He stroked her back in a gentle, soothing motion, and waited.

Finally, Amber quieted, her tears spent, and she drew a deep, wobbly breath as one last tremor swept through her body. Her mind drifted back from the private place of anguish where she had been, and she became acutely aware of Logan's rugged length pressed to her.

She inhaled his aroma, felt the steady rhythm of his large hand moving on her back, absorbed the heat of his body into her own. A liquid warmth crept from the core of her femininity and spread throughout her, causing her heart to beat a wild cadence.

"Amber?" Logan said quietly. "Do you think you've finished crying now? You can cry some more if you want to. I was just wondering if you thought you might be done."

"I'm done, I guess," she said, not moving. "I got your shirt all wet." She sniffled.

"Benny said I should tell you to blow your nose," he said, smiling slightly.

"I don't have a hanky."

"I don't either. Amber, I'm so damn sorry I made you cry."

"I couldn't help it, Logan. Everything just caught up with me. You talked so kindly to Benny, made him understand that he must never strap a gun low on his hip and . . . I wanted, I needed, to hear you say you'd never put your gun back on. At that moment, it was all I could think about; how badly I wanted to hear you say those words. I was dreaming, I suppose, being a little girl again, pretending things were the way I was fantasizing them to be in my mind. It's not your fault that I cried, it's mine."

"No. No, it isn't."

"It truly is, because I was holding fast to dreams that aren't mine to have. I wasn't thinking clearly because it's all happened so quickly, and it's frightening at times. Wonderful, but still frightening because it's all so new. I know deep within myself that you're going to strap that gun on again, then ride away from here, from me. But at that moment in the cabin, I just couldn't bear it. I couldn't, Logan, because I . . . I love you. With every breath in my body, with every part of me that is awakened now to womanhood, I love you, Logan Wade."

Sweet Jesus, no, Logan's mind screamed, as every muscle in his body tensed. No. Amber mustn't love him. He was the wrong man for her. She should love a good, decent man, who would give her pretty babes, and worship her for all his days.

"Maybe you just think you love me," he said, beads of sweat dotting his brow. "I'm the first man to have kissed you, and you probably confused it all in your mind."

"Oh, no, I'm sure I'm in love with you. I listened to my heart's song, and I know," she said, snuggling closer to him. Logan gritted his teeth as heated desire rocketed through his body. "Even Patricia could tell, when I was talking about you."

"Patricia knows that you . . . Forget it. Amber." He shifted slightly, and tilted her chin up with one finger. "Look at me, and listen to me. You can't love me, because I'm not the right man for you."

"I think you are."

"You're wrong."

"Why?"

"Because, damn it, I've killed four men. I killed them, Amber, with that gun that made you cry. I pulled the trigger, and shot them straight to hell!"

Eight

It was not so much the words that Logan spoke, but the chilling tone to his voice that caused Amber to stiffen as the color drained from her face. Logan felt and saw her reaction, and a shadow of haunting pain crossed over his features, his eyes turning a cold, winter blue.

"No," she said, seeing the harsh changes in him. "Logan, I . . ."

"It's true," he said, his voice gritty. "Your saying no, not wanting to believe it, isn't going to erase anything."

"You don't understand. Logan, I'm not a fool. I know you wore that gun, and I was the one who found you with a bullet in you. But I've told you that I don't care who you were before you came here. It doesn't matter to me. I heard you tell Benny that you'd killed men, but I know that you're not a gunfighter, that you didn't hire out to kill. There has to be a reason for what you did, and I'll listen if you want to tell me. But you don't have to if you don't want to, because who you were before has nothing to do with who you are now. I love you, Logan. Nothing is going to change how I feel about you."

"Sweet Jesus." He moved his arm from beneath her head and lay back on the grass, flinging his arm over his eyes. "You're playing childish games, Amber. You're pretending if you ignore something, it just won't be there." His voice was flat, had an empty, hollow sound. "That's not how life works."

Amber sat up and looked at him, willing herself not to start crying again as she stared at him, seeing the tight line of his jaw, hearing the weary quality to his voice.

He was like a man defeated, she realized, one giving way to the insidious ghosts of the past that were reaching out to snare him in their miscreant clutches.

She could feel him slipping away from her, retreating into his private hell where she would not be granted entry. It was as though Logan were teetering on the edge of a dark, bottomless pit that would swallow him up, take him away from her forever if he stepped further toward the abyss.

"Please, Logan," she said, her voice trembling, "tell me what happened to you. Tell me what drove you to strap on that gun."

Logan moved his arm to the grass and looked up at her, seeing the tears still glistening in her big, brown eyes, hearing the pleading in her voice. Her declaration of love hammered against his mind, filling him with an amalgam of joy and sorrow at the same time.

Amber loved him, his heart echoed over and over. And, merciful heaven, he loved *her*. She was everything that was good, decent, honest. And he was not. There, in that misty cove with the rainbow colors and gentle sounds of nature, it would be so easy to forget everything but his Amber, tell her of his love, and say he'd never leave her.

But beyond the cove was reality, and it wasn't going to go away. It was waiting there like a nefarious sentinel just outside the trees, the message of truth in its hand, the means to take Amber from him.

There was nowhere to run, nowhere to hide, for the sentinel was himself.

Logan would be the one to speak the words that would destroy the love of Amber Prescott, cause her to turn her back on him, but he had no choice but to tell her. She would hate him then, be free of him, could move forward and love again, find the right man to bring her happiness.

"Logan?"

He drew a deep breath that seemed to tear from his very soul, then shifted his gaze to the leaves above, and the multi-colored sky peeking through nature's umbrella.

"I had a brother," he said, his voice low. "Michael. He was three years older than me. Our parents died in a wagon accident when I was fifteen. We were living in the Canadian wilds because my father was a logger. Mike and I were big for our age, used to hard work in the logging camp, and they kept us on because we could do a man's share of labor. A few years later, Michael got restless, decided to move on, but I wanted to stay."

"But you went with him?" Amber said, her eyes riveted on Logan's face as he continued to stare up at the trees.

"I liked the sense of belonging, the feeling of security in that camp, being with people who cared about each other. There was a woman with a whole slew of babes who used to wrap apples in leaves and bury them beneath the campfire. Then she'd serve them up with sugar, milk, and cinnamon. She always made two for me. Damn, I sure did like those apples, and sitting there with that family as though I was one of them."

Logan stopped speaking as the memories flitted through his mental vision. Amber's heart ached as she pictured it all in her mind, seeing the young boy in the man's body, who had wanted nothing more than to belong.

"Couldn't you have stayed there?" she said.

"Mike was my brother. My place was with him. He was the only family I had left. So, we moved on; came down through New York, then started west. We could always find work because we were big, did whatever needed doing with no complaints, but Mike never wanted to settle in, stay in one spot for long. It was a part of him I didn't know existed, a wanderlust spirit that had been buried within him."

"But you weren't happy living that way," Amber said, more in the form of a statement than a question.

"Happy? I never thought about it much, I guess. As I got older I learned not to get attached to the folks we met, because I knew we'd be packing up later. We stayed in Oklahoma for a year once, and I thought maybe Mike . . . But one morning, he said we were going."

"Oh, Logan," Amber said, shaking her head.

"We went to California to try our luck panning gold, but lost everything we had working an empty stream bed. There was no gold for the Wade brothers so we pushed on—Arizona, New Mexico, here in Texas, Dodge City, Kansas, then back to Arizona. Damn, I was tired of it all. I just wanted to settle down, find my place, make roots somewhere. I felt torn in two, Amber, because Michael was my brother, but I knew I couldn't live like that anymore."

"Did you tell Michael? What did he say?"

"He just laughed, said we'd stay in Arizona until I came to my senses and realized there was nothing there to hold me, no one who cared if I came or went. But then . . ." A faint smile tugged at Logan's lips, then disappeared in the next instant, ". . . then Michael met Jude."

"Jude?"

"She was a young Apache girl . . . Well, woman, who had come into town with her brother, Chato, for supplies. There was an uneasy peace with the Apaches in that area. People were frightened of them, but were trying to accept them so everyone could live on the land, concentrate on working to survive. Jude was beautiful, she truly was. She had long, black hair, and big, dark eyes, and when she smiled at Mike that first time, I thought he was going to fall flat on his face."

"And Jude's brother? What did Chato do when he saw Michael's attraction to Jude?"

"He watched. He didn't say a word, just stayed close to Jude, and watched. The next week they came into town again, and Mike was waiting with a fistful of wilting wildflowers. I was standing next to him, and Chato moved in front of us, keeping Jude behind him."

"And then?"

"Lord, it was tense. Chato's eyes are so dark you can't see the pupils. He stared at Mike, me, then Mike again. Michael didn't flinch, just met Chato's eyes head on. Finally, Chato nodded, stepped back, and allowed Jude to take the flowers. We didn't know their names then, of course, but Chato suddenly opened his mouth and said, 'I am Chato. This is my sister, Jude.' "

"He spoke English?"

"Yeah, and so did Jude. The next week,

We've got your authors!

If you seek out the latest historical romances by today's bestselling authors, our new reader's service, KENSINGTON CHOICE, is the club for you.

KENSINGTON CHOICE is the only club where you can find authors like Janelle Taylor, Shannon Drake, Rosanne Bittner, Sylvie Sommerfield, Penelope Neri and Phoebe Conn all in one place...

...and the only service that will deliver their romances direct to your home as soon as they are published—even before they reach the bookstores.

KENSINGTON CHOICE is also the only service that will give you a substantial guaranteed discount off the publisher's prices on every one of those romances.

That's right: Every month, the Editors at Zebra and Pinnacle select four of the newest novels by our bestselling authors and rush them straight to you, even *before they reach the bookstores.* The publisher's prices for these romances range from $4.99 to $5.99—but they are always yours for the guaranteed low price of just *$3.95!*

That means you'll always save over $1.00...often as much as *$2.00*...off the publisher's prices on every new novel you get from KENSINGTON CHOICE!

All books are sent on a 10-day free examination basis, and there is no minimum number of books to buy. (A postage and handling charge of $1.50 is added to each shipment.)

As your introduction to the convenience and value of this new service, we invite you to accept

4 BOOKS FREE

The 4 books, worth up to $23.96, are our welcoming gift. You pay only $1 to help cover postage and handling.

To start your subscription to KENSINGTON CHOICE and receive your introductory package of 4 FREE romances, detach and mail the postpaid card at right *today.*

We have 4 FREE BOOKS for you
as your introduction to
KENSINGTON CHOICE
To get your FREE BOOKS, worth
up to $23.96, mail card below.

FREE BOOK CERTIFICATE

As my introduction to your new KENSINGTON CHOICE reader's service, please send me 4 FREE historical romances (worth up to $23.96), billing me just $1 to help cover postage and handling. As a KENSINGTON CHOICE subscriber, I will then receive 4 brand-new romances to preview each month for 10 days FREE. I can return any books I decide not to keep and owe nothing. The publisher's prices for the KENSINGTON CHOICE romances range from $4.99 to $5.99, but as a subscriber I will be entitled to get them for just $3.95 per book. There is no minimum number of books to buy, and I can cancel my subscription at any time. A $1.50 postage and handling charge is added to each shipment.

Name _____

Address _____ Apt. # _____

City _____ State _____ Zip _____

Telephone (____) _____

Signature _____

(If under 18, parent or guardian must sign)

Subscription subject to acceptance

KC 0894

We have
4
FREE
Historical
Romances
for you!

Details inside!

KENSINGTON CHOICE
Reader's Service
120 Brighton Road
P.O. Box 5214
Clifton, NJ 07015-5214

Mike was waiting for Jude again. The week after that, Chato said we were to come to their camp to share a meal with them, and to meet his wife, Lozen, and Naana, the grandmother who had raised Jude and Chato."

"Did you go?"

"I would have had to tie Mike to a tree to keep him from going. Anyone looking at Mike and Jude could tell they were in love, hardly knew what was going on around them. We were accepted in the camp because Chato was a brave warrior, and Naana was the widow of the chief. I was comfortable there, and Chato and I became very close. We talked for hours about the trouble between the white man and the Indians. We both were sickened by it, but knew it was far from over."

"And Jude and Michael?"

"A month later they were married there in the camp after following all the proper rules of courtship. Mike staked a claim on a homestead, and said he was going to settle down and live with Jude and their babes."

"And you?"

"It was a strange feeling, Amber. I suddenly realized I was free to do whatever I wanted to. Mike had his wife, his plans and, damn, they were happy, him and Jude. Homesteads were still being offered, and I started dreaming about getting one there in Arizona, or Texas, or Oregon, making a real home for myself and never moving again. I wanted a wife, babes, wanted to tend my land and die on it when I got old. Chato and I helped Mike build his barn and cabin, then I told Mike that I was pushing on to find my own place. He wished me well, said he'd come to see that he'd dragged me from one place to the next, and he'd been wrong to do it. Jude was expecting a babe by then, and they were counting the weeks until it came. But . . . Ah, hell," Logan said, running his hand down his face.

"What happened?" Amber whispered, feeling a knot tighten in her stomach.

"Mike, Jude, and Chato came into town with me when I was ready to buy my supplies to leave. I figured to go to Oregon and get a homestead. There were a bunch of wild men in town that day, causing trouble in the saloon, drinking, scaring folks. The sheriff was rounding them up and tossing them in jail. Four of them came into the store, loud and drunk. I heard voices from where I was out back with Chato loading my wagon, but I didn't realize the men were inside. Then I heard Mike yelling, telling someone to leave Jude alone, and Chato and I hightailed it in the back door."

"And?" Amber said, clutching her hands together in her lap.

"Mike threw himself at one of the men. It was all so damn confusing, but Chato and I just plowed straight in and took on the others. Next thing I knew, someone slammed something on my head and I was out cold on the floor. When I came to . . ." Logan stopped speaking as he clenched his jaw and a muscle twitched in the strong column of his neck.

Amber's heart battered wildly against her ribs as she saw the haunting pain settle deep in Logan's eyes, saw the tremor sweep through his body. She pressed her fingertips to her lips and waited for Logan to speak again, knowing she didn't want to hear what he was going to say. She could feel the tension emanating from his massive frame, and took his nearly palpable anguish into her own body.

"They were dead," Logan said, his voice echoing with a chilling quality. "Michael and Jude were shot dead. Chato was shot, too, but he was still alive."

"Dear God," Amber whispered. "Oh, dear God."

"I went crazy, wild. I didn't know what to do. I yelled at Mike and Jude, telling them to open their eyes and speak to me, say they weren't dead. I talked to the babe in Jude's belly, screaming to it to get itself born like it was supposed to. I cursed them for dying, then begged them not to be dead."

"Oh, Logan," Amber sobbed, as tears spilled onto her cheeks.

"The sheriff said he'd seen the four men running from the store, knew who they were, and told me their names. I took Chato to Lozen so she could tend to him. I took Mike and Jude to the camp, too, so they could be buried with the Apache rituals. Ah, Amber, I felt as though my heart and soul had been ripped to shreds."

"Logan, oh, my Logan," she said, curling up next to him and resting her head on his shoulder. He lifted his arm to pull her closer, turning his head to rest his lips on her forehead. "I'm so sorry, Logan," she said.

"I made up my mind that I would find those men and kill them if it took the rest of my life. There was a gunfighter in town, and I paid him to teach me how to handle a gun; a gun strapped low on my hip, tied down with a rawhide, a killer's gun. There was nothing inside me but raw hate. I practiced with that gun like a man possessed, then I set out to find those men. Chato was hurt bad, and I didn't know when I left if he was going to live or die. I still don't know if he lived, because all hell broke loose with the Indians after that, and I never went back to the camp. It was like losing another brother, the rest of my family. But I wasn't Logan Wade anymore, Amber. I was changed, different, nothing mattered but the burning need inside me to kill those bastards."

"And . . . and you did?"

"Yes. I tracked them down one by one, and called them out. I wanted them to know who it was who was sending them to hell. They drew first, I was faster, and I killed them. No sheriff found fault with what I'd done. Then

I'd move on to find the next. Five years. Five damn years I stalked them one after the other. Men came to fear me when I walked into a saloon. They saw the way I wore my gun, saw the hate in my eyes, on my face. No one would come near me or speak to me. In the most crowded room I was alone. So damn alone."

"But you were shot when I found you, Logan."

"I'd been nearly a year finding the last man. Jesse Turner, that was his name. I tracked him to Houston, then found out he'd left town a week before, so I set out after him. I found him about three days' ride from here. It was night, he was all alone, sitting by his campfire. I watched him through the trees and . . . and all of a sudden I couldn't see Mike and Jude's faces clearly, hear their voices, their laughter, nothing. I looked at Jesse Turner and realized he was young, couldn't have been more than a boy that day in the store. The others were men, but Jesse? I started shaking because I didn't know what I was doing there. None of it made sense anymore. In that moment I forgot how to hate and I was empty, a shell, because hate was all I'd known for five years. Hate and killing."

"Was it Jesse who shot you?"

"Yeah, I made a noise, I guess, because all of a sudden he was on his feet, going for his gun. I hesitated for a fraction of a second because I was confused, not sure what I was do-

ing, why I was intent on killing him. He fired
into the dark and hit me in the shoulder. On
reflex I drew, and shot him through the heart,
I saw him go down and I thought, No! No, I
don't want to kill him! Jesse's face got all
mixed up with Mike's; I saw them both, didn't
even know who I'd really killed. I pulled myself up onto Thunder and rode away. I got as
far as this cove. Amber, when you found me I
knew I was going to die and I didn't care, it
made no difference. My mission was over, finished, and so was I. I'd done what I had to
do, but toward the end I didn't even know why
I was doing it. Life had no meaning for me
anymore."

"But you did live, Logan," she said. "You
didn't give up, you fought the fever, willed
yourself to hang on."

"That was your doing. I heard you begging
me to fight and I did, not even knowing why.
I heard you singing so softly, felt your gentle
hands on me, knew I wanted to see you again,
and I couldn't see an angel if I died and went
to hell. You saved my worthless life; you, and
your pa, and Moses. But, Amber, I'm a killer,
a man who set out on a journey of revenge
and hate that took five years to finish. I don't
have the right to be here with decent, hard-
working people. I've kissed you, held you,
touched you. I've touched you with hands
soiled by men's blood, men dead from my gun.

I'm leaving here, Amber, just as soon as I'm able to ride."

"Logan, no. No, please, don't go. I love you so very much."

"I'm a killer, damn it. I tried to make it sound different for Benny's sake, but facts are facts. Just because my gun wasn't for hire doesn't make me less than what I truly am. I'm no better than the men who shot Mike, Jude, and Chato. Human life meant nothing to me. I wanted those men dead, and I saw that they died. Jesse? Hell, I don't know. I probably would have killed him even if he hadn't shot me, because that's all I know how to do now, just pull the trigger, then walk away not caring." He paused. "I'm sorry I kissed you, Amber."

"What?" she whispered, the breath catching in her throat.

"I kissed you, changed you, woke the womanly feelings in you, and I was so damn wrong to do that. You've waited such a long time to blossom like a beautiful flower, and it shouldn't have been me who took you from your innocent world. I'll never forgive myself for not leaving you alone. You've got to promise me you'll forget me, that you'll find your young buck in Waverly, and settle down, raising babes with a decent man."

"No, I can't promise you that. I love you, will always love you. What you told me about your life of the past five years makes me ache

inside for you, Logan, but it doesn't change
my feelings for you. It's over, you said that.
You never have to put that gun on again. You
can start a new life and . . ."

"No! I can't forget what I've done. It's never
going to go away, Amber. I can't change it, or
me, by pretending it never happened."

"I'm not pretending, I'm accepting. There's
a big difference between the two. I'm not passing judgment on you. Michael was your
brother, and you loved him, and Jude, and
Chato, too. There was so much involved, things
I can understand like honor, loyalty, pride."

"Revenge, hate, killing," he said, his voice
rough. "Do you understand those things, too?
No, because you haven't had to, and they
shouldn't be a part of your life. I shouldn't
have touched you but, God help me, I did. Forgive me for that much, Amber, please," he
said, his voice breaking slightly.

Amber slid her arm across Logan's chest,
then straightened her legs so that she was
stretched out next to him. Logan held her
tightly, wrapping his left arm around her waist,
and shifting so that their bodies met.

"Could you find it in your heart to forgive
me for kissing you, Amber?" he said quietly.
"I don't deserve it, I know, but . . ."

"To say yes would be to agree that it was
wrong, and I'll never believe that," she said,
drawing feathery circles on his shirt with her
fingertips. "There's no secrets between us now.

I know all about your past, and I'm so sad that
you've suffered. Forgive you? No. Love you,
cherish you, want you to kiss me again? Yes,
oh, yes. And it's even more than that, Logan.
I've listened to my heart's song, and I want
you to make love to me. I'm giving myself to
you, Logan Wade, woman to man, because I
love you."

"Sweet Jesus, no," he said, every muscle in
his body tensing. "Don't say that. Don't even
think it."

Amber leaned farther into him, her breasts
crushing against the hard wall of his chest. She
heard and felt his sharp intake of breath. "But
I *do* think about it," she said softly. "About
how glorious it will be to make love with you,
be one with you, be truly yours. I'll feel no
guilt or shame, because I know it's right and
good to become one with the only man I'll
ever love."

She began to unbutton his shirt. One button,
then two, then three.

"No." He grabbed her hand with shaking
fingers.

"I think it's only fair to tell you that while
I was sponging you when you had the fever I
didn't move the sheet from over your manhood. I didn't have the courage to do it, so
I've never seen a man, not really. But I'm not
frightened anymore, Logan. I want to see you,
all of you, and touch you. And I want you to
see me, because I truly belong to you now."

"Jesus. Would you quit saying things like that? I'm not going to make love to you. I'm carrying enough guilt over having kissed you. I'm sure as hell not going to take, steal, any more from you."

"You're not taking, I'm giving, all of me, here in our cove where I found you. It's so right that it should be here, where you first became a part of my life. I know I'm not experienced, Logan, but you could teach me all I need to know about pleasing you. I would please you, don't you think?"

"Yes. Ah, yes," he said, moving away and laying on his back. He closed his eyes, fighting for control as desire surged through his body, the blood pounding hotly through his veins. His arousal pressed painfully against his pants; heated, full, aching with the need and want of her. "Go back to the cabin. Now, Amber. Go," he said, his voice harsh with passion.

Amber got to her feet, then looked down at him, seeing his tightly closed eyes, the hard line of his jaw, the evidence of his arousal straining against the material of his pants.

A gentle smile formed on her lips as she quietly undid her dress and slipped it from her shoulders to fall in a heap at her feet. Full breasts pushed above the top of her thin chemise as she dropped to her knees beside him. She spoke his name in a husky whisper that matched the growing dimness of the gathering dusk.

"Logan."

His eyes shot open and his head snapped around to look at her, his heart hammering.

"Make love to me, Logan."

He gritted his teeth as his gaze swept over her, the eerie luminescence of the cove shimmering over her slender body outlined in the nearly transparent material of the chemise. A roaring noise echoed in his ears as his body warred with his mind.

Sweet Jesus, she was beautiful! Amber. Lord, how he loved her. Amber. He would be so gentle with her, give her pleasure, teach her the mysteries of her body and his. Amber. She'd have nothing to fear from him, because he'd make it good for her, just so damn good. No. God, no! He couldn't take her innocence. He couldn't.

Please, Amber's mind screamed, as she watched the play of emotions on Logan's face. Please, Logan. It wasn't wrong. She loved him, and that made it right and decent. Oh, Logan, please.

Amber lifted her hands and pulled the pins from her hair, then dragged her fingers through the silken tresses as they tumbled to her waist and over her breasts in a honey-colored waterfall.

Logan groaned deep in his throat. Beautiful, his mind whispered. Her hair was even more beautiful than he'd dreamed possible. Oh,

God, he wanted her . . . he wanted her . . .
he wanted her . . .

"Don't you want me, Logan?" Amber said,
leaning toward him, her breasts nearly spilling
over the top of her thin chemise.

"Damn you, yes," he said, lunging upward
and gripping her arms, his mouth coming
down onto hers in a punishing kiss.

Amber's eyes widened at the rough onslaught
of Logan's lips moving over hers, but in the
next instant the embrace gentled. His lips
never leaving hers, he lowered her to the lush
grass, covering her body partially with his as
his tongue delved deep into her mouth. She
circled his neck with her hands, inching her
fingers into the thick, night-darkness of his
hair.

Logan tore his lips from hers, his breathing
ragged as he trailed a ribbon of kisses down
the slender column of her throat, then across
the tops of her full breasts pushing above the
chemise. A soft purr came from Amber's lips,
heightening his passion further.

The fire within him raged, pounded, swirled
through his body. His hand seemed to move of
its own volition, pulling the straps of the chemise down, then away as Amber moved her
arms to allow his actions. He swept the material
below her breasts with trembling fingers, filling his vision with the sight of her ivory
breasts.

"Oh, sweet heaven above," he said, "you are the most exquisite woman I've ever seen."

"I'm *your* woman, Logan," she said. "I love you, and I'm yours."

The feel of Logan's mouth on her breast seemed to steal the breath from Amber's body. He suckled gently in a steady rhythm as his hand grasp the other breast, his thumb stroking the nipple to a hard button. A pulsing heat deep in the core of her femininity matched the pull of Logan's mouth, as desire rambled unchecked throughout her. Waves of sweet, aching pain rippled through her, and she closed her eyes to savor each wondrous sensation. His mouth found her other breast and a soft sigh of pure pleasure escaped from her throat.

Logan lifted his head to gaze at her flushed face, his eyes cloudy with desire. "I've got to stop," he said, his voice gritty with passion. "Now, before it's too late, I've got to stop."

"No, my love," she whispered, sliding her hands inside his shirt. "This is our cove, our world, you are mine, and I am yours. Come to me, Logan."

His control snapped. He was lost . . . gone . . . swept away on a tide of passion, of need, want, desire, like none before. The battle in his mind was conquered by the one in his body, the victor named.

"Amber," he said with a moan. His mouth swept down once more onto hers, his body shuddering with desire.

She pressed her hands to the back of his head to bring his mouth and tongue closer yet, her breasts crushing to his chest. His hand skimmed between them seeking, finding the soft mounds, bringing each bud to taut awareness.

Then his fingers moved lower to slip beneath the chemise crumbled at her waist. He shifted slightly, then drew the chemise and pantaloons down and away as she raised her hips to aid his task.

Amber lay before him in naked splendor.

"Dear God," he said, sucking in his breath, "an angel, my angel. Lovely. Beautiful. Just so damn beautiful."

Logan pushed himself to his feet and rid himself of his shirt and pants. As he looked at Amber again, he stopped, standing above her, watching the expressions of awe, wonder on her face as her gaze swept over him, lingering on his manhood, that was a bold announcement of his need of her. He searched her eyes for any flicker of fear, but saw none.

She lifted her arms to welcome him back into her embrace. "You're beautiful, too, Logan," she said, as he stretched out next to her.

"I'm going to hurt you, Amber," he said, his voice strained. "It can't be helped, but I'll be as gentle as possible. The pain won't last long, and it won't happen again, just this first time. Understand?"

"Yes."

"Do . . . do you want to change your mind? Tell me now, before I touch you again, because when I do I won't be able to stop. Please, Amber, be sure you want to do this. I'm going to take something from you that can never be replaced. This is the greatest gift you have to offer a man."

"And it's yours," she whispered.

"Ah, Amber."

In a sweet, slow, sensuous journey of hands, lips, and tongue, Logan kissed and caressed every inch of Amber's lissome form. His foray brought a moan from her throat and his name from her lips. It was sweet torture, heaven and hell, it was desire burning within her like an uncontrolled brush fire. It was Logan. And she loved him.

"Logan," she gasped.

"Soon. Soon," he said, his breathing labored as he strove for control.

His hand found the heated, moist core of her femininity, stroking her, making her ready for what he would bring to her. His muscles trembled from his restraint, but still he held back, wanting, needing to know she would be prepared to receive him.

"Logan. Oh, please. I feel as though I'm shattering into a million pieces."

"Yes. Yes, I'm here."

He moved over her then, hesitating above

her, gazing at her face, searching for the reassurance he needed.

And Amber smiled.

She smiled her gentle, womanly smile that spoke of love, and desire, and the willingness to go forward to a place she had never been to before. To go forward with Logan. Only him.

Logan entered her slowly, tentatively, watching her expression change once more to wonder and awe. He encountered nature's barrier, and stopped, every muscle in his body aching from forced restraint.

"Hold on to me," he said. "Hold on just as tight as you need to."

She gripped his upper arms as he thrust into her, covering her mouth with his to drink the sound of her sharp cry of pain. Then he waited, gritting his teeth with the knowledge that he'd hurt her, until he felt her relax beneath him.

And then it began; the rhythmic dance of lovers as old as time. With the instincts of her womanhood, Amber matched Logan's tempo, lifting her hips to meet him, to bring more of him into her, to fill her, consume her. Higher they soared as the cadence increased, thundered. Amber was searching for an elusive treasure that had no name, her body struggling to reach the summit of a climb of ecstasy.

She was there!

In a maelstrom of tempestuous sensations,

the spasms rocketed through her, hurling her over the edge of reality to a place without time or space.

"Logan!"

"Yes," he said, then joined her in the unearthly sphere, shuddering above her, calling her name; his seed, his virility, his strength, passing from him unto her. "Amber," he said, then collapsed against her, his energy spent. He pushed himself up on trembling arms, only then feeling the fiery pain in his shoulder. "Amber? I'm sorry I hurt you. Amber?"

"Oh, Logan," she said, cradling his face in her hands, "that was wonderful. I never knew it would be so wonderful. I love you, Logan."

He buried his face in the fragrant cloud of her hair for a long moment, before moving away and pulling her close to his side.

"We made love," he said quietly. "You were right about that. I've never made love before, and it was very special, rare. Thank you, Amber, for your gift."

"Is it always so wonderful, Logan?"

"It gets better and better."

"My goodness," she said, laughing softly, "just think what I have to look forward to."

Logan frowned as his hold on her tightened. The voices in his mind crept back, demanding their due, screaming louder, beating against his brain.

Dear Lord, what had he done? he inwardly seethed. Nothing had mattered but making love to Amber, to the only woman he had ever loved. He had taken her innocence because of his lusty nature, giving no thought to the moment beyond the one in which he had burned with the need of her.

Damn his soul! He would carry the guilt of his actions to his grave. He had taken a woman he'd had no right to have. He was Logan Wade, a man who had killed in hate and revenge, and Amber deserved better than what he was.

God, how he loved her!

And tomorrow he would leave the Prescott homestead.

Nine

The curtain of darkness dropped gently, slowly, as if warning the occupants of the cove that night would soon be upon them. Crickets began to serenade all who would listen, and a frog croaked as though having been asked to join the chorus.

Amber nestled closer to Logan's warmth as the last of the sun's rays faded, bringing a slight chill to the air. She was lethargic, contented, a woman fulfilled, and had no desire to move away from the protective embrace of the man she loved.

She felt no guilt for her actions, she realized—rather, she was registering a sense of peace, mingled with lingering awe and wonder at the glorious union she had shared with Logan. There was a foreign soreness in her body that was hers to savor, along with the knowledge that she was truly a woman. Her transformation was complete, and her heart's song was one of joy.

"Amber," Logan said quietly, "it's time we were getting back."

"I don't want to leave here, Logan. This is our place, our special place."

"Your pa is going to start worrying about you." He moved gently away from her and reaching for his clothes. "You . . . um . . . might want to wash up a bit in the stream, then we'll go."

Amber sighed. "All right, but I do wish we could stay here for the night. Wouldn't that be lovely? We could sleep, wake up together in the morning, and make wondrous love again."

Logan's jaw tightened. "Wash up," he said, pushing himself to his feet.

Amber rose and walked to the edge of the stream, where she washed away the evidence of her lost innocence. Logan watched her, telling himself that he shouldn't, but unable to draw his gaze from the beautiful picture she presented. Her hair tumbled forward as she bent over, and her skin had a dewy glow that beckoned to him once again to be touched. He swore under his breath and finished dressing, averting his eyes as Amber drew on her clothes.

"I'll never find my hairpins," she said, braiding the thick cascade into a single plait. "Well, it doesn't matter."

"Amber," Logan said, placing his hands on her shoulders, "listen to me."

"Yes?"

"I'm going to have to tell Nathan what happened in this cove."

"Why?" she said, her eyes widening. "This

was our private joining. Ours. It only concerns the two of us. Why would you tell my pa?"

"Because he has the right to know," he said gruffly. "You're his daughter, and you were an innocent. Nathan took me into his home, saved my life, trusted me. I betrayed that trust to-night in this cove."

"No, you didn't. You didn't force yourself on me, Logan, I came to you willingly. You kept trying to send me away, and I refused to go. I did what I knew was right and good, and I feel no shame, no guilt, for my actions. Pa needn't be told."

"Yes, he does need to be told. This is be-tween him and me now, man to man. I'll speak to him alone, and you'll stay out of it. Under-stand?"

"I still don't see why . . ."

"Amber."

"Land's sake, all right, Logan."

"You don't say one word. I'll talk to Nathan in private."

"Logan, you're not sorry we made love, are you?" she said, looking up at him anxiously. "You have that stormy expression on your face that says you're angry. Oh, Lord, you don't think poorly of me, do you? It wasn't wrong, Logan, because I love you and . . ."

"Shh," he said, gathering her into the circle of his arms. She wrapped her arms around his waist and leaned her head on his chest. "Mak-ing love with you was the greatest experience of my life," he said. "It truly was. I don't think poorly of you, Amber. I never will." Because he loved her with every breath in his worthless body. "I don't want you feeling guilty or ashamed about what happened." He carried enough guilt within him for the both of them. It was his fault, all of it. But he had to be careful as to what he said to her. He couldn't leave her, knowing she was filled with shame for her actions. "You did nothing wrong."

"I know that."

"Just don't forget it. No matter what happens, remember you did no wrong."

"What do you mean, 'No matter what happens'?"

"You let me worry about that. Come on now, let's go," he said, taking her hand.

"I love you, Logan," she said. "I just wanted to say it once more tonight, here in our cove. I love you, Logan Wade."

Logan forced a smile, then led Amber from the cove, her hand cradled in his. They reached the clearing and started toward the cabin, seeing the glow from a lamp within as darkness settled over the land. Amber began to hum softly as they walked, and the knot in Logan's gut tightened.

The further they went from the cove, the closer he came to reality and the truth of what he had done. Every muscle in his body was coiled, tense, his jaw set in a tight, hard line.

At the edge of the cabin, Logan stopped, and Amber looked up at him questioningly.

"Amber," he said, "when we go inside, walk into your bedroom and shut the door."

"But I haven't had my supper."

"Just do it. Go into your room, shut the door, and stay there. Don't come out no matter what you hear."

"You're frightening me, Logan."

"I have to speak with Nathan, and I intend to do it alone. Don't argue with me."

"It'll serve you right if I starve to death."

Logan smiled in spite of himself, then motioned her toward the open door of the cabin. Nathan was sitting at the table, but didn't turn his head in their direction as they entered. There was no sign of Benny or Moses.

Amber looked up at Logan and he pointed to her bedroom, shaking his head when she opened her mouth to speak. With one last glance at the unmoving Nathan, she crossed the room and went into her bedroom, closing the door behind her.

Logan studied Nathan's profile for a long moment, but could read nothing on the older man's face. Logan walked to the cot, slid the gun from the holster, then moved to the table, sitting down next to Nathan, and placing the gun by Nathan's hand.

A heavy silence hung in the air, beating against Logan, causing sweat to trickle down his chest and back. Nathan slowly lowered his eyes to look at the gun glistening in the glow of the oil lamp.

"You have every right to use that gun," Logan finally said, his voice low. "I won't be making any move to stop you."

Nathan shifted his gaze to meet Logan's. "You saying I have just cause to kill you, Logan?"

"Yes, sir, you do," he said, looking directly into Nathan's eyes.

"I've never killed a man without knowing why I was doin' it. You best tell me what reason I have to pick up that gun."

"Damn it," Logan said, shaking his head, "do you actually want to hear the words? Have them echo in this cabin, your home?"

"I do," Nathan said, nodding.

"Sweet Jesus, Nathan, I've had your daughter, your sweet, innocent Amber! I took her, I made love to her in that cove. There, I've said it. Now pick up the gun, and get it over with."

Nathan leaned back in his chair and crossed his arms over his chest, his eyes never leaving Logan's. A muscle twitched in Logan's jaw, pain throbbed in his shoulder, but he made no attempt to avert his eyes from Nathan's scrutiny. The seconds ticked by in agonizing slowness.

"Do you take me for a fool, son?" Nathan said, breaking the oppressive silence.

"There's not a lawman in Texas who would find fault with your gunning me down."

"That's not what I mean, Logan. I could shoot you dead, bury you in the desert, and no one would be none the wiser. I know that. So, I'll ask you again. Do you take me for a fool?"

"I don't know what in the hell you're talking about," he said, his voice rising.

"I sent you to the cove after Amber. I did it knowin' what the outcome would be. I knew, Logan Wade, that you'd be havin' Amber."

"What?" Logan said, his voice hardly more than a whisper. "What did you say?"

"You heard me, boy."

"I don't believe this." Logan frowned. "What in the hell kind of father are you?"

"One filled with guilt. A father knowin' I've kept my daughter on this homestead to tend to woman's work, because I needed her here, and Benny needed her to be a ma to him. I've cheated my own girl out of havin' a husband, a home of her own, babes, like she deserves. And I have to keep on doin' it, 'cause I've got no choice."

"Keep talking," Logan said, his voice harsh. "So far, I'm not liking this one damn bit."

"Don't be gettin' your back hair up, boy. I'm not lookin' to trap you into bein' Amber's husband. There's no man that can force another to marry 'gainst his will. No, Logan, that wasn't what I set out to do when I sent you to the cove after Amber. I've seen the changes in her since you've come, heard her tell of 'em, too. She's discovered the woman within herself and it was time, long overdue. She deserved to have what you gave her tonight."

"Jesus," Logan said, running his hand down his face. "This is crazy. A father doesn't handpick a man, especially a man like me, to take his daughter's innocence."

"He does if he knows she's not to have her own life to lead. He does if he feels he can give her at least a glimpse of what she would have had. He does if he sees himself in the man he chose."

"You see yourself in me? Nathan, I've killed four men with that gun."

"And I killed more than a dozen with the one I wore."

"What?"

"Did you hire out as a gunfighter, Logan?"

"No. They shot my brother and his pregnant wife. It was raw hate and revenge that sent me after them. Five years. It took me five years to find them all. But I did it. I didn't stop until they all were dead," Logan said, a bitter edge to his voice. "Jesse was the last, and he put a bullet in me before I could gun him down. I called the others out so they'd know who was sending them to hell, fair and square. But I'm a killer, Nathan."

"No more than me. Having a deputy's badge pinned to my shirt doesn't change the fact that I ended men's lives. We do what we have to. It wasn't till I met my Mary that I hung up my gun for good. Yes, Logan, I see myself in you, includin' the loneliness I suffered in those days. I looked deep within myself, and knew you were the man to give my Amber a taste of happiness, as brief as it might be."

"Damn you," Logan said, "what gave you the right to make these decisions? You may feel just dandy about all of this, but I sure as hell don't. I took something from Amber that wasn't mine to have. I don't care what fancy thinking you've done, but what happened in that cove was wrong. I've got guilt twisting in me like a hot knife. Amber deserves better than what I am. I'm leaving here, Nathan. Come dawn, I'm going."

"That's your choice to make, son," Nathan said quietly.

"And if there's a babe? What then? Did you think about that?"

"I'll be prayin' there's a babe."

"Good God, Nathan, are you totally insane?"

"No. I'm facin' life head on, trying to do what's best for my son and daughter. I need Amber here, but it's only right she have as much as she can. There'll be no shame in her havin' your babe if it's meant to be. Will be a blessin' for all of us. I'm not askin' you to carry that guilt within you. I'm not askin' anything of you at all."

Logan pushed himself to his feet and walked around the table to the hearth, bracing his hands on the edge of the mantel, and staring down at the glowing embers of the fire.

A thousand voices screamed in his mind. Never, *never*, had he met a man like Nathan Prescott. Nathan had set out to have his daughter's innocence taken by a gun-toting, lusty buck, who was just passing through. But yet, as Nathan sat there explaining his reasons in that calm, quiet voice of his, it all seemed to make sense. Nathan had a wisdom like no one Logan had ever known. Amber had been robbed of her chance to live her own life, and so Nathan was giving her as much as he could to make up for it. It was right, and good, and decent.

But Nathan had made one mistake, Logan thought. He'd picked the wrong man to awaken the woman in Amber. There was nothing Nathan could say that would change Logan's mind about that. Nathan had the peace within him to live with what had happened that night, but Logan didn't. It twisted his insides and caused his grip on the mantel to tighten.

He was a killer, the voices echoed. There'd been no badge on his shirt to justify his actions. He could have found the four men and turned them over to the law, but he'd chosen the path to hell instead, and pulled the trigger on that gun time and again.

Logan lifted his head, his glance falling on the bullet resting on the mantel. He picked it up and stared at it, the battered metal seeming to burn the palm of his hand. It was tangible evidence of what he was, proof of his past. He slipped the bullet into the pocket of his pants, and drew a weary breath.

"I'll be leaving in the morning," he said, his voice flat.

"You do what you must," Nathan said. "Every man has a right to find his place, his peace."

"There will be no peace for me, Nathan. I understand the reasoning behind your decision made for Amber, but it doesn't erase my own guilt."

"Then I did you an injustice by sending you to the cove after her."

"No. You did what you thought best for the people you love. I can't find fault with that. One man's thinking doesn't always work for another, that's all."

"You're too hard on yourself, Logan. You killed men who killed your brother. There's no shame in that. Any man with a sense of pride would have done the same."

"It started out like that, but something changed, *I* changed. The hate ate at me, turned me into someone I didn't know. When I came upon Jesse Turner that last night, I could hardly remember why I was hell-bent on killing him. But I knew I was going to do it, because that was what I was, a killer."

"I've been that road," Nathan said, "but I turned back, started over with my Mary."

"It's too late for me. The hate is gone, the guilt isn't. And now I have the guilt of what I did to Amber to add to it."

"That guilt for Amber isn't yours to carry, son. If there's any to be placed, it's on me, and I don't see it that way. You gave Amber something she deserved to have, and I'm grateful. It eases my own burden some, because I know I have to keep her here, especially for Benny. I'll be sincerely prayin' there's a babe, but that's up to the good Lord to decide."

"A babe," Logan said, shifting his gaze to the rocking chair. "Yeah, Amber would be a wonderful mother. She'd sit in that chair and sing softly as she . . ." He stopped speaking as emotion choked off his words.

"You could stay, you know. You'd be welcome here, Logan."

"No," he said, his voice husky, "I can't."

"I'm truly sorry if I caused you grief. Lord knows I never meant to do that."

"I know you didn't."

"Where will you go?"

"Doesn't matter," Logan said, looking at the rocker again. "I'll just get on Thunder and head out."

"You don't have your full strength back yet."

"I'm all right. Nathan, I should say something to Amber before I leave but, God help me, I don't know what it would be. She thinks she's in love with me. Ah, damn, she's going to cry again."

"I'll tend to her. Her tears of tomorrow are more my fault than yours. When she calms down, I'll explain it all further, hope she understands why I did it. Just bid her a gentle good-bye, and I'll deal with the rest. She's strong, my Amber. I best get to bed. Morning comes too fast as it is. Night, Logan," Nathan said, getting to his feet.

"Yeah," he said, watching as Nathan walked slowly across the room. "Nathan?"

"Yes?" he said, turning his head to look at him.

"I love her. I didn't tell her that I do, but I want you to know. I do love Amber."

"Logan, if I hadn't known that to be a true fact, you never would have gone to that cove tonight," he said, then entered the bedroom and shut the door behind him.

"You're a helluva man, Nathan Prescott," Logan said under his breath. "I'm honored to have met you."

He turned, his glance once again coming to rest on the pretty rocking chair. A baby, his mind whispered. His and Amber's. Had it happened? Had a new life begun to grow as he'd buried his seed deep within her? Was she, at that very moment, carrying his child? He'd never know. Damn it, he'd never know!

Logan blew out the lamp, then stretched out on the cot, staring up into the darkness. He wanted to sleep, escape from the turmoil in his mind and soul, but he knew he wouldn't. He'd just lie there, replaying it all in his mind, torturing himself with visions of Amber, and waiting for the dawn that would take him out of her life forever.

Amber lay huddled in bed wide awake. She'd been stiff with tension as she'd heard the murmur of Logan's and Nathan's voices, had strained to hear what they were saying, but nothing had been clear.

They had talked for so long, she thought. And said what? A moment ago the voices had stopped, then the lamplight creeping under the door had darkened. What words had passed between the two men? What had been Nathan's reaction to Logan's telling of what had happened in the cove? Had Nathan thought poorly of her, or did he believe in her enough to realize that she had gone to Logan out of love? It didn't seem right somehow that she had been sent to her room like a child, while they discussed what she had done as a woman.

"Not right at all," she said.

Well, she'd best get some sleep, she mused with an inner sigh. She'd know when she saw her pa in the morning how he felt about her. And she'd see Logan in the morning, too. Her wonderful Logan. How magnificent his body was, how strong and powerful was his manhood that had thrust within her, moved against her softness, then taken her to that place of ecstasy.

She truly belonged to Logan now, and her heart sang with joy.

Amber closed her eyes and gave way to the somnolence that drifted in around her. A gentle smile was on her lips as she slept.

Just before dawn, a cadence of thunder rumbled across the sky, followed by another, then yet another. Wind howled against the sturdy cabin as Logan jerked up and swung his feet to the floor. He reached under the cot for his boots, and tugged them on, gritting his teeth as the pain grinded in his shoulder. The thunder roared again, and he got to his feet just as Nathan came out of the bedroom, a sleepy-eyed Benny behind him.

"Storm comin' in," Nathan said.

"Seems so," Logan said.

"Latch the shutters, Benny," Nathan said. "Temperatures droppin'. We'll have to hurry if we're goin' to . . ."

"Pa?" Amber said, opening her bedroom door. "I heard thunder."

"Get dressed," Nathan said. "Then come to the barn for the tarps. Hurry, Amber."

"Yes, Pa," she said, then slammed the door.

"I don't understand," Logan said. "I thought you'd be glad of a rain for the crops."

"Not when the temperature drops this fast," Nathan said. "This means *hail*, Logan. We've got to cover as much of the corn as we can. If the hail is like some I've seen, we'll lose everything we don't tarp over. Come on, Benny," he said, heading for the door.

"I'll help," Logan said.

"Your shoulder isn't up to this, Logan," Nathan said. "The tarps are heavy, and have to be flung over the stalks. They break the stalks, but we can save the harvest. That corn is near ready for market now."

"I said I'm helping," Logan said. "Forget my damn shoulder."

Amber came running out of her room clad in a brown dress, her hair still hanging down her back in the single braid.

"I'm ready, Pa," she said.

"Then let's go," Logan said.

"Logan, no," she said. "Your shoulder is . . ."

"Hell," he said, heading out the door.

"Stubborn son of a gun," Nathan muttered.

The first drops of rain were just beginning to fall as the four reached the barn. Moses had hitched a horse to a wagon, and was hauling the heavy tarps from the back of the barn.

"It's rollin' in fast," Moses said. "Goin' to hail for sure. Benny, crawl up there and hold those reins so the horse don't spook from the thunder."

"Yes, Moses," Benny said, scrambling up onto the seat of the wagon.

Nathan and Amber ran to the far end of the

barn as Logan's gaze met Moses's across the wagon bed.

"You're goin' to tear that wound open, Wade," Moses said. "You best go back to the cabin."

"I want to help," Logan said, his voice low. "I need to be here, Moses."

Moses studied Logan's face for a seemingly endless moment, then nodded. "Yeah, I can see that you do. The tarps are in the back."

The group worked in silence, all ears straining to listen for the sound of hail beating on the roof. The rain and wind increased its fury, but the ominous thud of the damaging hail didn't come.

Moses carried four tarps to Logan and Nathan's two, while Amber dragged one at a time across the barn floor. The animals moved restlessly in their stalls, and Benny talked in a soothing voice to the horse hitched to the wagon. As Moses flung the last tarp onto the pile in the wagon bed, the hail began to drum down.

"Dear God, no," Amber whispered.

Moses picked up Amber and set her on top of the tarps, then climbed up onto the seat, taking the reins from Benny.

"Git up, horse," Moses yelled. "Go, boy."

The horse took off like a shot, Amber clinging to the tarps to keep from being flung off the wagon.

Outside, Logan and Nathan ran after the

wagon, the dark sky dropping its heavy burden on the ground below. The hail was large, landing with stinging blows on Logan's head, shoulders, and back.

"Jesus," he said, as he ran. "I've never seen anything like this."

"We need that crop," Nathan yelled. "Damn it, we need that crop."

Logan picked up his speed, ignoring the pain in his shoulder as his boots landed with pounding intensity as he ran. He arrived at the cornfield before Nathan, and reached in the back of the wagon for a tarp. Amber was dragging one with Benny toward the field.

"Amber! Benny!" Logan called. "Get under the wagon. The hail is too big, you're going to get hurt."

Amber shook her head and continued her task, straining against the weight of the tarp.

"Damn it," Logan said, yanking a tarp off the pile.

Time lost meaning.

The hail beat down relentlessly as the wind whipped with increasing fury. It was difficult to see, to move, impossible to think. Logan felt a hot, searing pain rip through his shoulder, then warm blood running down his chest beneath his cold, rain-soaked shirt. But he worked on. One row of corn stalks was covered. Then two, then three. Benny fell to his knees in exhaustion, and Amber led him to safety beneath the wagon before she reached for another tarp.

Muscles and lungs begged for mercy, but still they pushed forward. Four rows, five.

And the hail continued to fall.

Suddenly, Nathan stopped, the tarp in his arms slipping unnoticed to the ground.

"Nathan?" Logan yelled, over the noise of the storm. "What's wrong?"

"It's over," he said, his voice flat.

"What? There's still tarps left. We can . . ."

Nathan shook his head and pointed to the remaining rows of corn. Logan turned, then sucked in his breath in shock. It was gone, all of it, beaten into the muddy ground, and destroyed.

There was nothing left.

"No!" Amber screamed. "No. We'll cover it. Please, Pa? Please?"

"It's no use, missy," Moses said.

"You can't give up." She sobbed, beating her fists against Moses's chest. "I won't let you. You've got to help me."

"Easy, missy, easy now," Moses said, wrapping his big arms around her.

Logan looked at Amber and Moses, then turned to Nathan. The older man stood statue still, oblivious to the hail battering against him. His shoulders were slumped, and exhaustion was etched on his pale face as he stared out over the land. Logan felt a hot coil of anger start churning within him, along with the emotions of frustration and helplessness.

Why? his mind clamored. Why had this happened to these good and decent people? They'd worked so damn hard, and for what? In the breath of a moment it was gone, destroyed, wiped away as though it had never been there. Damn it to hell, it wasn't fair.

"Pa? Amber?" Benny said, his voice shaking as he crawled from beneath the wagon.

"Come here, Benny," Logan said, drawing him close to his side.

And then the hail stopped.

As quickly as it had come, it stopped.

The wind gentled, and the first streaks of a colorful dawn inched across the horizon. An eerie silence fell, broken only by the sound of Amber's sobs as Moses continued to hold her tightly in his arms. No one moved. No one spoke. Their clothes were torn, bodies bruised, exhaustion and shock numbed their senses.

And then, as if in slow motion, Nathan Prescott crumbled to the ground.

"Pa!" Benny shrieked.

Before Logan could move, Moses had set Amber away from him and hunkered down beside Nathan.

"Oh, God, Pa," Amber said, dropping to her knees beside her father.

"Nathan?" Logan whispered, tightening his hold on Benny's shoulders. "Come on, Nathan, open your eyes. Nathan?"

Moses pressed his ear to Nathan's chest, then placed his large hand on the older man's neck.

"Moses?" Amber said. "Moses, what's wrong with him? Why is he so still? Talk to me. Moses?"

The big, black man lifted his head to reveal tears streaming down his face. "He's . . . he's left us, missy," he said, choking on the words. "His heart gave out. He's with his Mary now."

"Don't you say that to me," Amber said, sobbing. "Don't you tell me my pa is dead. Do you hear me, Moses? Do you? You've got no right to say my pa is dead."

"Amber," Logan said quietly. "Amber, please, listen to me."

"No," she said, scrambling to her feet. "Come away from Logan, Benny, before he says it, too. Our pa isn't dead, Benny. He can't be. He just can't be."

Amber's eyes widened in horror as Moses lifted Nathan's body into his arms and began to walk slowly toward the cabin, tears still streaming down his face. Benny began to cry in great, gulping sobs as he clung to Logan's leg.

"Amber," Logan said, his own throat tight, "Benny needs you. Come get him, Amber, he needs you."

A rushing noise echoed in Amber's ears as she turned slowly to look at Logan. His lips were moving, but she couldn't understand what he was saying to her. Something terrible had happened, but now she couldn't remember what it was. She was cold and wet, but didn't know why. All she knew was that thousands of bees were buzzing in her head. Buzzing and buzzing.

And then everything went mercifully black.

Ten

Chato planted his hands on his thighs and pushed himself slowly to his feet, his dark brows knitted in a frown.

Logan Wade, he thought incredulously, the brother of his soul was . . . possibly . . . alive. The signs he had found where Logan had been shot showed that he'd managed to struggle onto his horse and leave. He was bleeding badly, Chato might yet come across his body, but for now there was hope that he lived.

Chato swung smoothly onto the bare back of his horse, then started slowly forward, his dark eyes riveted on the ground.

If Logan lived, he vowed, he would find him, and together they would return to camp to say a final farewell to Naana. Logan would see Lozen again. Logan would smile upon little Jude, the child of the hearts of Chato and Lozen. And Chato and Logan would talk far into the night as brothers, as they'd done years before.

If Logan was alive.

"So be it," Chato said, with a decisive nod.

He nudged his horse onward, following the trail of dried blood.

"Amber! Amber!" Benny screamed, running to where she lay on the wet ground. "Don't be dead, too, Amber."

Logan covered the distance between them in two long strides, and quickly scooped Amber up into his arms. "Amber?"

"Don't be dead, Amber," Benny said, sobbing hysterically.

"She's not dead, Benny," Logan said. "She fainted, that's all. She'll come around in a few minutes."

"Are you sure?" he said, in a wobbly voice.

"I'm sure. Let's get to the cabin."

Benny had to run to keep up with Logan's long-legged stride as they made their way through the puddles. Logan held Amber tightly in his arms, oblivious to the pain in his shoulder. He glanced down at her often, seeing her pale, still face, and his heart battered against his ribs.

Ah, Nathan, he thought fiercely, why'd you have to go and die? He'd been one of the finest men Logan had ever known. And now he was dead, was going to be buried in the same cold, wet ground that held the evidence of the ruined crop. What was to become of them all; Amber, Benny, Moses, without Nathan there to guide them with his quiet, wise ways? He wouldn't think about all of that now. He had to see to Amber.

Moses came lumbering out of the cabin door and hurried toward them, concern etched on his face.

"Missy?" he said. "Missy, are you all right?"

"She fainted," Logan said, not slowing his pace. "Let's get her inside."

Moses swung Benny up into his arms, and they all entered the cabin a few moments later. Logan stopped, staring down at Amber where she lay nestled against his chest.

"Moses," he said, "she needs to get out of these wet things."

"Then you best take her into her room and tend to her, Logan," Moses said.

"Me? But . . ."

"You're the only one left that has the right to do for her," Moses said, a sad quality to his voice. "I'll stoke the fire and help Benny get into dry clothes. I put Nathan on his bed. I'll keep Benny out of there for now. Tend to Amber, Logan, 'fore she catches a chill."

"Yeah," Logan said, frowning as he turned toward Amber's room.

Moses knew, his mind clamored. He knew what had happened in the cove. Jesus. Maybe Moses wouldn't refuse the offer to shoot Logan dead with his own gun.

Logan kicked the door shut behind him with his foot, then placed Amber gently on the bed.

He pulled off her shoes, then reached for the buttons on her dress.

"Amber?" he said. "Damn." Why was he hesitating? He'd seen Amber naked before. But this was different somehow. It just didn't seem right to be stripping off her clothes when she didn't even know it. "Amber?"

"Pa?" Amber murmured, not opening her eyes. "That you, Pa?"

"Yeah, it's me," Logan said.

"I had a bad dream, Pa," she mumbled. "I thought you were . . ."

"Shh," Logan said, undoing the buttons. "I'm going to get you out of these wet things."

"So tired, Pa."

"Then you sleep. Just sleep, and don't worry about anything."

"I love you, Pa."

"I know you do, Amber," he said quietly. She'd loved her pa, and now he was dead. Ah, man, his poor beautiful Amber. "Sleep."

Logan worked as quickly as possible, pulling away the sodden dress, chemise, and pantaloons from Amber's limp body. He swore under his breath when he saw the ugly, purple bruises beginning to form on her ivory skin from where the hail had beat down upon her.

Before he could think about the fact that she was naked before him, he picked up the cotton nightgown from where she'd tossed it across the bed, drew it over her head, worked her arms through the sleeves, then pulled it down to her ankles. He tucked the blanket across her shoulders, then gazed at her.

"Sleep, pretty Amber," he said softly, then turned and left the bedroom, leaving the door halfway open.

"Logan?" Benny said anxiously.

"She's fine, Benny, just tired. She's going to sleep for a while now."

"My pa's dead, Logan," Benny said, brushing his arm under his nose.

"I know," he said gently, hunkering down to look Benny directly in the eyes. "You can cry all you want to, because you've got the right. Nathan Prescott was a fine man, probably the finest I've ever known. We're going to miss him, all of us. You cry, and when you're done, you'll feel better. Then we'll talk about all that needs to be tended to."

"Well, I guess I'm done cryin'," Benny said, sniffling. "I'm not no babe, I'm a big, strappin' boy, and I can do lots of things."

"You bet you can," Logan said, smiling at him. "How about getting me a dry shirt out of my saddlebags? I sure would appreciate it."

"Right now," Benny said, running across the room.

Logan pushed himself slowly upward, his hand clutching his shoulder. He turned to see Moses setting out clean rags on the table.

"Let's get that wound tended to," Moses said. "Coffee will be ready soon."

Logan unbuttoned his shirt and pulled it

gingerly away from the raw, bleeding wound. He slipped the shirt off, then sat down on a chair by the table, gripping his thighs with his hands.

"Mmm," Moses said frowning, as he looked at Logan's shoulder.

"Just do it," Logan said gruffly.

"Mmm," Moses said, wiping the fresh blood away with a warm, wet rag.

"Moses," Logan said, his voice hushed, "we've got to bury Nathan."

"I know that. I'll put together a coffin soon as we eat somethin'."

"Amber's going to take this really hard, Moses. She . . . Ow! Damn it, ease up a little. 'Less, of course, you're trying to kill me."

Their eyes met and Moses's hand stilled for a moment.

"No," the huge man said, shaking his head. "I've got no cause to kill you, Wade. Nathan did what he thought best, and I respect that."

"I respect it, too, but I don't agree with it," Logan said quietly. "I feel guilty as hell about . . . I told Nathan I was leaving."

"Here's your shirt, Logan," Benny said, running to the table. "I took out your shavin' stuff, too."

"Fine," Logan said. "Now you stand there and protect me from Moses while he tends to my shoulder. This giant man here does *not* have a gentle touch."

Benny crawled up on his knees on a chair

and rested his arms on the table, a serious expression on his face, as though he was indeed making sure that Moses did a fine job of tending to Logan's shoulder.

Benny would be all right, Logan mused. As long as there was someone to hold him, hug him, reassure him, he'd come through this, accept the death of Nathan. But Amber? What of her? Damn, what a mess.

"Done," Moses said. "Wasn't all that bad, just bled a lot. Hurts plenty, I imagine."

"You imagine right," Logan said, reaching for his clean shirt. "At the rate I'm going, I'll run out of shirts."

"Get the mugs, Benny," Moses said. "I'll slice up some bread and dried beef. We best get some food in us."

"I'll check on Amber," Logan said.

Amber appeared to be sleeping peacefully, her hand curled next to her cheek, making her look like a very young girl. Logan frowned and shook his head, then walked back to the table. The three ate in silence for several minutes.

"How come my pa had to die?" Benny finally said, in a small voice choked with tears.

Logan's head snapped up and he looked quickly at Moses, hoping the black man was prepared to answer Benny's question. But Moses shook his head, as quick tears filled his dark eyes.

Damn, Logan thought. "Benny, I think maybe God needed your pa to do something important for him somewhere else. And I also think he's doing that special job with your ma, because she's been waiting for him in a place we don't know about. It's hard for you to be without your pa, but you have to believe that he's doing fine, he's happy."

"Who else is in that place, Logan?" Benny said, then sniffled.

"I don't know for sure. Maybe my brother Michael and his Jude."

"Oh," Benny said, nodding slowly. "That doesn't sound so bad, I guess. I just wouldn't want my pa to be all alone."

"He's not, I'm certain of that," Logan said.

Moses cleared his throat roughly. "Benny, we best be goin' down to the field and get the wagon. The cow needs milkin', the stock has to be fed. You finish up that meal, then we'll go. I'm surely goin' to need those muscles of yours."

"*My* muscles?" Benny said, staring at his thin arms.

"That's a fact," Logan said, nodding. "Here I sit with a bum shoulder. I'm stuck with woman's work, washing up these dishes, setting stew on to simmer. I swear, Benny Prescott, you tell a soul that Logan Wade did woman's work, I'll tan your butt."

Benny laughed in delight. "No one will hear it from me, Logan. It'll be between us men folks, private like."

"I should hope so," Logan said, draining his

coffee mug. His gaze met Moses's over the rim, and Moses smiled, nodding in approval. "I'll tend to Amber if she wakes," Logan went on.

Big talk, he thought dryly. She was going to cry for sure about Nathan. Dealing with a little boy's sorrow was one thing, but a woman's tears? He already knew how Amber's tears ripped him right through to his soul.

"We best be goin', Benny," Moses said, getting to his feet.

"I'm ready, Moses," Benny said, sliding off his chair. "I'll be helpin' you plenty, you'll see."

After Moses and Benny had left the cabin, Logan poured himself another mug of coffee, checked on Amber, then stood in the open doorway of the cabin.

His gaze swept over the tattered land, then up to the sky, that was now a bright blue—fluffy white clouds moving rapidly across the heavens.

The early-morning storm seemed like a nightmare, a make-believe happening that hadn't really taken place. But it had been real, and Nathan Prescott was dead.

Logan shook his head and frowned. It seemed like an eternity since he'd sat in the glow of the oil lamp talking with Nathan about what had taken place in the cove. And at dawn, Logan was to have gotten on Thunder and ridden away from the Prescott homestead. Ridden away from Amber. Forever.

Now what in the hell was he going to do? he asked himself. He still had to leave, he knew that. But not today. Definitely not today.

"Wash the dishes, Wade," he said, tossing the dregs of his coffee onto the ground.

He gathered his shaving supplies and went out the back door to shave in front of the mirror hung on the cabin. Back inside, he heated water, then washed the dishes. Deciding they could dry on their own, he replaced them in the cupboard.

In the smokehouse, he found a small beef roast and set it to simmer in a pot over the fire in the hearth. He rinsed off two handfuls of potatoes and carrots, wondered absently if they were supposed to be peeled, then dismissed the idea and tossed them into the pot.

Woman's work, he mused, was boring as hell.

Logan's glance fell on the closed door of Nathan and Benny's bedroom, and he walked slowly toward it, then entered the quiet room. He sat down on Benny's cot, resting his elbows on his knees and lacing his fingers loosely together as he stared at Nathan.

"Damn it, Nathan," he said quietly, "I wish to hell you hadn't gone and died on us. I'm supposed to be half a county away from here by now. I'm still leaving, I hope you know that. Nothing has changed. I have to go. But I'll hang around a bit, till things settle down. You were a helluva man, Nathan Prescott, you truly were."

Logan jerked in surprise as he felt the moisture on his cheeks, and only then realized that he was crying. He ran his hand down his face in a quick, angry motion, then got to his feet. After one long, last look at Nathan, he left the room, pulling the door closed behind him.

"Logan?"

"Amber."

She stood across the room in her nightie, her hands clutched tightly together. Her face was pale and drawn, and her hair was in wild disarray, the braid having worked loose. She looked young, and frightened, and Logan's heart ached with an actual physical pain.

"Logan," she whispered, "is my pa dead? Is he truly dead, Logan?"

Logan stared up at the ceiling for a long moment to control his own teetering emotions, then looked at Amber again.

"Yes," he said, his voice husky.

"I see," she said softly, then walked to the table and sank into one of the chairs. "Is Benny all right?"

"He's doing fine," Logan said, coming across the room and pouring her a mug of coffee. "Drink this. Would you like some bread and meat?"

"No. No, thank you," she said, staring into the mug as she wrapped her hands around it.

Logan sat down opposite her, a deep frown on his face. "Don't hold back your tears," he said gently. "It's not good to do that. I'll leave you alone, if you like, and you can cry, or I'll stay. Whatever you want."

"Crying won't bring my pa back," she said, her voice flat, empty sounding. "Nothing will."

"That's true, but you can't keep your sorrow bottled up inside you."

"Logan, was Pa angry about what happened in the cove? I have to know. I have the right to know."

"No, Amber, he wasn't angry, not at all. He . . ." Logan stopped speaking, his mind racing. He couldn't tell her the whole story, not now. She had enough to deal with at the moment. "I swear to you he wasn't angry. We talked, man to man, and he . . . understood."

Amber lifted her eyes to look at him, and he returned her gaze steadily. "I believe you. I couldn't bear it if he'd died thinking poorly of me."

"Oh, no, no, he didn't."

"Where is he? My pa?"

"In the bedroom."

"I don't want to see him dead. Would that be all right, if I didn't want to see him dead?"

"Of course, Amber. You do whatever feels best. We'll bury him this afternoon. You decide on where, someplace he would have liked."

"Not in the cove. I don't want death in the cove. Beyond the cornfield, maybe."

"That's fine."

"We lost the crop."

"Don't think about that now. Why don't you go back to bed and rest?"

"I have chores."

"I did them," he said, smiling at her. "Wait until you taste my stew."

"Oh. Did you hurt your shoulder in the storm?"

"Don't worry about me. You go rest."

"I loved him, Logan. I loved my pa so much."

"I know," he said, his throat tightening. "I know. And he loved you and Benny more than any father I've ever met. That should be some comfort to you, how much Nathan loved you."

"Yes, of course, it is, but . . ." Tears filled her eyes. "But . . . oh, dear God, I don't want him to be gone from me forever. Not my pa. Not my pa, Logan."

She began to tremble, and covered her face with her hands as sobs consumed her. Logan lunged to his feet and went to her. He lifted her into his arms, then settled back onto the chair with Amber held tightly to him.

And she cried.

A feeling of helplessness swept through Logan, and he clenched his jaw in angry frustration. He didn't know what to do or say to ease Amber's pain. Ah, damn, he was a big, strong man, and she was a fragile woman crying as though her heart was breaking. Hell, why wasn't there something he could do?

Amber cried until she had no more tears to

shed, then drew a wobbly breath. She lifted her head to meet Logan's troubled gaze.

"Thank you, Logan," she said softly. "Your comforting me means more than I can say. I'll be fine now. I'll just rest a bit more, if that's all right." She brushed her lips over his, then slid off his lap. "Thank you."

"I didn't do anything."

She looked at him again. "You were here, for me." She managed a small smile. "You were here." She crossed the floor, went into her bedroom, and closed the door.

Logan stared after her. Just his being there had been enough? he thought. That didn't make much sense. How would she feel if she knew he'd been planning to be gone at dawn's light? Well, there was no use dwelling on that. He was staying . . . for now.

"Logan," Moses said, coming in the door, "I'm goin' over to Hunters' to tell 'em 'bout Nathan, see if they want to follow me back for the buryin'. I set the wood out for the coffin and cut it to size. Don't figure Benny should be seeing his pa's coffin bein' put together. Think you could nail it?"

"Yeah."

"Missy wake up yet?"

"Yeah, she came out here. She cried her tears for Nathan. She says I was a comfort to her, but I don't see how. I just hope she's really all right."

"She says you were a comfort, then you were.

Won't hurt none, though, for her to have a woman with her. Mrs. Hunter will know what to do. Benny's comin' with me. You did good with that boy, Logan, real good. Those things you said about Nathan havin' something special to do for the Lord . . . Well, it sounded mighty fine, eased my heart some, too. We'll be goin' on to Hunters' now."

"I'll tend to the coffin. Think Benny wants to see his pa?"

"No, he says not."

"Then I'll move Nathan out of the bedroom and . . . I'll have it done before you get back. Amber wants to bury him beyond the cornfield."

"Not in the cove?"

"No, not in the cove."

"She's right," Moses said, nodding. "The cove is a place of life, not death. Be back shortly."

"Yeah," Logan said, as Moses left the cabin.

The cove was a place of life? he mentally repeated. A new life? A babe? Had it happened last night in the cove? No, he wasn't thinking about that. Last night was a million years ago.

Logan walked to Amber's door and knocked quietly. When there was no response from within, he turned the knob and pushed the door open a bit, peering in. Amber was asleep, huddled in a ball beneath the blanket on the bed.

Should he wake her to tell her he'd be in the barn if she needed him? he wondered. No, better to let her rest. He'd go to the barn, and get back as quickly as he could. Hell, he kept making decisions like he knew exactly what he was doing, which was a far piece from the truth.

In the barn, Logan constructed the coffin while ignoring the jarring pain in his shoulder that came with each swing of the hammer. The wooden box was heavy, and he faced the dilemma of trying to move it to the cabin, or bringing Nathan's body to the barn. He had no intention of waiting for Moses, and forcing Benny to witness what the boy didn't need to see.

Logan settled on a plan of wrapping Nathan in a blanket, hoisting him over his right shoulder, and bringing him to the barn. Without, he hoped, Amber coming out of her bedroom as Logan passed through the cabin.

His dreary chore was just barely completed, the last nail driven into the top of the coffin, when Logan heard the approach of the wagon.

He stepped out of the barn into the bright sunlight, then made his way toward the cabin. A second wagon followed Moses, and Logan recognized Patricia Hunter. A man was driving the Hunter wagon, and five boys rode in the back. When Logan met them at the cabin, Patricia made introductions in a subdued voice.

"How's Amber, Logan?" she said.

"Doing all right, I guess. She cried. She's sleeping in her room."

"I'll go to her," Patricia said. "Dustin, watch the babe. Boys, you stay in the shade by the side of the cabin, and be quiet. Amber's in no mood for noise. Benny, quit using your sleeve for a handkerchief. Hankies were made for a purpose, young man. Logan, smile. You're enough to put anyone in a gloomy mood."

"Hell's fire," Logan said grinning, as Patricia marched into the cabin. "The army could use her."

"She's something, she is," Dustin said, chuckling. "Keeps us walking a straight line."

"Hunters lost their whole crop," Moses said quietly. "Everything."

"That's rough," Logan said. "I'm sorry."

"I was mighty depressed, I'll tell you that," Dustin said. "Was feelin' real sorry for myself till Moses drove up and told us about Nathan. Made me count my blessings. I lost none of my loved ones in that storm. But I'm wiped out, finished. We'll be headin' back to Virginia in a few days' time."

"You're giving up your homestead?" Logan asked.

"Have to. Can't make it through another winter without the supplies we'd have gotten in Waverly with the crop. We'll give you folks our chickens. Damn, it's a shame about Nathan. He was a fine, fine man."

"That he was," Logan said. "I've never met anyone like him before."

"You stayin' on here, Logan?" Dustin asked.

"I . . ."

"Amber's finishing dressing," Patricia said, coming out of the cabin. "Dustin, when you speak over Nathan, keep it short. Amber isn't up to much strain. God rest Nathan's soul. It just doesn't seem right that he was taken. Well, ours is not to question." She sighed. "I hated to tell Amber that we're leaving for Virginia soon, but I thought she should know. I'll miss her so. I'll miss all of you. Move, move, before I start blubbering like a babe."

"Coffin is in the barn," Logan said quietly.

Logan, Moses, and Dustin took the wagon to the barn and loaded the coffin into the back.

"You're not diggin' the grave, Logan," Moses said. "I'm gettin' mighty tired of patchin' your shoulder back together."

Logan climbed up onto the seat next to Moses, as Dustin sat in the bed of the wagon. They walked the horse to the cabin and arrived just as Amber came out of the door. She stared at the coffin for a long moment, then turned and went to the Hunter wagon.

Logan's jaw tightened as he watched her, saw her pale face, the stiff set to her shoulders. Her hair was wound into a tight coil at the nape of her neck, and she wore a severe black dress. Her features softened when Benny ran to hug her, then her solemn mask settled back into place.

Beyond the cornfield the group stood in stony silence, even the Hunter boys keeping still. Moses and Dustin made short work of digging the grave in the rain-soaked soil, then the coffin was lowered into the ground by ropes. Benny buried his face in Patricia's skirt and wept.

Amber didn't take her eyes from the coffin, and Logan's gaze was riveted on her. Dustin spoke of the goodness of Nathan Prescott, the kindness in his heart and soul, and said he would be greatly missed.

The grave was filled in.

It was over.

"Amen," Patricia said, wiping a tear from her cheek. "God bless you, Nathan." She hugged Amber, then hustled the boys into the wagon. "We'll see you before we leave for Virginia," she said. "Moses, Benny needs a nap. He's all tuckered out. Take care now."

"Come on, Benny," Moses said, lifting him up onto the wagon seat as the Hunters drove away. "We'll unhitch this horse, then get you bedded down for a bit. Logan, will you . . ."

"I'll bring Amber," Logan said. "You go ahead."

As Moses clucked to the horses and the wagon creaked forward, Logan turned to Amber. She had wrapped her hands around her elbows as though she was chilled despite the blazing sun, and stood staring at the mound of freshly turned soil that marked her father's grave. Logan searched his mind for something to say to her, something meaningful, but he drew a blank.

"Good-bye, Pa," Amber whispered, as two tears slid down her cheeks. "I love you, Nathan Prescott. Rest easy in the place you've gone to. Good-bye."

Logan swallowed past the lump in his throat, then placed his hand gently on her shoulder. "Let's go back to the cabin. It's too hot out here. I . . . yeah, I have to check on my stew."

Amber dashed the tears from her cheeks and they started toward the cabin.

"Hunters are going back to Virginia," she said quietly.

"Yeah, I know."

"Pa is dead. The Hunters are going. Everyone is leaving."

"That's not true."

"Oh, Logan, I'm going to miss my pa so much."

"I know," he said gently, "but you have Benny, who really needs you now more than ever, and Moses."

"And you, Logan?"

"I'm right here," he said, forcing a smile.

She halted her step, causing Logan to do the same. She looked up at him.

"I love you, Logan."

"Yeah, well," he said, then stopped speaking

for a moment. "Benny is probably due for a hug, so let's get back to the cabin."

"To check on your stew?" she said, smiling.

"Yeah, my stew. It'll be great." He paused. "Amber, Nathan wouldn't want you to grieve too long for him. He'd want you to get on with living; smiling, laughing, singing softly like you do."

"Loving?"

"Come on," he said, starting off again.

Oh, yeah, he thought dryly, Nathan saw loving and making love, as part of Amber's world. Jesus in heaven, what would she say if she knew that Nathan had sent Logan to the cove last night with the sole purpose of having him make love to her? Nathan had even been praying there would be a babe from that coming together. Would she understand her father's reasoning, or feel betrayed?

Amber glanced over her shoulder for another look at Nathan's grave.

"Give it time," Logan said. "The pain will go away, and then you'll have all the nice memories to think about."

"It didn't work that way for you about Michael and Jude."

"No, it didn't, because I allowed the hate to fill me. I took the wrong road, but you won't let that happen. You're a Prescott, and that's something to be proud of. And you've got a fine homestead here, a purpose, a reason to get up in the morning. Everything is going to work out fine, Amber, you'll see."

"We've got to get those ears of corn from beneath the tarps before they spoil," she said. "We'll dry and shuck them, then use them for seed in the spring. There won't be money now for beans, but that can't be helped. Unless . . . Yes, I could finish my quilt, and try to trade it in Waverly for bean seeds. Patricia is giving us her chickens. Oh, I wish the Hunters weren't leaving. So much has changed so quickly, Logan. So very much."

"Don't think about anything today. Tomorrow is soon enough to tend to what needs doing. Just rest and be there for Benny."

"I suppose you're right," she said, as they approached the cabin.

Moses came out of the door. "Missy?"

"Oh, Moses," she said, hugging him tightly. "I'll miss Pa every day of my life, but I'll smile, I promise. Where's Benny?"

"He's sleeping. He wouldn't go into the bedroom, so he's on Logan's cot. Benny says he can't sleep in that room without his pa, and I guess we'll respect that for a while. I'll take Nathan's cot to the barn to use. You can sleep on Benny's, Logan."

Logan frowned. "No, I don't think so, Moses. You sleep in there, I'll take the barn."

"No, sir," Moses said, shaking his head. "I have my things around me out there. It's home to me. Amber and Benny need a man in the cabin to protect them at night. That man is you."

But he wasn't staying there, damn it, Logan's mind thundered. He'd told Moses that. Nothing had changed. He was leaving. He was still Logan Wade, killer. He still didn't deserve to stay among these people, or to have the love of Amber Prescott.

And how in the hell was he supposed to sleep under the same roof with Amber and not touch her, without going straight out of his mind?

Eleven

Inside the cabin, Amber hurried to the cot to check on a sleeping Benny. Her gaze fell on the open saddlebags lying on the end of the cot, and she turned to look at Logan questioningly.

"Benny got a clean shirt out for me," Logan said. "I've got no big secrets in those saddlebags, Amber. Just a few things I own, nothing fancy."

Amber nodded, then walked to the hearth to peer at the stew. She stirred it, but made no comment regarding the unpeeled vegetables.

Logan had allowed Benny to go in his saddlebags, her mind whispered. It was a sign that Logan was relaxing, coming to view them as his family, this as his home. Wasn't it? He'd worked so hard to save the corn crop, been with them, side by side.

And her pa, her wonderful pa, she mused, had accepted and understood what had taken place in the cove. He hadn't thought poorly of her. He'd believed in her enough to know that she'd gone to Logan as a woman in love with her man.

And Pa had liked Logan, had seen himself in Logan Wade. There was no guilt nor shame to be had from what they had done. She loved Logan and he . . . No, he'd never said that he loved her, but surely he did. He'd said they'd made love, not had plain old sex. And he'd said he'd never made love with anyone but her. He loved her, she knew he did, and he would tell her when he felt the time was right.

"I'm goin' to go take the tarps from the corn," Moses said.

"I'll help you," Logan said. "With one hand. Believe me, Moses, I'm tired of you jabbing around on my shoulder, too. I can pull them free with one hand."

"All right then," Moses said, heading for the door.

"We'll be in later, Amber," Logan said. "You just rest while we're gone. There's nothing you need to be doing."

"I'll rest," she said, smiling.

The two men left the cabin and Amber sank onto the rocker, moving it slowly back and forth. She was so tired, so very tired. She felt old, as though she'd aged years in just hours.

"Oh, Pa," she said, her eyes filling with tears. He was really gone, and she had to accept that, just as she'd had to deal with losing her ma. But, dear heaven, it hurt, just hurt so much. Count your blessings, Pa would say. Yes, she should do that. She had many blessings in Benny, Moses, their fine homestead. She had a roof over her head, clothes on her back, meat in the smokehouse. And then there was the blessing that was so special, wonderful, rare; Logan. Her Logan. Pa was with his beloved Mary again. Amber was with Logan.

"I'll miss you, Pa, I truly will," she said, her voice hushed. "But I'll make you proud. I'll care for Benny, Moses, tend to my chores as the woman of this homestead, and love my Logan. Until I draw my last breath, I'll love my Logan."

Out in the field, Logan removed his shirt, and began to drag the tarps from the crumbled corn stalks. Moses had once again hitched the horse to the wagon, and the tarps were folded and stacked in the bed. Each time Logan forgot and yanked with both hands, the shooting pain in his shoulder pulled him up short, and made him swear a blue streak. The men worked in silence until the last tarp was in the wagon.

"Now what?" Logan said.

"Pull the ears of corn off, and put them in those wicker baskets," Moses said.

"Amber says she's working on a quilt she could trade for the bean seeds."

"I suppose," Moses said, nodding. "Be the

best thing to do gettin' those beans goin' in the spring but . . . well . . ."

"But what?"

"Mr. Prescott, well, Nathan planned to have missy trade that quilt for something real special for her birthday. He was goin' to tell her when we went into Waverly next trip. He even had the storekeeper set it back for her. Nathan gave the man a dollar to save that surprise, told him Amber made the finest quilt in this county. Well, so be it. I'll tell the storekeeper we can't be gettin' it. Suppose he'll keep that dollar, though."

"What was it? The surprise for her birthday?"

"A music box. Prettiest little thing you ever saw. Lift the cover and it plays a tune just as nice as you please. She sure would have liked that music box."

"Yeah, I'm sure she would have," Logan said quietly.

"Logan," Moses said, "you told me this mornin' that you're leavin' here. That's your business and none of mine, but I can't say that I know why you're goin'. You said yourself that you got no family, no one waitin' on you to get back. There's a place here for you, if you want it. And I know our missy loves you, she sure enough does. You could have a good life here."

"With good and decent people," Logan said frowning. "I have no right to be here, Moses.

I'm not like all of you. I killed men out of pure hate and revenge. I carry a burden of guilt about that that weighs me down. And now I've got the guilt about Amber twisting my insides."

"Nathan never intended you to feel . . ."

"I know that. He told me. But it doesn't change how I feel about it. Amber deserves better than me, Moses. I can see it all in my mind, those past five years, what I did, how I lived. I can't pretend it didn't happen, and no one else should, either. You'll be here, you'll take care of Amber and Benny. She'll meet some young buck in Waverly, who will be proud to be a part of this homestead, be Amber's husband, and raise Benny as a son."

"And if she has your babe? What then, Logan?"

"Jesus, Moses, don't do this to me," Logan said, staring up at the sky for a long moment. "Do you think I like the idea of riding out of here not knowing if she's carrying my child?"

"I don't know."

"Damn you, what kind of man do you think I am?" Logan roared.

"Only what you're tellin' me you are," Moses said calmly.

"You're just like Nathan, do you know that? You talk quiet and low, you look straight into a man's soul, you reason things through just like he did."

"Well, thank you," Moses said, smiling and

nodding. "To be compared favorably with Nathan Prescott is one of the finest things ever said to me."

"And you drive me crazy," Logan bellowed. "Just the same as he did."

"Mmm," Moses said. "Yeah, I expect that I do. To me, a man's past is his to deal with. What he does today is what's important."

"Oh, yeah? Well, on that one we agree. I'm dealing with my past, and it tells me I can't stay here."

"Makes no sense to me, Wade. It truly don't."

"Good Lord above," Logan said, "you're Nathan in a bigger body and darker skin." Moses laughed. "If you say you're praying for Amber to have my babe, I'll lose my mind, standing right here in front of you."

"I'm not prayin' for that."

"Well, thank God for that much," Logan muttered.

"I *already* prayed for it. Got down on my knees in the barn, folded my hands, and asked the Almighty to . . ."

"That's it!" Logan said, pointing a long finger at Moses. "Don't say another word. We'll pick the damn corn, but don't speak to me while we're doing it."

Moses chuckled. "You're not actin' too friendly, Logan."

"Crazy men don't have to be friendly," he

said, glaring at Moses. "Everyone just keeps out of our way."

Moses whooped with laughter. Logan's frown deepened. They worked in silence for the next hour, their backs aching from the tedious chore of bending over to pick the corn from the broken stalks. The sun began to inch its way westward, a cooling breeze bringing welcome relief from the scorching heat. Moses straightened and glanced up at the sky.

"Looks peaceful enough," he said, "but I don't trust it none. We best load these baskets into the wagon and get them in the barn."

"We're a long way from finished," Logan said, drawing his forearm over his sweaty brow. "This corn is exposed now. We'll lose it if it hails again."

"We'll lose it to spoil if we leave it under the tarps," Moses said. "Chance we'll have to take."

"Well, I don't know much about how all this works."

"You're learnin'."

"Doesn't matter if I do. I'm leaving here, remember?"

Moses swung a basket of corn on top of the tarps in the wagon bed. "Just when you plannin' on goin'?"

Logan's head snapped up. "Oh, well, I . . ." He ran one hand over the back of his neck. ". . . I haven't decided for sure. I thought I'd be certain that Amber and Benny are all settled down about Nathan."

"That's mighty considerate of you," Moses said, grinning.

"Well, I owe Nathan my life. I think it's the least I can do."

"Yep."

"By the way, Mr. Moses," Logan said gruffly, "I don't appreciate the way you arranged for me to sleep in that cabin."

"That a fact? Why not?"

"Because Amber's in there."

"Yep."

"Damn it, man, I'm not touching her again. I'm carrying a lifetime of guilt as it is. Do you have any idea what it's going to be like trying to sleep when she's . . . Ah, hell, forget it."

"Yep, I'd say you got a bit of a problem there," Moses said, chuckling softly.

"I'm glad you realize that. I'll take the barn."

"Nope. The barn is my home, I told you that."

"Yeah? Then what fancy plan are you going to come up with when I leave? It's not good thinking to leave a woman and boy alone in a cabin at night."

"I figure to worry 'bout that when the time comes. No sense in bringin' on troubles 'fore they get here."

"Thank you, Nathan Prescott," Logan said dryly. "He'd have said that."

"Yep. Let's haul this load to the barn. It'll take us an hour to get these tarps put away. Be suppertime by then."

Logan suddenly smiled. "I wouldn't be in an all-fired rush about eating that meal. I made the stew, remember?"

The two men looked at each other and burst into laughter, the boisterous, masculine sound carrying through the gathering dusk. Moses gazed out over the land in the direction of Nathan's grave.

"He would have liked this, you know," Moses said quietly. "Hearin' laughter on this homestead on the day he died. He'd have been the first to say it was fine to cry, to wash away the sorrow, then he'd be listenin' for the laughter."

"And for Amber to sing softly," Logan said.

"That, too. Let's get movin'."

It was dark by the time Logan and Moses left the barn and headed for the cabin. The welcoming glow of the oil lamp beckoned to them to enter, but they washed up first, going in through the back door. Benny was peering over Amber's shoulder as she ladled the stew into a bowl.

"That don't look so good, Amber," Benny said. "What's wrong with those potatoes?"

"Nothing's wrong with them. They have the peels on, that's all. Peels never hurt anyone," Amber said, turning to the table. "Oh, Logan, Moses, I didn't hear you come in. You surely put in long hours in that field. Come sit. You must be starving."

"Finest looking stew I ever saw," Logan said, ruffling Benny's hair.

The group sat down, filled their plates, then a silence fell as one by one their gazes were pulled to Nathan's empty chair.

"Oh, dear," Amber said, brushing a tear from her cheek. "I'm sorry, but it just isn't natural yet that Pa isn't here."

"That chair," Logan said, "is for the Prescott man of the house. It seems to me that Benny should be sitting in it."

"Me?" Benny said, his eyes widening. "Sittin' in my pa's chair?"

"Yes," Amber said firmly. "Absolutely. You are the Prescott man of the house now, and that's where you belong. Here's his plate, Logan. Benny, you go on and take your rightful place."

Benny walked slowly to the head of the table, then looked at Amber, Logan, and Moses. Each nodded their encouragement. The little boy slid onto the seat, then took a deep breath.

"Are you sure that Pa . . ." he started, his lower lip trembling.

"He'd want you there, Benjamin," Amber said gently. "He truly would."

Benny drew himself up to his full height. "Then here I'll sit," he said, smiling.

The gloomy mood that had settled over the cabin dissipated, and the meal was consumed.

No one complained about the stew, but no one had second helpings. Moses and Benny went to the barn to tend to the stock. Logan sipped another cup of coffee as Amber washed the dishes.

"That was lousy stew," Logan said, laughing softly.

"It certainly was, Mr. Wade," Amber said, smiling, "but it's the thought that counts."

"I suppose."

"Logan, I saw the blood-soaked rags. Is your shoulder all right?"

"No worse. I tore it open a bit, but not enough to worry about."

"You'll be careful with it, won't you?"

"Yep. The faster it heals, the less misery I suffer from Moses poking on me."

"Logan, you're so good with Benny. You seem to know, sense, just what he needs, what to say to him. You're going to make a wonderful father someday."

Logan stiffened in his chair, every muscle in his body tensing. He searched Amber's face as she wiped up the table, but saw no hint that she was doing anything but idly chatting.

Sweet heaven, he thought, hadn't it crossed her mind at all that she could be carrying his child within her? No, maybe not. So much had happened since they'd been in the cove, she probably hadn't thought of that yet. Lord knew everyone else had.

"I'll be doing the wash tomorrow," Amber

said. "Thought I'd tell you in case you were working up to another tantrum about your pants."

"Doing the wash is a big job, Amber. Maybe you should rest another day."

"No need," she said, sitting down opposite him at the table. She yawned.

"You're tired," Logan said. "Why don't you go on to bed. I'll tuck Benny in when he comes."

"Logan, would it be disrespectful for us to make love on the night of the day my pa died?"

He choked on his coffee. "What?"

"Are there rules about that?"

"How in the hell should I know?" he said, his voice rising. "But rules or not, we're not making love tonight." Or any other night, his mind screamed. Never again. He was never touching her again.

"We're not?"

"No!"

"Why not?"

Because he couldn't bear the guilt. Because he was leaving her, damn it. "Because you're tired," he said.

"I'm not *that* tired."

"Well, I am. And my shoulder's throbbing like a toothache. I just want to fall onto that cot and sleep 'til morning."

"Oh. Well," she said, sighing, "I guess that's that."

"Damn right, it is," he said, scowling at her. "Go on to bed now."

Benny came in the door at that moment, his steps dragging.

"Oh, Benny, you're so worn out," Amber said, getting to her feet. "Let's get your nightshirt on, and I'll tuck you in."

"Moses said I could sleep on the cot out here."

"That's fine," Moses said, coming in the door. "I just came for the spare cot in the bedroom."

"Fancy that," Logan said, giving Moses a stormy glare. Moses hooted with laughter. "I'm going outside for a while."

The sky was an umbrella of twinkling stars, the moon a silvery globe in the heavens as Logan walked leisurely toward the cornfield, the way clearly lit by the spectacle of beauty overhead.

He filled his lungs with the fresh, cool air, drinking in the aromas of the homestead. The turmoil in his mind gentled, the land once again giving its gift of peace.

He veered to the right and went on, soon finding himself at the edge of the cove. Hesitating a moment, he worked his way through the trees to come to the clearing by the stream, stretching out on his back on the lush grass.

Memories of Amber assaulted him, and he granted them entry, reliving in his mind the lovemaking they had shared in that special place. He saw her naked before him, her breasts full, hips gently sloped, her hair a golden cascade tumbling to her waist.

How sweet, innocent, and trusting she had been as she'd given herself to him, declaring her love, offering him her treasure. She had filled the empty chill in his soul with love and warmth, and their joining had been like nothing he had ever experienced before. He loved her with an aching intensity, which seemed to grow with every passing hour.

Logan's body reacted to his vivid memories, and he shifted slightly to ease his discomfort. It was worth an ache in his gut, he decided, to replay in his mind each exquisite moment of what he had shared with his Amber. The memories were all he was to have.

He had to leave, he knew it, but the question was . . . when. But, sweet Jesus, how he wanted to stay. Stay and love his Amber. Stay and work with Moses dawn to dusk with a purpose, a reason for being. Stay and be a friend, a substitute father for Benny, who had staked a claim on Logan's heart. Logan wanted it all, every bit of it. But he didn't deserve any of it.

Logan thought suddenly of the bullet that still rested in his pocket, and he drew it out, turning it between his fingers as he stared at it. With a surge of anger, he sat up and threw the battered metal into the stream, watching the circle of water grow bigger and bigger around where it had landed. The bullet had

had the same kind of far-reaching effects on his life. It had brought him to this cove, to Amber, and he would never be the same again. Nathan had dug that bullet out of him, but the knife had not sliced away the past five years of his existence.

When should he go? he thought, sinking back onto the grass. The question was beginning to torment him nearly as much as the reality of the thought that he would be leaving his Amber forever. So, yeah, he'd see the work through on the cornfield, help build the chicken coop, and repair the fence. That was it. He would stay for as many days as those chores took, then he'd go.

"Damn," Logan said, rolling up to his feet in a smooth, powerful motion. It had been a helluva day, and he was tired, bone weary. He couldn't think any more tonight, not tonight. The problem of how long he was staying had been solved. That was something at least. All he wanted to do now was get some sleep.

He walked back to the cabin and entered through the front door, which he closed and latched behind him. He checked to see that the shutters were firmly in place, then gazed down at a sleeping Benny. The little boy had his arms flung above his head in the abandon of childish slumber, and a gentle smile tugged at Logan's lips.

Benny was a nice kid, Logan mused, one any man should be proud to call his own. He might

not grow up to be very big, but he had
Nathan's blood in his veins, and Benny could
walk tall among any he chose. He was a
Prescott, and that made him a cut above the
rest.

Logan turned and walked to the table to
blow out the lamp, but he hesitated, his gaze
coming to rest on Amber's closed bedroom
door. She was in that room, his Amber, in that
bed, wearing her pristine nightie, her hair in
heavy braids over her full, lush breasts. Breasts
he knew, had touched, kissed, suckled. The
dewy silk of her skin was like velvet beneath
his callused hands, the liquid heat between her
thighs a haven of ecstasy for his pulsing manhood, that now stirred, ached with the need
and want of her. Amber. Good God, how he
loved her.

Logan drew a sharp, painful breath, striving
for control, willing his body to cool its ardor
and rising passion. He damned his lusty nature, registered disgust at his randy thoughts.

His glance fell on Nathan's empty chair.
Damn that Nathan Prescott and his reasoning
born of love for Amber, Logan fumed. Damn
the guilt Nathan had heaped on Logan's soul.
And damn that Amber for causing Logan to
fall in love with her.

Rage and sexual frustration pounded
through Logan's veins, clouding his touch with
reality. He wasn't thinking clearly, knew it to
be true somewhere in the deep recesses of his

mind, but he didn't care. He was filled with cold fury at all that had taken place, and ached with the need of his woman. His hands curled into tight fists at his sides, as a tremor swept through his coiled body.

And then Amber was there.

She stepped from her room and seemed to float toward him, a vision of loveliness in her white gown, the oil lamp flickering its glow over her lissome form. She came to him, standing before him, looking up at him with a serene, gentle, womanly smile on her face.

"Damn you," Logan said, then gripped her arms and hauled her up against him, his mouth coming down hard onto hers in a punishing kiss.

Logan jerked his head away and lifted Amber into his arms, striding across the cabin, and into her bedroom kicking the door closed behind him. He dropped her onto the bed, then stripped her nightgown up and away to leave her naked before him. His jaw was set in a tight, hard line, and a muscle twitched in the strong column of his neck. She stared up at him with wide eyes that registered a flicker of fear.

"Logan, what . . ."

"Shut up," he said, unbuttoning his shirt.

Love and hate tumbled together in his mind; screaming, pulling at him, driving him on. He sat on the edge of the bed to remove his boots in jerky motions, then stood again to shed his pants. His glistening, naked body was a bold announcement of his masculinity.

"Logan," Amber said shakily, "why are you so angry? You're frightening me. You said we weren't going to . . ."

"Don't talk, damn it," he said, covering her body with his. "This is what you wanted. This is what you all wanted, all of you. I can't fight you all. And I can't fight this fire burning in me."

"Logan, I don't understand what you're talking about."

"Damn you, Amber Prescott," he said, with a strangled moan, then claimed her mouth in a searing, feverish kiss.

No, Amber's mind screamed. There was something wrong. This wasn't Logan, this angry, brutal man. Why was he doing this? Where was the gentle kiss, the stroking hands, the . . . But, oh, dear heaven, she wanted him.

Amber circled Logan's neck with her arms, increasing the pressure of his ravishing mouth on hers. Her breasts were crushed to his chest in a sweet pain, his massive form heavy upon her. The honeyed warmth in the core of her femininity was kindled from an ember to a raging flame of desire that rambled throughout her, igniting her passion as it went.

She moved her hands to his muscled back, his buttocks, then gasped in pleasure as he ground his hips against her, his manhood strong and heated, holding the promise of ecstasy.

He tore his mouth from hers and found her breast, drawing the nipple deep into his mouth, his tongue flicking roughly over the taut bud. He moved to the other, his hand skimming down her stomach to her secret place of darkness.

"Logan," she gasped, as his fingers sought and found her womanly heat.

He lifted his hips and in the next instant drove deep within her with a powerful thrust that stole the breath from her body. She took him into her, all of him, sheathing him in velvet heat, arching her back to bring him closer yet. Logan thundered within her with a cadence that echoed in her ears. She met his tempo, matched his raging rhythm, felt herself be lifted away to soar above time and space. Spasms rocketed through their bodies, spilling them over into the glorious place they had traveled to.

"Logan!"

"Sweet Jesus . . . Amber."

And then all was still, quiet, strangely quiet.

Logan stiffened and moved away, rolling onto his back and flinging his arm over his eyes, his chest heaving. "Dear God," he whispered, "what have I done?"

Amber drew a deep, steadying breath, then sat up, turning her head to look at him. "You made love to me," she said, a thread of breathlessness in her voice. "Yes, you certainly did."

He shot up and gripped her by the arms. "I raped you," he said, his voice harsh. "Are you so dumb you can't tell the difference?"

"Don't be silly," she said, smiling at him. "It was, well, slightly rougher than in the cove but, oh, Logan, you took me to that wonderful place again. It was glorious."

Logan swung off the bed and began to dress, his hands trembling.

"Logan," Amber said, "why are you so angry? I'm glad we made love. You frightened me at first, but I don't pretend to understand yet all there is to know about this. Didn't I please you?"

"Listen to me," he said, through clenched teeth. "I didn't make love to you, that was plain old sex like with the whores in the saloons. I took from you, I didn't give. That was barnyard rutting, Amber."

"It was not. Don't you dare say such a thing, or utter words like rape, and whores, and . . . I swear, Logan, you're not making any sense at all. If I'm not upset, then why should you be?"

"Damn it, because I was never going to touch you again."

"What?" she whispered.

"I planned to help Moses with the corn, the chicken coop, the fence, then I was leaving here! Leaving, Amber, and never coming back."

"Dear Lord, no," she said, scrambling to her knees.

"Oh, yes," he said, a bitter edge to his voice, "I was going because I didn't deserve to be here, I wasn't good enough, decent enough. But there were too many of you to fight, too damn many. Well, you won, all of you. Nathan, Moses, you."

"I don't understand," she said frantically. "I love you. I . . ."

"I don't have space in my soul for what happened in this room tonight, Amber," he said, his voice suddenly flat, empty-sounding. "I was already overflowing with guilt, and there's nowhere to put this. The only chance I have of saving my sanity is to stay here and work. I'll work until I'm too tired to breathe. Maybe then, maybe, if I give to the land, to this homestead, I'll ease some of the pain of my guilt. Maybe."

"Oh, no, Logan, that's the wrong reason to stay. I thought you wanted to be here. I thought you loved me. Logan?"

He picked up his boots and stared down at her, an unreadable expression on his face. Then, without speaking, he turned and left the room, closing the door behind him.

Twelve

When Amber woke the next morning at dawn, a wave of sadness washed over her. She opened her eyes and wondered in her foggy state if she had had a disturbing dream. But then she remembered. Her pa was dead. Logan didn't love her, and had been going to leave the homestead.

She mustered every ounce of her determination, pushed aside her gloomy mood, and slid off the bed. After washing with her lavender soap, she dressed in a yellow-and-white gingham checked dress, then wound her hair into a bun at the nape of her neck. Her breasts were tender from her less-than-gentle lovemaking with Logan, and a smile tugged onto her lips.

Logan was staying, her mind and heart whispered. For a while and for the wrong reasons, he was staying. And with that knowledge came the glimmer of hope that he would step away from his past and into the future, with her.

Amber left the bedroom to find sunlight streaming in through the open doors and shutters. Muffled voices came from the rear of the cabin, and Amber went to the back door and looked out.

Logan was stripped to the waist, lather covering his face as he shaved. He bent his knees slightly to see in the mirror hanging on the cabin, and the action caused his pants to strain against the muscles of his thighs. His pants rode low on his hips, his belt still looped through the pair Amber planned to wash that day.

As he dragged the straight-edged razor over his jaw, the corded muscles in his arms bunched from the motion. The dark hair on his chest was damp and curly, and Amber's gaze followed the path it took as it narrowed to a strip that disappeared below the waistband of his pants.

He was only shaving, she told herself, but there was something just so masculine about the entire scene she was witnessing. Every move he made spoke of power, strength, virility, and her heart fluttered wildly beneath her breast.

She knew that body. It had meshed with hers, become one with hers, taken her to that glorious, ecstasy-filled place. And she knew that man. He could bellow in rage, speak kindly in concern, whisper hoarsely in passion. He was Logan. And she loved him.

Benny was leaning against the wooden table, his arms crossed on the top as he stared up at Logan. The little boy was dressed, his hair slicked down. He watched every move that Logan made, an expression of awe on his face.

"I never saw a man grow so much beard overnight," Benny said.

"That a fact?" Logan said, swishing the razor in the pan of water. "I'm just a hairy bear, I guess."

"My pa shaved, but I never paid no attention. Moses has his own mirror in the barn. Doesn't that hurt, scraping on your face like that?"

"Nope," Logan said, tilting his chin up to draw the razor along his throat.

"You're welcome to move the mirror higher," Amber said.

"Jesus," Logan said, jerking as he turned to look at her where she stood in the doorway. "I nearly slit my throat. Don't sneak up on a man when he's shaving, Amber."

"Yeah," Benny said, frowning, "don't do that." He ran his hand over his smooth cheeks. "A man could cut himself real bad."

Logan chuckled as he glanced down at Benny. "Don't be in a rush to start shaving. Once you get a stubble, you have to do this every day, like it or not. I saw a man once who had a beard that went all the way to his belly. He . . ."

"I'll start breakfast," Amber said stiffly, then spun around and went to the side cupboard. She scooped coffee beans from the sack and dumped them into the grinder, turning the handle with more force than was necessary.

Logan Wade was being rude again, she silently fumed. He'd barked at her, then ignored her like she was a bug on the wall. It would have served him right if he'd slit his throat. There he'd stood, half naked, his chest glistening in the morning sun, shaving with that slow, steady motion that reminded her of when his hands were stroking her breasts and . . . Oh, he was just so rude.

Amber pursed her lips and set the table. Then she broke eggs into a frying pan and placed it on the grate after stoking the fire. She sliced bread, ham, and dried beef, then made the coffee.

Logan's stew, she decided, was going to be finished at noon. It simply was not meant for empty stomachs first thing in the morning.

Logan came in the back door buttoning his shirt, Benny close on his heels, as Moses came in the front door.

"Mornin'," Moses said.

"Hello, Moses," Amber said, smiling at him. "Breakfast is ready. Benny sit down. Oh, you, too, Logan," she said, not looking at him.

Moses glanced at Amber then Logan. "Mmm," the big man said. "Everyone doin' all right this mornin'?"

"Just dandy," Logan said gruffly, sitting down at the table. Benny slid onto Nathan's chair. "I don't suppose anyone knows where my belt is," Logan said. "I'd hate to have my pants fall off at an inappropriate time." Benny giggled.

"Your belt, Mr. Wade," Amber said, plunking the platter of eggs onto the table, "will be retrieved from your filthy, dirty pants when I do the wash today. Moses, I'd appreciate your bringing my washtubs up from the barn, along with what you need washing."

"Sure thing, missy. I'll stretch the hanging ropes for you, too."

"Thank you. Now, eat while it's hot."

"I figure you want us to pick the rest of that corn, Moses," Logan said, heaping eggs on his plate.

"Yep. We need to get that done. You feelin' up to workin' today, Benny?"

"Yep," Benny said. "Can I have some coffee?"

"No," Amber said. "You drink your mug of milk like you always do."

"I'm not a babe, Amber. I want some coffee."

"No, Benjamin, you may not have coffee."

"You can have coffee," Logan said, "if you don't mind staying the size you are. It makes you stop growing if you drink it before you're at your full height."

"That a fact?" Benny said, his eyes wide.

"Truly is," Moses said. "Know why I'm so big? Didn't get no coffee in me till I was way past the time I shoulda stopped growin'. Lucky for me someone poured a mug in me 'fore I got any taller. I'd never have fit in a cabin like this if I hadn't got that mug of brew when I did."

"I think I'll just drink this milk," Benny said. Logan and Moses exchanged smiles.

Amber, however, frowned. Rude, her mind repeated. All of them. They were ignoring her. There they sat, eating the food she'd prepared without so much as a glance in her direction. Benny had been ready to argue his head off for that mug of coffee until Logan stepped in with his ridiculous tale, which Moses went along with. Had anyone asked if she felt up to working today? No. They'd just pile up their dirty clothes and expect her to . . .

"Amber," Logan said quietly, "maybe you should wait another day on that wash. You should rest up after last . . . after yesterday."

A warm glow started in the pit of Amber's stomach and traveled throughout her, showing itself in the form of a lovely smile on her face.

"Thank you for your concern, Logan," she said, "but I'm fine, I truly am. There's not a thing wrong with me."

Logan looked at her for a long moment, a deep frown on his face, then redirected his attention to his plate without commenting.

"You sure look pretty as a picture," Moses said. "Not every homestead in Texas has such a pretty woman at the head of the table."

"Amber's prettier than any girl I seen in Waverly," Benny said.

"Why, thank you," she said. Oh, weren't they all just the sweetest things? "Gather all your dirty clothes, and I'll wash them squeaky clean. I'll get your belt for you now, Logan," she said, getting up from the table.

"No need. I can wait for it."

"It's no trouble at all," she said cheerfully. "I should have thought of it before now."

"Fine breakfast, missy," Moses said, getting to his feet. "Come on, Benny, you can help me bring up the washtubs."

"I'll go on to the field," Logan said, quickly pushing back his chair and rising.

"Just a minute, Logan," Amber said, rummaging through a wicker basket of clothes. "I'll give you your belt."

Logan's jaw tightened as he glanced over at Amber then back to the doorway that Moses and Benny were disappearing through.

Damn it, he thought, he didn't want to be alone with her. He couldn't face her after what he'd done to her last night. Now he could add the title of coward to his long list of worthless attributes. He was such a bastard. He'd taken his Amber with no regard for her, her pleasure. He'd been rough, brutal, had no doubt left his mark on her delicate body. And she'd still told him that their joining had been wonderful, because that was how much she loved and trusted him. Damn, he didn't deserve to be in the same room with her.

"Here you are," Amber said, walking to where Logan stood and handing him the belt.

"Thanks," he said gruffly, starting toward the door, then turning back toward the cot. "Think I'll get my Stetson. That sun gets damn hot." He reached under the cot for the Stetson, then straightened, settling the hat on his head.

Beautiful, Amber thought dreamily. Logan looked so rugged with that Stetson casting shadows over his tanned face. Just so male. "Oh," she said, snapping herself back to attention. "Don't you want a fresh bandage on your shoulder?"

"No," he said, starting toward the door again.

"But you got it wet this morning."

"I said no, Amber," he said, through clenched teeth.

"Logan?"

He stopped, his back to her, his shoulders ramrod stiff. "What?"

"Nothing," she said softly. I love you, her mind whispered.

"Are you sure you're all right?" he said, his voice hushed. Had he hurt her? Dear God, had he? He'd been so damn rough with her.

"Yes, I'm fine. I told you last night that I was. What we shared was . . ."

Logan spun around, his blue eyes flashing.

"We didn't 'share' anything. I took from you, pure and simple."

"That's not true."

"I was there."

"So was I."

"You're doing it again," he said. "You're pretending if you ignore something it will go away. Well, it won't work, any of it. You'll be a lot better off if you face the truth as it is."

Amber smiled. "I intend to, Logan Wade."

He narrowed his eyes. "Meaning?"

"Meaning I love you with every breath in my body. Meaning I will cherish the memory of last night right along with the memory of our time in the cove."

"Damn it to hell," he roared, turning and stalking out of the door.

"I still say he swears too much," Amber said, beginning to clear the table.

And in the next moment she began to sing softly, the husky sound floating through the clear morning air.

Outside, Logan stopped dead in his tracks, his head snapping around. Now she was singing? his mind raged. Singing, for God's sake? Hell. He started off again in the direction of the field, his boots thudding against the dusty ground as he went, a deep frown on his face.

By the time Amber had cleaned up from breakfast, the water in the washtub was boiling, having been set over a fire prepared by Moses in front of the cabin. The second tub contained cool, clear rinse water.

She added the lye to the hot water, then stirred it thoroughly with a stick. She poked the soiled clothes beneath the surface, tears springing to her eyes as she touched Nathan's things.

She would wash them clean, she decided, then store them in her hope chest to be used for rags and scraps for her quilt. She'd done the same with her mother's dresses, so nothing would go to waste, but it brought an ache to her heart to know she was washing her father's clothes for the last time.

The sun climbed higher in the sky, and Amber felt the perspiration run down between her full breasts. She rinsed the clothes in the cool water, wrung them out, then draped them over the ropes Moses had strung from nails in the side of the cabin to stakes set in the ground.

Her arms ached from her efforts, and her dress began to stick to her skin. On and on she worked, until the last shirt was flung across the ropes. The sun was directly overhead, and she sighed, realizing it was time to prepare the noon meal.

Inside the cabin, she scrubbed her hands and face, then set out the food. She was just too hot to eat, she decided. All she wanted to do was go to the stream, bathe, and wash her hair. She gathered clean clothes, a towel, her lavender soap, and headed for the cornfield.

"Logan, Moses, Benny," she called, as she approached.

All three straightened from where they were bent over the stalks, and started toward her.

"Where you headed, missy?" Moses said.

"I'm going to the stream to bathe. Your meal is ready on the table."

"Wait a minute," Logan said, coming to where she stood. "You're going to bathe in that stream naked?"

"That's usually how one bathes, sir," she said, frowning up at him. "It's a little difficult to do with one's clothes on."

"Don't get sassy," he said. "It's not good thinking to be naked in that stream alone. What if someone comes along? What about renegade Comanches?"

"Don't be silly. No one is going to go into that cove."

"*I* did," he said, thumping his chest with his thumb. "What if you'd been naked *that* day?"

"You were too weak to do anything about it."

"Mercy," Moses said, chuckling.

"What? Too weak for what?" Benny said, appearing totally confused.

"Hush, Benny," Moses said, grinning. "Missy and Logan are workin' up to a real wing-dinger of a fight here. Don't interrupt."

"Oh, all right," Benny said, shrugging.

Logan glared at Moses.

"Well, I'm off," Amber said. "Go eat, and I'll see you later."

"Hold it, Miss Prescott," Logan said, grabbing her arm. "Maybe I didn't make myself clear. You're not going into that cove alone, and stripping down to your bare bottom." Benny giggled. "Shut up, Benny," Logan said.

"Yes, sir," Benny said, then clamped his hand over his mouth.

Amber smacked Logan's hand away. "Don't tell me what to do, Logan Wade. You're not my father."

"Damn right, I'm not. I'm your . . ." Logan stopped speaking and looked quickly at Moses, who had a pleasant, all-innocence expression on his face. Lover, Logan finished in his mind. And the man who loved her. "Hell," he said, throwing up his hands, "I give up."

"Well, you know," Amber said slowly, gazing up at him from beneath her lashes, "if you're all that concerned, you could come stand guard while I bathe."

"No," Logan said, then swallowed heavily. "No, absolutely not."

"Just a suggestion. Ta-ta," she said, waggling her fingers at him as she walked away, a definite sway to her hips.

Logan tugged his Stetson roughly forward on his head, then planted his hands on his hips as he stared up at the sky in an attempt to control his temper. "I should tan her butt," he muttered.

Moses laughed. "She'll be all right in that

cove, Logan. She bathes there all the time. Quit frettin'. Let's go eat."

"I still don't like it," Logan said.

"That wasn't much of a fight," Benny said.

"Oh, there was a lot more said than you heard," Moses said, grinning.

"Don't start in on me, Moses," Logan said, a warning tone to his voice.

"Wouldn't dream of it. We all know, what we all know."

"I don't understand nothin' nobody is sayin'," Benny said. "I'm hungry." He took off at a run for the cabin.

Logan turned his head to see Amber disappear into the trees of the cove. A muscle jumped in his jaw.

"You love her, Wade," Moses said quietly.

"Yeah," Logan said, slowly meeting Moses's gaze, "I do."

"Does she know? Did you tell her?"

"No."

"Are you gonna tell her?"

"No. Moses, I . . . Maybe you can't understand this because you're not carrying the guilt I am. It's eating me alive, tearing me apart. I'll be staying on here for now, to work. I'll do whatever needs doing, you just tell me what you want done. Maybe the guilt will ease some if I give something back to this homestead."

"That's why you're stayin'?" Moses said, frowning.

"Yeah," Logan said, running his hand over the back of his neck, "that's why."

"That's not good reasonin', Logan. You don't owe a debt here. It's Amber you should be stayin' for."

"Amber's not mine to have," Logan said, his voice hushed.

"Merciful Lord, you are a stubborn mule. Let the past go."

"There's more than the past churning in me now, Moses. I . . . Look, I'm staying, all right? When, if, the day comes I feel freed enough from what I've done to leave, I'll tell you. I won't just disappear. That's how things stand, and I don't want to discuss it again. Ever."

"But . . ."

"Damn it, no more," he said, striding off in the direction of the cabin.

"Stubborn as a mule," Moses said under his breath, following after Logan. "He truly is."

Before entering the cabin, Logan looked once more in the direction of the cove, then swore. Damn that Amber, he thought, as he went inside.

". . . don't you think so, Logan?" Benny said.

"What?"

"I'm taller than I was when you came here."

"Oh, you bet you are," Logan said, sitting down at the table. "Any fool could tell that you've grown."

"Wait till you see how big I am a year from now," Benny said.

"We'll be thinkin' 'bout pourin' that coffee in ya," Moses said, sliding heavily onto a chair, " 'fore you bump your head on the ceilin'."

Benny laughed in delight.

A year from now, Logan mused, as he filled his plate. Where would he be? Still there on that homestead? Long since gone, and long since forgotten by those he'd left behind? A year. Damn, there could be a babe in a cradle in that cabin by then. His baby, his and Amber's. Sweet Jesus, he could have harmed his child last night as well as Amber.

Amber said she was all right, his mind rambled on. She looked all right. Hell, she looked beautiful, so beautiful. And at that very moment she was naked in that stream and . . . Damn it. Didn't his lust ever cool? What kind of an animal was he? If he thought of her, he wanted her. Bastard.

"You're goin' to curdle Benny's milk," Moses said. "That look on your face is somethin' to behold, Logan."

"Just thinking about things."

"Mmm," Moses said.

"I need to get Thunder some fresh air," Logan said. "I'll tether him in that stretch with the cattle, then meet you back at the cornfield."

"This stew don't taste no better today than it did last night," Benny said.

"Thanks," Logan said, smiling.

"We should feed this to our pig," Benny said.

"If we had one," Logan said. "In the meantime, you'll do. Eat up."

"Pa said we was to get a pig in Waverly next trip," Benny said. "We still gonna get one?"

"We'll see," Moses said. "Logan and me gotta figure things out fresh since we lost the corn crop. We've got winter provisions to get in. Won't be anythin' left over for extras, but we'll see."

"When we goin' to Waverly, Moses?" Benny asked.

"Don't know for sure. Missy has to finish that quilt so we can trade it for beans. When we do go, that will be the last trip 'til spring. We . . . Say now, we have to think this through 'fore we go. Hunters won't be here to tend to the milk cow. One of us will have to stay here. Well, no matter. There's nothin' in Waverly I need to see."

"No, I'll stay here," Logan said.

"No use arguin' it now," Moses said. "Don't even know when we're goin'. I'll ask missy how she's doin' on her quilt. Well, we still got us corn to pick."

"I'll be there as soon as I tend to Thunder," Logan said, getting to his feet.

"Fair enough," Moses said.

In the barn, Logan smiled as he ran his hand down the nose of the sleek horse. "How

are you, boy? I'm going to take you outside
for some fresh air and sunshine. Hope you're
getting used to this place because we're going
to be here a while. How long? Don't know. Really don't."

Well, there he was talking to his horse again,
Logan thought dryly. Just like all the other
lonely cowboys. Lonely? Was he? No, maybe
not. Not like before, during the past five years.
There, on that homestead, he was part of
something real, good, solid, and decent. There
was a purpose, a reason, for every hour of
backbreaking labor. And there were fine people there, the finest he'd ever met.

And in spite of everything Amber knew
about him to be true, she loved him.

"She's not using the good sense God gave
her," Logan said to the horse.

Was it possible to pay a debt of guilt with
hard labor? Logan wondered. He didn't know,
but it was the only hope he had of lessening
his heavy inner burden. What if the guilt were
slowly chipped away, until it no longer existed
and he was free? Free to love his Amber.

"Ah, Thunder," he said, "I'm dreaming, I
guess, but I love her so damn much."

With a weary sigh, Logan slipped the bridle
over the horse's head, settled the bit in the animal's mouth, then led him from the stall. He
scooped up tethering straps from a hook on
the wall, then left the barn. Thunder pranced

impatiently, straining against Logan's hold on the reins.

"Easy, boy, easy," Logan said. "I know you want to run. Whoa, boy."

The horse calmed under Logan's soothing tone as Logan led him around the side of the barn to the fenced area in the rear.

Suddenly a flash of light caused Logan to stop, and his head jerked up. There, on a small rise in the distance, a lone Indian sat on a horse. Logan's heart raced and every muscle tensed as he watched the Indian raise his rifle straight above his head.

In the next instant, the light flashed in Logan's eyes again in a quick off-and-on rhythm. Memories slammed against Logan's mind, and images danced before his mental vision.

"Chato," he whispered. "Dear God, it's Chato."

With no regard for his injured shoulder, Logan swung onto Thunder's bare back, the reins tightly in his hands as he kneed the horse into action. Thunder bolted forward, and Logan sucked in his breath as pain radiated from his chest down his leg.

As Logan moved, so did the Indian. They raced their horses toward each other to meet in the open field.

"I am Chato," he said, a wide smile on his face.

Logan held Thunder in check. "I am Logan.

Holy hell, it's good to see you. I can't believe this. What are you doing here?"

Chato's smile faded. "I have come for you, brother of my soul. It is Naana's wish to speak with you, touch you, thank you from her heart."

"Thank me? For what?"

"We must talk, my brother."

"Yes, of course. Look, come with me. I need to tell the people of this homestead that you're not to be feared." He paused. "Chato, have you seen Comanches around here?"

"There were some, but they moved on when the soldiers came. There's nothing for them this far north but death from the soldiers' guns."

"Good, good. Damn, I still can't believe you're here."

"I thought you were dead. I have sought you often in these five years, Logan. I've watched as you did what was needed, that which I could not do in these troubled times. My heart is grateful to you for what you have done, brother of my soul. We can all rest in peace now because of you."

"Peace?" Logan said, frowning.

"You executed justice in all our names, and did it with honor. Each man you found was given a fair chance to defend himself. I saw. I am proud to be your brother. Comanches drove me away before I could take your body to Naana to be buried with the highest rituals given to brave Apache warriors. Such joy Naana will have when I bring you to her alive and well. Lozen, too, will weep with happiness."

"You were watching me during those five years?" Logan said incredulously. "Why didn't you approach me, talk to me?"

"No. You were on a mission that was mine as well. I could only wait until you had freed us all from the ghosts of the past. It is done. Michael and Jude rest in peace in their eternal sleep. We owe you much, my brother."

"I'm a killer, Chato," Logan said quietly.

"What words are these? You are a warrior, who has done great honor to your people and mine. The peace within Michael and Jude is ours to have as we walk our land. Because of you, we are all free now of the burden in our souls."

Logan met Chato's gaze for a long moment.

"I'll think on this," Logan said, finally. "We'll talk some more."

"So be it."

"Let's head for that battered cornfield before Moses decides to shoot you."

They walked their horses forward, side by side. They were two men of strength and purpose. Two men of different cultures and heritages, sitting tall on the backs of gleaming horses. Two men . . . brothers.

"Moses," Logan called, as they neared the field. "I'm coming with a friend."

Moses straightened and squinted against the sun.

"An Indian," Benny shrieked. He leaped at Moses, literally crawling up the big man's body, forcing Moses to hold tightly to him.

"Hey, Benny," Logan said, laughing, "this is Chato, my brother. Well, he's like a brother to me." He pulled up his horse. "He isn't going to hurt you."

"I am Chato. Apache. Friend."

"Oh," the little boy said. "I am Benny. This here is Moses."

Moses set Benny on his feet. "Howdy. You're full of surprises, Logan, but if you say Chato is your friend, your brother, it's fine by me. You're welcome to share what we have, Chato. This is the Prescott homestead, and what's ours is yours."

"I'm the Prescott man of the house," Benny said, puffing out his chest. "I wasn't really that scared of you or nothin', Chato. I just gotta look out for my own."

"Brave warrior," Chato said, nodding.

Logan chuckled, and Moses smiled.

"You move, and I'll shoot you deader than a post."

Logan's eyes widened as he saw Amber advancing toward them with a rifle in her hands. She was coming from the direction of the cabin and had, he surmised, seen Chato, circled behind the cabin from the cove, and was ready to blow Chato into the next county.

"Amber, no, wait," Logan said. "You don't understand."

"Get off that horse," Amber said, jerking the rifle toward Chato.

"Amber, damn it," Logan said. "Put that rifle down before you shoot someone. This is Chato. I told you about him, remember? He came looking for me. Put the damn gun down."

"You have a brave woman, Logan," Chato said. "You have chosen well. Naana will be pleased."

Logan's head snapped around to look at Chato. "She's not my . . . What I mean is . . . Never mind." He looked at Amber again. "Drop the rifle."

"Chato?" Amber said, slowly lowering the rifle. "Oh, my goodness. I thought . . . Oh, I'm terribly sorry. He came looking for you, Logan? Why?"

"Logan must return to camp with me," Chato said. "Naana, who sees Logan as the grandson of her soul, wishes it to be so."

Return to camp? Amber's mind echoed. The Apache camp? Leave the homestead, leave her? Oh, no, please no.

"Let's tether the horses," Logan said, "then we'll talk, Chato."

They walked their horses slowly away, and Amber watched them go, her heart aching.

"Easy now, missy," Moses said. "You don't

have the whole story yet, so don't be lookin'
for grief that isn't here."

"He's leaving," she said, her voice trembling.
"He'll go with Chato, I know he will."

"Could be," Moses said, nodding, "but that
don't say he won't come back."

Amber turned and started toward the cabin,
tears blurring her vision.

At suppertime, Logan entered the cabin,
filled two plates, and went back outside. Amber
looked at Moses, who only shrugged. Amber
poked at the food on her plate, her appetite
gone. While Amber, Benny, and Moses were
still at the table, Logan reentered the cabin.

"I'm leaving with Chato before dawn," he
said quietly, "so I'll say goodbye now."

No! Amber's mind screamed.

"Chato's grandmother, Naana, is dying, and
she wants to see me."

Moses nodded. Amber's gaze was riveted on
Logan.

"That's somethin'," Benny said, his voice
filled with awe. "You know an Indian who
doesn't kill nobody, and you're goin' to his
camp, and . . . When you come back, will you
bring me a real Apache arrow? Could you do
that, Logan?"

Silence hung heavily in the cabin.

"Yeah," Logan said finally, "I'll bring you an

arrow." He shifted his gaze to Amber. "When I come back."

She got to her feet. "Logan?"

"I'll be back. I have a debt to pay here, remember?"

"No," she said, lifting her chin, "you don't."

Their eyes held in a timeless moment, then Logan spun on his heel and left the cabin.

"Patience, missy," Moses said. "He says he'll be back, and he will. Logan's a man of his word."

And Logan Wade was the man of her heart, Amber thought, fighting against her tears. Forever.

Thirteen

Logan sat cross-legged on the dirt floor of the tepee and watched Naana sleep. Her breathing was shallow, the slight rise and fall of her chest barely discernible.

Naana was close to death, Logan knew, and she no longer fought against the spirits who would carry her to the place of eternal sleep. During the four weeks that Logan had been in the Apache camp, Naana had held on, asking for him each day so that they could talk.

The words had flowed from him, Logan recalled, like a rushing river too powerful to stop. He had told her of the five long years spent seeking and finding those who had killed Jude and Michael. He'd bared his soul about his inner guilt about the men dying at his hand.

On and on he'd talked, telling Naana about his love for Amber, and the added burden of guilt he now carried because of what he'd done to her. He spoke of his plan to work on the Prescott homestead with the hope of gaining some inner peace.

Naana had listened, and then she had spoken

to Logan in return. She'd declared him to be a man of honor for having avenged the deaths of their Jude and Michael. She spoke softly, with the wisdom of her years, and inch by emotional inch, peace began to touch Logan's soul.

With a knowing smile, Naana asked if Amber had voiced outrage at their rough coupling, or had Amber known with her own womanly wisdom that a man is a complex creature needing much love and understanding?

The days passed, and with each one Logan felt the weight that had been crushing him begin to lift, then be swept into oblivion.

"Logan," Naana whispered, opening her eyes, "you are free."

"I am free, Naana."

"So be it, my grandson. May your God guide your steps. Go home, Logan Wade. Amber waits for you. Send Chato and Lozen to me with the babe Jude, so I may say my good-bye. It is time."

Logan leaned over and brushed his lips across the old woman's forehead. "Thank you, Naana, for giving me back my life. Sleep well."

With tears glistening in his eyes, Logan got to his feet and went in search of Chato.

Naana would leave this world for another place that night, Logan knew. In the following days, he'd help Chato prepare the people of the camp to move to the reservation.

And then, Logan thought, he was going home, to Amber.

* * *

Amber usually enjoyed the changing of summer to autumn, the crisp mornings and evenings, the shortening of the days. But this year it only hammered home to her that time was going rapidly by.

Six weeks. It had been six, long and lonely weeks since Logan had ridden away from the Prescott homestead with Chato, and she felt as though her heart was slowly but surely shattering into a million pieces.

She wanted to see Logan smile, hear his laughter, be aware of how his vibrant masculinity seemed to fill the cabin to overflowing when he entered.

She ached for the feel of his strong arms pulling her to the hard wall of his chest. Ached for the softness of his lips claiming hers, his callused hands on her body, and ached to be consumed with his manhood, carried away to the place he took her to, then feel him shudder above her as he joined her in ecstasy.

But the days and nights passed, and Logan didn't return.

So, knowing that Moses was not comfortable sleeping in the cabin, Amber had assured him that she'd lock up after the nightly chores, and she and Benny would be fine.

* * *

Six weeks and three days after Logan had gone, Amber sat by the fire working on the quilt. Benny, who had suddenly announced that he would be sleeping in his own room again, had moved his cot back into place several weeks before.

The night was chilly, as autumn crept closer to winter, and Amber postponed leaving her cozy spot by the hearth to secure the cabin for the night. She must sleep soon, she knew, as tomorrow would be another long day. Another long day without Logan.

Logan stopped outside the cabin door. He'd taken Thunder to the barn, spoken to Moses, and now there he was, staring at the door as though it were the most fascinating thing he'd ever seen.

Within that cabin, he knew, was the woman he loved, wanted, needed, for all time. The next few minutes would mark his destiny, determine his future, his remaining days.

And Logan Wade was scared to death.

"Do it, Wade," he muttered, then reached for the doorknob.

Amber was sitting in her rocker by the hearth sewing on the quilt when he stepped inside, closing the door behind him. The firelight cast a golden halo over her, and his racing heartbeat echoed in his ears.

"Did you forget something, Moses?" Amber said, not glancing in his direction.

"Hello, Amber," he quietly.

Amber's head snapped around and her eyes widened. "Logan?" She made no attempt to rise, knowing her trembling legs would never support her.

"I'm back, Amber. I'd like to talk to you."

"Yes, of course," she said. Talk about what? How he'd found his peace, was there only to say one last good-bye? Oh, dear Lord, he was so magnificent in his sheepskin jacket and . . . She had to stay calm, hold onto her dignity, wait and see what he had to say to her. Oh, God, Logan was back. "Take off your jacket, if you like. There's hot coffee here over the fire."

He took off his jacket, dropped it across a chair, then poured a mug of the steaming liquid. He pulled up another chair and set it in front of her, straddling it backwards, and resting his arms across the top as he wrapped one hand around the mug of coffee.

"Quilt sure is pretty," he said. Hell, he had to be the biggest coward in the State of Texas. Get on with it, Wade. "Real nice."

"Thank you. It's almost finished. We can go into Waverly soon and trade it for the beans," she said. Dear heaven, why was he there? What did he want? He'd been gone over six weeks, and there he sat just as calm as you please, chatting about the quilt. Damn the man.

"Amber, I really do need to talk to you," he said.

"About?"

"Could you stop sewing for a moment and look at me?"

Amber wove the needle through the material, then clutched her shaking hands together on top of the bulky bundle on her lap. She slowly lifted her head to gaze into the blue pools of Logan's eyes.

"What is it you wish to speak to me about?" she said, hearing the unsteady quality to her voice.

"I'm sorry that I was gone so long, Amber. Chato insisted we take it slow because of my shoulder. Then when we reached the camp I spent a lot of time with Naana, Chato and Jude's grandmother. She'd been waiting for me, holding onto life, and when she sensed that I was troubled, it was as though she refused to die until she knew I was at peace."

"Oh, Logan," Amber said softly, "she sounds like a very special person."

"Yeah, she was. She's gone now. They're all special; Chato, Lozen, their little girl, Jude, the people in the camp. Saying good-bye to them was hard because they're going to the reservation. I just hope they'll be happy there."

"Yes, so do I."

"You know that I've been carrying a heavy burden within me, Amber, and that I hoped to work it through by laboring on this homestead. Naana made me see that my guilt was misplaced, was wrong, very wrong. Amber, that night in your bed I was too rough, and I'm more sorry than I can say, but we *did* make love. We shared. You gave yourself to me, I didn't just take. That's true, isn't it?"

"Yes, oh, yes. I tried to tell you then that it was, but you wouldn't listen."

"Then that's the last of it, of all the guilt. I'm free, Amber."

"I see," she said, willing herself not to cry. "Then you've accomplished everything you set out to do."

"Not quite. There's one more thing I need to say to you."

"Yes?"

Logan placed the mug on the hearth then stood, swinging the chair around and sitting back down, his knees pressing against hers as he leaned forward and covered her hands with his.

"I love you, Amber Prescott," he said, his voice gritty with emotion. "I truly do love you."

Amber's heart began to beat a wild cadence. "You . . . you what?" she whispered.

"I love you. I've loved you since that night in the cove, since *before* we made love. I didn't feel I had the right to tell you, but thanks to Naana's patience and wisdom, I've come to understand that . . . Amber? Are you all right? You're as white as bleached flour."

"Say it once more. Tell me you love me. Please?"

"Ah, Amber, I do. I love you with my mind, my heart, my body, and my soul that is finally free."

"Oh, Logan." She launched herself at him, flinging herself against him, nearly toppling them over in the chair. The quilt fell to a forgotten heap of bright colors on the floor. "Oh, my Logan, I love you so," she said, smiling through her tears.

He swung her around to sit on his lap. "Will you marry me? When we go into Waverly, will you become my wife?"

"Your . . . Yes. Oh, yes."

Logan's mouth melted over Amber's in a soft, gentle kiss. In the next instant he groaned deep in his chest and the kiss intensified. Tongues met, passions soared. The hurt, confusion, the chill of loneliness within them was pushed into oblivion and forgotten, replaced by the warm glow of love that burst into a heated flame.

"I want you," he said, beginning to pull the pins from her hair. "I want to make love to you."

"And I want you. I do. Oh, Logan, I love you so very much. I missed you these weeks more than I can say."

"You smell so damn good," he said, nuzzling her neck. He inhaled her sweet, lavender scent.

"Are we going to make love on this chair?"

"What?" he said, lifting his head to look at her.

"Are we?"

"No!"

"Can't be done, huh?"

"Well, yes, it could, but . . . You ask the damnest questions."

"How else am I going to learn anything?"

"I'll teach you all you need to know," he said, getting to his feet with her held tightly to his chest.

"Thought you might," she said, laughing. "It's about that chair. How . . ."

He halted her chatter with a long searing kiss, then carried her into the bedroom and set her on her feet. The flames from the fire in the living-room hearth cast a faint glow over the room. Clothes seemed to float away, then they tumbled onto the bed, reaching eagerly for each other.

Hands and lips, teeth and tongues explored and rediscovered the glorious mysteries of the one within their reach. Their breathing became labored in the quiet room, hearts beat a wild cadence, bodies glistened.

"Oh, Logan, come to me," Amber gasped. "I need you. I want you."

"Not yet, my love," he said, his voice vibrant with passion. "I have to be sure you're ready for me. I don't want to hurt you, not ever again."

With womanly instinct newly born, Amber

knew there was still a lingering shadow of guilt in Logan's soul for what had happened at their last joining. She slid her hand over the moist plane of his stomach, then beyond.

"Amber!"

"Love me," she whispered. "You won't hurt me, Logan. You never have. There's such a heat, a fire in me. I need you, now. Now, Logan."

"Jesus," he said, with a groan.

But he gave up the battle and came to her. Came to her honeyed warmth and velvety softness that welcomed and received him. The last ghost of guilt in Logan Wade's soul vanished. He was free, whole, and gave all of himself to the woman he loved.

He filled her with his manhood, moved within her with the strength of his powerful body tempered with gentleness. Executing every ounce of self-control that he possessed, he held himself in check, assuring Amber's pleasure; waiting, waiting, until he felt her close tightly around him, her spasms sweeping through her like crashing waves on the sought-after shore.

"Logan!"

"Yes." And then he joined her. "Amber." He shuddered within her time and again, then collapsed against her; spent, sated, and totally at peace. "I love you. Good Lord, how I love you."

"And I love you, Logan."

He moved away, then tucked her close to his side, his hand coming to rest on her flat stomach. He absently noted the difference in color between his darkly tanned hand and her dewy white skin, then another thought slammed against his mind. The baby! Was his child nestled deep within her, there beneath where his hand rested at that very moment? Was there a babe? Had Amber had her monthly flow? Lord, he couldn't ask her a question like that. Could he? After all, he was going to be her husband so . . .

"Been feeling all right?" he asked, with what he hoped was a casual tone to his voice. Damn, he was such a coward. What had happened to the question he was *supposed* to ask her?

"No."

"What?" he said, his muscles tensing.

"No, I haven't felt all right. I've been miserable while you've been gone. Miserable, and lonely, and sad. But now I'm fine. I'm marvelous. I'm loved. Oh, Logan, I'm so happy."

"And I'm going to see to it that you stay that way," he said, kissing her on the forehead. "Amber . . . um . . . have you had your . . . your . . ."

"My what?"

"Your supper." Hell.

"Yes, of course, I have. Maybe I should ask if *you're* all right. You're behaving rather strangely."

"Me? Oh. Well, it's not every day that a man proposes marriage, you know."

"That's true. Amber Prescott Wade. Oh, I

adore how that sounds. I'd like to name our first son Nathan after my pa, if that suits you."

"Son? What son?" he said, shifting up on his arm to peer down at her.

"Well, surely we'll have babes."

"Speaking of babes, have you had your . . ."

"Did you hear Benny cry out in his sleep? He has nightmares sometimes."

Logan left the bed and pulled on his pants. "I'll check on him. Then I'm going to lock up the cabin and bed down in Benny's room."

"You're spending the night in the other bedroom? Why?"

"Because there's an impressionable young boy in this house. Benny isn't to wake in the mornings to find us in bed together until we're married proper."

"Well, land's sake, Mr. Wade," Amber said, smiling.

"I love you, Amber. I'm going to tell you that every day for the rest of our lives. Tell you in the day, show you how much at night."

"Oh, Logan," she whispered. "Welcome home, my love."

Later, Logan lay on the cot next to Benny's, staring up into the darkness. He missed Amber, he realized. She was only a room away, and he missed her. He missed her soft curves, and lavender scent, and the way her hair floated over his body like a silken waterfall.

Amber. His wife. Damn, it sounded good. He would spend the rest of his life making her happy, watching her smile, hearing her sing softly. He was the luckiest man on the face of the earth to have been given so much, when he gave so little in return.

He would work hard on that homestead, use every ounce of muscle he had to help turn it into a fine, fine spread. He would labor at the side of his friend Moses, and count the big man among his many blessings. He'd be a father-figure to Benny, but never presume to take Nathan Prescott's place. It was good. All of it.

"I love you, Amber," he whispered to the night, and then he slept.

A man at peace.

Fourteen

The following week was busy as plans for the trip to Waverly took shape. Hugs and handshakes had been exchanged when Logan announced that he and Amber were to be married in Waverly.

Moses was to be at the wedding, Logan had decreed, so that milk cow would simply have to make the journey with them. They could sell the fresh milk in Waverly while they were there, Logan had added, and Benny could have the money to buy himself a special present. Everyone agreed it was a marvelous plan.

Amber worked on the quilt in every spare moment she could find, knowing the sooner she finished, the quicker she would become Logan's wife.

He came to her each night in her bed, then crept away later to sleep in the narrow cot in Benny's room. She longed for when she would wake at dawn's light to find Logan, her husband, at her side. She glowed with happiness, and her husky voice was bursting with song through the hours of the day.

Logan and Moses made a careful list of supplies to be purchased and bartered for. While the trip to Waverly could be made in the winter, it would be a cold two days of travel, and it was safer not to go again until spring.

The chickens the Hunters had left behind as they departed for Virginia were producing more eggs than Amber could possibly use in her cooking. The extra chickens would be traded in Waverly for the long-awaited pig.

Amber announced that she needed one more day to work on the quilt, and the excitement on the homestead grew. The next morning Amber rose earlier than usual to sew the quilt before it was time to start breakfast.

She dressed, then walked to the bedroom door, only to stop, her eyes widening. In a rush of panic, she ran to the bed, reached under it for the chamber pot, and became violently sick to her stomach.

"Land's sake," she said, sinking to her knees on the floor, and wiping cold beads of sweat from her brow. "Oh, Lord," she shrieked, as Logan came bursting in the room, clad only in his pants.

What happened?" he said, "I heard weird noises. What . . . You've been sick."

"Please. Don't say that word," she said, dragging herself up to sit on the edge of the bed. "Don't even suggest it."

Logan sat down next to her, a deep frown on his face as he studied her pale face. He took her hand in his. "Has this happened before?"

"The last three days my stomach felt wobbly when I got up, but this is the first time it did anything about it."

"This time I'm going to ask," Logan muttered. "I have to. I've put it off for as long as I can."

"Logan, what are you mumbling about? I'm really not in the mood."

He took a deep breath. "Amber, have you had your monthly flow in the last weeks?"

"I beg your pardon? You can't ask me something like that. That's personal."

"Damn it, answer the question."

"No."

"No, you won't answer the question, or no, you haven't . . ."

"No, I haven't had . . . what you asked me if I'd had."

"I'll be damned," he said, a wide grin spreading across his face.

"Logan," she said crossly, "I really don't see what . . ."

"Amber," he said, gripping her by the shoulders and smiling at her, "I think you're carrying my babe."

Amber hardly remembered what transpired during the hours of the day. When Logan had made his startling announcement, her eyes had widened and her mouth had dropped open.

Before either could respond further, the voice of a sleepy Benny calling for Logan reached their ears. Logan had kissed her quickly, told her that they would talk later, then hurried from the room, his broad smile still firmly in place.

To Amber, it seemed as though she were moving in slow motion as she prepared breakfast, but since no one commented, she'd assumed she appeared to be behaving normally.

Logan smiled at her continually, until she finally blushed a pretty pink and refused to look at him again. She announced that the quilt would definitely be finished within the next few hours, and Benny cut loose with a loud yell of delight. They would leave for Waverly at dawn the next day.

The noon meal was hurried as Logan and Moses needed every spare minute to prepare for the trip. The wagon was loaded with what they planned to sell and trade, plus the provisions needed to camp out overnight on the way.

Amber sewed on the quilt until her fingers were numb, then sighed in relief when it was finished an hour after supper. She wrapped it carefully in a blanket, then set it by the door to be loaded into the wagon in the morning.

She was so sleepy she voiced no objection when Logan kissed her good night at her bedroom door. They still had to talk, he said, but tomorrow would be soon enough, as what she needed now was to rest up for the two-day trip ahead.

Amber fully expected to fall asleep the moment her head touched the pillow, but instead she lay wide awake in the darkness, her mind whirling.

A babe. A baby, she thought. Logan's child. Was it true? Was it there, within her?

She pressed her hands onto her flat stomach as her heart quickened. She'd never even thought about a babe when she'd given herself to Logan. Somehow, in some childish, foolish place in her mind, she'd associated babies with being married, having a husband. It was the natural order of things, and that was how it would be.

She'd felt no shame at having made love with Logan while not being his wife. But a babe? That changed things, brought what they had done into reality with a resounding thud. They had created a child, and they weren't even married.

"Stop it, Amber," she scolded herself. She and Logan were to become husband and wife as soon as they arrived in Waverly. Everything would be fine then, be proper and right. Besides, a wobbly stomach didn't necessarily mean she was carrying Logan's child. It might not be true at all.

"Go to sleep," Amber whispered in the darkness. "You've got a big day tomorrow. You, too," she said, patting her stomach. Now she was talking to a babe she didn't even know for certain existed. She had to get some rest.

An hour before dawn the next morning, there was no doubt whatsoever in Amber Prescott's mind that she was carrying a babe within her. She was violently sick to her stomach once again, and sat weak and shaking on the floor next to the chamber pot. Logan did not hear her misery, apparently, as he didn't come barreling through her door, and she was grateful. At that moment, she could have very happily punched him right in the nose.

By the time Amber had washed and dressed, she was feeling fine, and beginning to tingle with excitement over the trip. She was setting the table when Logan came in the back door, shivering as he buttoned his shirt.

"You can start shaving in here, Logan," Amber said, glancing up at him. "Never could understand why Pa stood out there freezing all winter."

"Good thought," he said, coming to her and pulling her into his arms. He kissed her until her knees trembled, then finally lifted his head. "Were you sick this morning?" he said still holding her tightly to him.

"Yes."

"I didn't hear you. I'm sorry. I should have been there to help."

"I don't need any help," she said dryly. "I do a very good job of it on my own."

"I really think you're carrying . . ."

"And I really think you're right."

"You're not upset, are you?" he said frowning. "That's what I wanted to talk to you about. I'm so damn happy about this, Amber, but it's important that you are, too."

"I am. Well, I will be once we're married."

"I missed you last night," he murmured, his mouth sweeping down onto hers.

Amber melted against him, returning the kiss in total abandon, all rational thought pushed to a dusty corner of her mind. She drank in the taste, the feel, the aroma of Logan Wade.

"When you're done doin' that, can I have some breakfast?" Benny said, then yawned.

Logan put his head back and roared with laughter, as Amber's cheeks blushed crimson. She wiggled out of Logan's arms, shot Benny a stormy glare he was totally oblivious to, then she turned to the hearth to break eggs into a pan.

"When you get older," Logan said, smiling at Benny, "you'll get your priorities straight."

"My what?"

"Never mind," Logan said. "All in good time. Ready to go to Waverly?"

"You bet. Yes, sir, Logan, I can hardly wait. I'm gettin' me the finest surprise ever with my money from that milk."

"And I'm gettin' me a wife," Logan said quietly.

Amber turned to look at him, and their eyes met for a warm, telling moment that spoke of love.

Northern Texas seemed to be encased in an invisible tunnel that brought chilling winds and a sharper contrast in seasons than the lower portion of the state. It was not uncommon in the dead of winter for a blanket of snow to fall, transforming the land into a white fairy-tale world of beauty.

But with the snow, came the danger of being unable to venture off a homestead. It was safer by far to lay in provisions for the entire winter rather than risk the trip to Waverly in the unpredictable weather. More than one weary traveler had lost his way in a swirling sea of white, and frozen to death, sometimes within shouting distance of his own cabin.

A chill, biting wind accompanied the group leaving the Prescott homestead, and no one spoke for the first two hours of the journey as they huddled against the cold. Logan rode high in the saddle on a prancing Thunder, while Moses drove the wagon, Amber next to him on the seat, and Benny tucked among the supplies in the bed. The milk cow was tied on behind, bellowing its complaints.

Amber had registered a flash of fear when

Logan had reached into the side cupboard where he'd placed his belongings. He withdrew the saddlebags and the gleaming rifle, but nothing more. Amber's heart had quieted as she realized that Logan had no intention of strapping on his holster.

She had had the irrational thought that Logan should throw the evil weapon in the stream, banishing it from that homestead and their lives. But the decision of what he would do with that gun was his to make, and she knew it. Nathan Prescott had hung up his gun forever for his beloved Mary. Amber could only pray that Logan would do the same for her. But until the day he no longer owned it, she wouldn't be truly sure.

"Are you doing all right, Amber?" Logan said, moving Thunder close to the wagon.

"Yes, I'm fine," she said. She pulled the blanket more tightly around her over her wool coat. "Just cold."

"I'm hoping those clouds will clear off so we'll get the warmth of the sun. We could shift things in the bed of the wagon, and you could sit back there."

"No, I'm really fine."

"Positive?"

"Logan, please, stop fussing at me."

"Well, I worry about you. It's part of my job as a husband," he said. Moses hooted with laughter. "Damn it, Moses," Logan said, "shut up. I intend to do this husband thing right."

"No doubt in my mind 'bout that," Moses said, shaking with laughter. "No doubt at all."

"Hush, both of you," Amber said, lifting her chin.

"You're supposed to say, 'Yes, ma'am,' " Moses said, grinning at Logan.

"Like hell," he said, tugging his Stetson further forward. Amber laughed in loving delight.

Time passed and the sun won the battle against the thick clouds. The warming glow was welcomed and the miles seemed to disappear more quickly. At noon they stopped to eat some of the food Amber had packed, then set out again, spirits high.

Conversation was casual, lazy, consisting of little more than comments on the scenery, what changes they might find in ever-growing Waverly, the hope that they would be able to barter for the sought-after bean seeds and pig.

Logan left the decision as to where they would camp for the night to Moses, and they arrived at the designated spot at dusk, with Amber and Benny once more shivering and wrapped in blankets. Logan quickly made a fire, while Moses milked the cow and tethered the horses.

"I'll unload some things from the wagon bed," Logan said to Amber. "You and Benny will sleep in there."

"Don't be silly," Amber said. "We've always slept on the ground."

"Not this time. It'll be warmer in the wagon.

"But I don't want . . ."

"Too bad," he said, kissing her quickly, then grinning at her. "You're going to. Now you say, 'Yes, sir.' "

"Like hell," she said. Logan laughed and hugged her until she yelled for mercy.

The night was long and cold, and Amber greeted the dawn by stumbling from the wagon and being sick to her stomach. Logan ran to her side, holding her head as she retched, murmuring comforting words in her ear. To Amber's relief, Benny and Moses slept through her humiliating performance.

"How much longer?" Benny said, in the middle of the afternoon. "My butt is numb."

"Another hour, give or take," Moses said. "Decided yet what you're gettin' with your money from the milk?"

"Yep."

"Gonna tell us?" Moses asked.

"Nope. My surprise, my secret. Logan said I could have anythin' I wanted, and I know what it is."

"Maybe we should talk about this a bit, Benny," Amber said.

"Nope."

"Logan?" Amber said.

"It's Benny's business," Logan said, shrugging.

"Yep," Benny said.

"Oh-h-h, dear," Amber said, rolling her eyes to the heavens.

Waverly, Texas. It was an oasis in the desert, a bustling, beehive of activity, a mixture of cultures and people. It grew steadily, the sound of nails being hammered into fresh wood reverberating continually through the air.

It offered something to everyone who came; a church, school, rows of stores, saloons with the painted women to service the randy cowboys passing through. Waverly was busy and noisy, and to those who visited from the isolated homesteads, it represented a temporary glimpse of excitement, people, treasures brought in from the railroad-fed cities beyond.

Due to the ongoing traffic of homesteaders moving in and out of Waverly to sell, barter, lay in supplies, men were for hire to stand guard over possessions in the wagons where they were left behind the livery stable. It was with one of these men that Logan shook hands, having reached an agreement on price for the tall Irishman to sleep under the wagon and milk the cow morning and night.

"There's no man big enough to be getting past Sean O'Malley," the Irishman said. "Well, there may be one," he added, his gaze sweeping over Moses.

Logan chuckled. "And this is Benny. That's his milk in that cow. He plans to sell it."

"Is that a fact?" Sean said. "I'll be puttin'
in a word for you at Rosie's Cafe, lad. I'll be
gettin' you a fair price, I will. What you plan
to do with a pocket full of pennies?"

"It's a secret," Benny said.

"Aye, is it now? Well, then I won't be askin'
again," Sean said, nodding solemnly.

"Let's get to the hotel," Logan said, smiling.
"I'll check in with you later, Sean. Moses and
I will spell you a bit."

"Fair enough," Sean said. "You show that
bonnie lass a fine time in Waverly."

"I intend to," Logan said, circling Amber's
shoulders with his arm.

"Aye," Sean said grinning, as he winked at
Logan.

Amber's eyes were sparkling with excitement
as they collected their clothing parcels and
started down the wooden sidewalk. There was
so much to see, to hear, to smell! New build-
ings had sprung up since the last trip, and Amber was anxious to explore.

"We'll see everything, I promise," Logan
said, smiling at her warmly. "But do you think
we could get our rooms first? Then there's the
little matter of finding out when and where
we're to be married."

"Oh, of course, she said. "Yes, married.
Land's sake, I'm getting nervous."

Their rooms were on the second floor of a
clean, fairly new hotel. Logan ordered a bathtub and hot water to be delivered to Amber's

room, and she smiled in delight. He left her
after a lengthy kiss, telling her he would return
shortly, and she was to keep the door securely
locked while he was gone.

A short time later, Amber sank up to her
chin in the warm water of the promised tub,
a sigh of pleasure escaping from her lips. She
lathered with her lavender soap, lifting first
one leg, then the other, to cream the fragrant
suds over her soft skin.

She'd never had a tub brought to her room
before, she mused, and she felt elegant and
pampered, the warm water soothing away her
aching muscles from the hours spent on the
rough trail.

She leaned her head back on the edge of
the tub and closed her eyes, deciding not to
move from her delightful watery expanse until
the cooling water forced her to budge. She had
nearly dozed off into a dreamy sleep, when a
knock sounded at the door.

"Oh," she gasped, sitting bolt upward.

"Amber? It's Logan."

"I'm in the tub still. I'll . . ."

"Can you be ready in a half an hour?"

"Ready for what?" she called, frowning
slightly.

"To get married."

Amber's eyes widened and her heart
thrummed beneath her breast. Married? her
mind echoed. In a half an hour? Well, yes, of
course, that's why they'd come to Waverly. No,

they'd come for winter supplies and a pig. No, no, she was to marry Logan Wade, become his wife. His wife. She was carrying his babe within her at that very moment and . . .

"Amber?" Logan said, knocking again.

"Yes, a half an hour. I'll be ready."

"Good. I'll come back for you."

Amber pressed her trembling hands to her flushed cheeks and took a deep steadying breath. What was wrong with her? she wondered. Why was she so nervous? She felt as though a swarm of butterflies were swooshing through her stomach, and her heart was hammering. She was marrying her Logan, and she loved him with every breath in her body. It wasn't as if she had to fear what would take place when he claimed his husbandly rights. It was heavenly when he . . .

"So, get out of this tub," Amber said, laughing. "You're about to be married."

She brushed her hair until it shown, then twisted it into the bun at the nape of her neck. She'd chosen a simple white dress with lace edging the sleeves, neck, and hem. It wasn't a fancy dress, she knew, but was the newest one she owned, and had no mends or patches to mar it. When Logan's knock sounded again she hurried to the door.

"Logan?" she said, before turning the lock.

"Yeah, it's me."

Amber flung the door open, then blinked once slowly, her eyes sweeping over Logan from head to toe. He was dressed in dark pants that had a new sheen to them, a pristine white shirt, and a black vest. His black Stetson was wiped clean of trail dust and was tucked under his arm. His hair was thick, shiny, slightly damp, and neatly combed. And in his hand was a small bouquet of pink and white flowers.

"Oh, Logan," she whispered, "you look beautiful."

He frowned. "That's not the type of thing you say to a man."

"Oh," she said, smiling. "Then you're very handsome. How's that?"

"Never mind," he said gruffly. "These are for you," he said, thrusting the flowers at her. "I thought you should have flowers, because brides have flowers. Well, Jude was the only bride I've ever seen, but she had flowers. Anyway, I got you flowers."

Amber pressed the pretty bouquet to her nose and inhaled the delicate fragrance, hiding her smile in the satiny petals. Logan was babbling, was actually a nervous bridegroom. Oh, mercy, how she loved him.

"Do I look all right?" she said, gazing up at him.

"What? Oh, yeah, you're lovely, beautiful. But I told you that. Didn't I? Well, I was thinking it. You're the prettiest bride to ever be married in Waverly. Hell, in the whole state of Texas."

"Oh, how sweet. Thank you. I'll get my

shawl. It belonged to my ma, and I only wear it on very special occasions."

"This is definitely a special occasion," he said, pulling his Stetson roughly forward. "Let's go."

Again Amber suppressed her smile as she gathered the white shawl and draped it around her shoulders. She gave Logan the key to the room, and he locked the door behind them. At the next room, he knocked briskly, and a moment later, Benny and Moses stepped out into the hall. Both were dressed in fresh clothes, and Benny had his hair plastered down with water.

"What funeral we attendin'?" Moses said with a grin, looking at Logan's surly expression.

"We'll do without your sense of humor, thank you," Logan said, grabbing Amber's arm and hauling her down the hall. Moses's rumbly laughter bounced off the walls. Logan shot him a murderous glare over his shoulder.

"Logan don't seem too happy, Moses," Benny whispered.

"He'll be fine," Moses said, grinning. "If he doesn't pass out cold on his face, that is."

"I heard that," Logan bellowed.

Amber laughed. Logan glared at her, too.

The church was at the edge of town, set back off the street, and surrounded by a white picket fence. The preacher and his wife were short, round, and had continual smiles on their faces. They ushered the group in, placed everyone where they wanted them, then the preacher opened his Bible and began to speak in a rapid flow of words, which tumbled one into the next.

"Say 'I do,' " he finally said to Logan.

"Huh? Oh, I do."

The mumbo-jumbo started again, and Amber smiled pleasantly, having no idea what the man was saying.

"Now you," he said, nodding at Amber.

"I do," she said merrily.

"The ring?" the preacher said to Logan.

"The what?" he said, frowning. "Oh, the ring." He fumbled in the pocket of his vest and produced a thin, gold band. "Here," he said, pushing it at the preacher.

"No, no, you put it on your bride's finger."

"I know that," Logan said, scowling at him. Moses coughed. "I'll deal with you later, Moses," he muttered. Logan lifted Amber's left hand and slipped the ring on her third finger.

"Oh, Logan," she said, sudden tears filling her eyes, "it's beautiful. I never dreamed I'd have a ring."

"I now pronounce you man and wife," the preacher said, snapping the Bible closed. "Kiss the bride. You are Mr. and Mrs. Logan Wade."

"I'll be damned," Logan said.

The preacher rolled his eyes heavenward in response to Logan's choice of words, then scurried off, his plump wife close on his heels and still smiling.

Logan lifted his large hands and cradled Amber's face, a warm glow in the blue pools of his eyes. "Hello, Mrs. Wade," he said, his voice strangely husky.

"Hello, Mr. Wade," she said, tears shimmering in her eyes.

"I love you, Amber," he said, then lowered his head to claim her mouth.

The kiss was tender, and soft, and sweet at the onset, but as Logan began to gather Amber close to his chest, another voice was heard from.

"When you're done doin' that," Benny said, "can we eat supper? I sure am hungry."

Logan jerked his head up and looked down at Benny, who had a scowl on his face. Logan burst into laughter. "Supper, it is, Benny. The finest Waverly has to offer."

Amber glanced up to see Moses smiling at her. She moved to where he stood and hugged him tightly.

"Be happy, missy," he said, his voice choked with emotion. "This is a mighty fine day for all of us."

"I'll be happy, Moses," she said. "I truly will."

Logan and Moses shook hands, exchanged meaningful smiles that spoke of friendship and trust, then the group left the church. The first streaks of a colorful sunset were inching across the sky, and Amber pulled her shawl closer around her against the chill.

Logan circled her shoulders with his arm and kissed her on the temple. She moved to his side, relishing his heat, his strength, his aroma. As they walked, Amber held her left hand out in front of her, tilting it back and forth, the rainbow colors of the sunset glittering on the shiny gold band. A gentle smile formed on her lips.

She was married.

She was married to Logan Wade, and her heart was filled with immeasurable joy. She would stand at his side for the remainder of her days, work with him, love with him, have his babes. She was truly blessed.

Amber's eyes widened when they entered the restaurant Logan had chosen. She had never eaten in a place that had cloths on the table and fancy fabric on the seat of the chairs. Where Logan had gotten the money for her ring, and now for the dinner they were to have, Amber didn't know, and wouldn't ask.

The meal was a festive event. The food was served by a cheerful waitress who saw Amber's flowers and asked if a wedding was being celebrated.

"Yep," Benny said, puffing up with importance, "we did all that talkin' stuff over at the church, then Logan kissed Amber, and that was that."

The waitress beamed, then produced a bottle

of wine compliments of the owner, who happened to be her husband. Moses proposed a toast to the bride and groom, and Benny was allowed an inch of the wine.

"Well," Moses said finally, "Benny and I will be goin' down to spell Sean so he can have his supper. We'll see you in the mornin'."

"Logan's cot is in our room," Benny said. "We'll see him 'fore mornin'."

"No, Benny," Logan said, "I'll be sleeping in Amber's room."

"Why?" Benny said.

"Because we're married now. Married folks sleep in the same bed."

Benny frowned. "Well, all I got to say is, I sure hope Amber don't snore, or you won't be gettin' no sleep at all, Logan."

"Benjamin Prescott," Amber said indignantly. "I do not snore."

Logan whooped with laughter. Amber jabbed him in the ribs with her elbow.

The foursome left the restaurant and walked to the hotel. Darkness had settled over Waverly, but the streets were still busy with riders on horses, and those driving wagons. Laughter and music drifted through the air from the saloons. Moses and Benny left Amber and Logan at the door of the hotel and headed for the livery stable. Logan led Amber inside and up the stairs to their room, neither speaking.

Amber looked up at Logan from beneath her lashes as he inserted the key in the door, and realized she felt suddenly shy. Ridiculous, she told herself. Childish. She was no longer an innocent, whose mind centered on where noses went when people kissed. She was a woman. A woman, who had given herself to her man, and rejoiced in their union. It was just that so many folks had seen her flowers, knew she was a bride, and knew exactly what was going to take place in that room tonight. Mercy.

Inside the room, Logan snapped the lock into place. "Stay there while I light the lamp," he said. Amber leaned back against the door.

Logan made his way across the dark room and lit the oil lamp, turning the wick up only enough to cast a dim, rosy glow over the expanse. The bathtub had been removed in their absence, and fresh towels were on the dresser, along with a pitcher of water and a pretty china bowl. Logan removed his Stetson, set it on the dresser, then turned to Amber, walking slowly toward her. He stopped directly in front of her and placed his hands flat on the door on either side of her head. She gazed up at him; not smiling, not speaking, just looking at him.

"You," he said, his voice gritty, "are my wife, my life, my reason for being. I will devote the remainder of my days to making you happy, so that I can see your smile and hear you sing softly. Amber Wade, you are mine."

Desire swirled throughout Amber, and a soft moan escaped from her lips as Logan's mouth melted over hers. He inched closer, pressing

against her, his body announcing his need, his
arousal, his want of her. His lips never leaving
hers, he pulled the pins from her hair, and
dragged his fingers gently through the golden
tresses.

Amber slid her hands inside Logan's vest
and up his back, feeling the muscles under his
shirt move beneath her palms. His tongue
plummeted deep into her mouth, sending
shockwaves of desire coursing through her.
Their breathing became labored as heartbeats
quickened, and Logan's hands were trembling
when he lifted his head and reached for the
buttons on her dress.

"Damn," he muttered.

"I'll do it," she whispered. "I want you so
much, Logan. I hope it's not wanton to want
you so much. I think about how it's going to
feel when you're inside of me and I . . ."

"Jesus," he said, stripping off his vest and
shirt. "We're never going to make it to the bed
if you keep talking like that."

"Oh, but what I'm saying is true," she said,
her dress falling to the floor. "And then when
you start to move in me, wonderful sensations
travel all through me. Then when . . ."

"Amber!"

"Yes?"

He pulled the chemise up over her head and
dropped it onto the floor. "I love you. And
it's not wanton for you to want me, it's won-

derful, but please don't say any more until we get to that bed."

"Oh. Well, do you think we could hurry and get over there?"

Logan chuckled deep in his chest and lifted her into his arms, carrying her to the bed and laying her down. She sat up long enough to remove her shoes, stockings, and pantaloons, then watched as Logan tugged off his boots and pants.

"Now, Logan?" she said, smiling.

"Now, Amber," he said, covering her body with his.

Logan Wade did not get much sleep that night, but it wasn't because Amber snored.

Fifteen

Amber was sick in the morning right on schedule and Logan was by her side, holding her head and murmuring soothing words as hot tears stung her eyes.

"Oh, I hate this," she said. She moaned, sinking back against the pillow.

"I know," he said, smoothing the hair away from her face. "It kills me to see you so sick, but I don't think it lasts too many weeks."

"Weeks? Weeks! I'll be dead by then."

"No, you won't. Listen, why don't you go back to sleep? There's no chores to be tended to. I'll come back for you later, and we'll see the sights."

"Couldn't you stay just a few more minutes?"

"Sure thing," he said, tucking the blankets around her.

Amber snuggled close to Logan's naked warmth, her hand sliding between them to rest on her stomach.

"Feeling better?" he asked, his lips resting lightly on her forehead.

"Yes. Logan, I . . . I was just thinking about

my pa. I know you said he understood about
what happened in the cove that night, but I
can't help wondering if he'd think poorly of
me because I was carrying your babe before
we were married."

"No, he wouldn't think poorly of you. He
was praying for a babe to come of that night."

Amber frowned. "What?" she said, moving
her head back so she could see Logan's face.

"Amber, I can't begin to say things, find the
words like Nathan could. He explained it all
to me, I was angry at first, but then I understood why he sent me after you that night."

"He sent you? I thought you'd come on your
own," she said, her frown deepening.

"You were crying, and I didn't know how to
deal with your tears. Nathan said I had caused
you to cry because of my gun, and I was the
one to go to you. He sent me, knowing that
I'd . . . that we would . . . He knew we'd . . .
Ah, hell."

Amber sat bolt upward, clutching the sheet
to her bare breasts as she stared at Logan with
wide eyes, shock evident on her face. "My pa
planned for us to make love? He planned it?
Why? Why would a father do such a thing?"

"Calm down, all right?"

"No, I won't calm down. Tell me, Logan.
Tell me why he did it."

"He felt guilty because you didn't have a
husband and babes of your own. He needed

you there on the homestead to do woman's work and tend to Benny."

"So he was trying to trap you into marrying me?" she shrieked.

"No! That was never his intention. He just wanted you to have . . ."

"A little plain old sex while a lusty buck was on the property? My God, I can't believe this."

"Damn it, Amber, I told you I couldn't explain things the way Nathan could. He wanted you to have some happiness, even if it was only for a short time. And he was praying for a babe so you'd have it to love, fill your life."

"Dear heaven. And you? You said you were angry when he told you."

"At first, yes. I didn't think he had the right to control people's lives the way he had. But then I came to realize he'd done it out of love for you. It didn't erase my own guilt but . . ."

"Your guilt?"

"Even with Nathan's blessings over what had happened, I had a knife of guilt twisting in my gut. I'd taken your innocence, and I'd been wrong to do it. Nathan and I just didn't view it the same way. I still respected him more than I can say, but I felt he'd made a mistake. Then when I took you so roughly that night in your bed, it was more than I could bear."

"So you stayed on the homestead," she said, her voice hushed. "You stayed to labor, to pay your debt, work through your guilt. You were seeking a way to find your peace, and you did.

You found it by talking with Naana at the Apache camp."

"Well, yeah, I . . ."

"Then you eased the last of your conscience by marrying me, telling me that you love me, that you want this babe."

Logan sat up and gripped her tightly by the shoulders. "Damn you," he said, his jaw tight, "don't you say such a thing. I rid myself of the guilts so I *could* tell you that I love you and ask you to be my wife. I'm not using you to ease my conscience. I love you, Amber."

"I don't believe you," she said, quick tears filling her eyes as a tremor swept through her body. "You, my pa, you're two of a kind. Men filled with guilt and using me to rid yourself of it with no regard for my feelings."

"No. Nathan loved you. *I* love you."

"Damn you both," Amber said, sobbing. She covered her face with her hands.

"Amber, please," Logan said. "You've got it all wrong. Listen to me. I . . ."

"No," she said, shaking her head. "I've heard enough. Leave me alone. Just leave me alone," she said, sobbing uncontrollably.

Logan clenched his jaw so tightly his teeth ached. Damn it to hell, he fumed. She'd taken every word he'd said all wrong. If only Nathan were there to explain things in his gentle, wise way. Maybe if he left Amber alone for a while, let her sort it through, she'd come to understand that she was viewing things backwards.

"Amber," he said quietly, "I'll be back for you later. You rest, just stay in bed. You've mixed everything up in your mind, and you're not thinking straight." He moved off the bed and began to dress.

Amber slowly lifted her head to look at him, tears streaming down her face, a haunting sadness in the dark pools of her eyes. "No wonder my pa saw himself in you," she said, a bitter edge to her voice.

Logan opened his mouth to reply, then closed it again, shaking his head as he strode to the door. "I'll be back for you later," he said, tugging on his Stetson. "I love you, Amber. I truly do love you."

As the door closed behind Logan, Amber sank onto the pillow and gave way to her tears. She cried for shattered dreams. She cried as one betrayed, used as a stepping stone for two men to reach their sought-after goals.

She cried for the babe within her, who had been conceived in deceit, and she cried for herself, for childhood lost and the womanhood found, that had brought her such chilling misery. She wept until there were no more tears, and then she slept, huddled in a ball beneath the blankets.

The hours of the morning passed quickly as Logan, Moses, and Benny bought and traded at various stores in Waverly. The quilt was exchanged for the precious bean seeds, and the chickens for a young, squealing pig that was sealed in a louvered, wooden box.

Benny had not questioned Logan's explanation that Amber was still sleeping, but Logan had felt Moses's penetrating gaze on him many times during the morning. Trip after trip was made to the livery stable, where Sean helped make room in the wagon for the winter provisions.

"Did you be gettin' your surprise yet, lad?" Sean asked Benny.

"Not yet. I'm gettin' it tomorrow mornin' at dawn, just 'fore we leave for home."

"Mmm," Moses said. "Care to tell us what it is?"

"Nope."

"This finishes the provisions," Logan said. "Damn, that pig is loud. It's going to be a long trip back. I have one other stop to make, but the supplies are tended to."

"Thought I'd take Benny through town this afternoon," Moses said. "Give you and missy a chance to be on your own."

"Yeah," Logan said, not meeting Moses's gaze.

"Benny," Moses said, "run in there and say howdy to Thunder so he won't be spookin' none. See you later, Sean."

Benny ran into the livery stable, and Moses walked to the edge of the building out of Sean's hearing, Logan following slowly behind.

"Wanna talk 'bout it?" Moses said quietly. "You're coiled like a bullwhip again, Logan. I'm not pressin' into your business with missy, but somethin' sure isn't right. Every other trip to Waverly she was up at daybreak, flutterin' around, seein' all there was to see. Not like her to be holed up in her room. I'll help if I'm able, shut up if you tell me. Take your pick."

Logan sighed. It was a sigh that seemed to tear at his soul, and a tormenting pain was reflected in his blue eyes. "I'm Amber's husband now," he said, his voice low, hoarse. "She's in my safe keeping, such as it is. Whatever trouble I've created, sorrow I've caused her, is mine to deal with. I sure as hell didn't mean to hurt her, make her cry, but I did. Again. I didn't hurt her physically, but in her heart and mind. Words, Moses. Words spoken, but misunderstood. I'm praying that she's sorted it through, that she'll be smiling when I walk back into that room."

"And singin' softly?" Moses said, placing his hand on Logan's shoulder.

"And singing softly," Logan said, hardly above a whisper.

But she wasn't.

Amber was neither smiling, nor singing, nor crying, when Logan reentered their hotel room. She stood staring out the window, wearing her faded pink dress, her arms wrapped tightly around her elbows in a protective gesture. She didn't acknowledge his arrival.

"Amber?" he said, coming up behind her. He lifted his hands to place them on her shoulders, then hesitated, shoving his hands into his pockets instead. "Amber?"

Silence.

"Would you like to talk about this now? You misunderstood what I was trying to say. Couldn't we sit down and discuss it?"

"No," she said, not moving. "I sorted it all through, piece by piece, everything you said, and it's perfectly clear to me."

"Meaning?"

She turned slowly to face him, her features pale and drawn. "Meaning both you and my pa used me to rid yourself of inner burdens of guilt. I would hate you, Logan, if I could, but I don't have the energy left," she said, her voice trembling. "I'm going to concentrate on my babe now. *My* baby, Logan Wade."

"Damn it, it's mine, too. I planted the seed in you. That's my child you're carrying, Amber. You're not closing yourself off from me. I'm your husband. You're acting as judge and jury over me and your pa, who is dead in his grave and can't even defend himself. You've sentenced us to hang in hell, and your verdict is unfair. Nathan loved you, and so do I. You've twisted everything around, and you're viewing it all wrong. I'm getting you out of this room. You wanted to see Waverly, and that's what we're going to do."

"No!"

"Yes," he said, grabbing her arm.

"Yes, sir," she snapped, pulling her arm free. She stomped to the door and flung it open.

"Sweet Jesus," Logan said, under his breath as he followed her. "What in the hell am I going to do?" He locked the door behind them, then automatically lifted his arm to circle Amber's shoulder, only to drop it back to his side. "I just realized you haven't had anything to eat."

"There's dried beef in the basket in the wagon."

"No, I'll take you to Rosie's Cafe. I want you to have a good, hot meal."

Amber's head snapped up. "Logan, all this is costing so much money. This hotel, the bathtub sent up, my ring, the . . ."

"Don't worry about it," he said gruffly, starting off down the hall.

Amber hurried to catch up with him. "But I do worry."

Logan stopped and frowned down at her. "We got the provisions, plenty of everything. Plus, we traded your quilt for the beans, and the chickens for the pig. A damn loud, squealing pig, by the way."

"We didn't have any corn to trade. Where is all this money coming from?"

"Look, I had some money in my saddlebags. I offered it to Nathan in exchange for him keeping me under his roof, but he refused to take it. We have winter provisions, Amber, everything we need, because I won't see my family go hungry. Now if you want to view that as my trying to ease my guilt in some way, go right ahead. You'll think what you want to, anyway. Come on. I'm getting some food in you." He started off again down the hall.

Amber scrambled to keep up with Logan's long-legged stride, her mind whirling. His family. That was how he had said it. His family. The provisions were for all of them; Amber, Benny, Moses, Logan, and, yes, the babe within her. Logan's family. He had said it with pride and possessiveness in his voice. He'd seen to it that she'd had a real wedding ring and a bouquet of flowers and . . . Oh, damn him, he was confusing her.

She knew the truth, had heard it from Logan's own lips. She had been nothing more than a . . . a tool to Logan and Nathan, that they had used to free themselves of their inner guilts. Yes, a tool, like a hoe or spade struck against the ground to rid corn stalks of choking weeds. How gullible she'd been, and childish, foolish.

And how very much in love with Logan Wade.

And now? her mind whispered. Oh, merciful heaven, she still loved him, would always love him. Logan had betrayed her, lied in words and actions, but it was too late. She couldn't quiet her heart's song, stop her flow of love like a stream gone dry. But she would hide that love for him from that moment forward. She would muster her pride, and not be used again as Logan's tool against his guilt. She'd concentrate on the babe, her babe, and not show any evidence of her love for Logan Wade.

"Here's the cafe," Logan said, bringing Amber from her tormented reverie.

Amber blinked several times as they entered and she realized she'd been unaware that they'd left the hotel and walked down the sidewalk. The aroma of food reached her, and her stomach rumbled in response.

"Hungry?" Logan said, smiling slightly.

"Yes, I guess I am."

"There's a table. Order anything you want."

The eggs, fried ham, flaky hot biscuits, and steaming coffee were delicious, and Amber ate every bite. Logan said he'd eaten earlier, and settled for sipping a cup of coffee as he watched her eat. A smile tugged onto his lips as he saw the thick layers of jam she lathered on her biscuits.

Lord, how he loved her, Logan's mind echoed. He felt as though he were teetering on the edge of a deep, dark pit. Teetering, with the fear of falling in and disappearing into the depths of hell. Sunshine was on the other side. Sunshine, and Amber, their babe, the life they could share. Amber was hurt, angry, confused, and if he lost her and her love, he would topple over the edge of the pit into the chilling, empty world of loneliness where he'd been for so long before.

Logan sighed. What could he do, say, to make her understand? He had to be careful, tread softly. His own temper, frustration, over the situation was growing, hovering just below the surface. He wanted to shake her until her teeth rattled, and demand that she believe he loved her. Hell.

"Oh, I'm so stuffed," Amber said, sinking back in her chair.

"You did put away a morsel or two," Logan said, smiling. "Ready to see the sights of Waverly?"

"Well, I . . ."

"There's a store that has bonnets and shoes. That's it, just bonnets and shoes. Oh, and those parasol things. The place just opened up a few weeks ago, and the women are flocking in there. I looked in the window, and saw a pair of red shoes. Can you imagine that? Red shoes."

"Really?" Amber said, her eyes dancing with excitement. "Red? Where would a woman wear such fancy shoes? And parasols? Patricia Hunter saw a parasol once. She said it was beautiful. Could we go look at them, Logan?"

"Sure thing," he said, pushing himself to his feet. "I'd never pass up a chance to see pretty parasols and red shoes."

Outside the store, Logan changed his tune. He peered in the window and saw the many women inside, laughing and talking as they tried on the bonnets and shoes. He stepped away from the door.

"Aren't you coming in?" Amber said.

"I think not," he said, frowning. "Looks a little crowded in there. You take all the time you need, but I'll wait out here."

"Saloons are more crowded than this."

"With men."

"Well, land's sake, Logan, since when don't you like women?"

"Women are fine, but not a bunch of them together twittering."

"Twittering?" Amber said, bursting into laughter.

"Yeah," he said gruffly, "twittering. Just go in the damn store, and I'll wait here. Go."

Amber laughed again and entered the store. Logan leaned against the building, his arms crossed loosely over his chest. Amber had laughed, he realized. Ah, man, he loved that sound. It touched his heart gently, just like when she sang softly.

Two young women came out of the store and glanced at Logan. He lifted his fingers to the brim of his Stetson in polite greeting, then cringed as the women giggled.

Twittering—he reaffirmed in his mind.

A deputy sheriff strolled by and Logan stiffened, only to relax in the next instant. The lawman hadn't given Logan a second look. There was no gun strapped low on Logan's hip, no

cold glint in his blue eyes. He was no longer a
man to be watched, feared, steered clear of. He
was simply a husband waiting for his wife. A
homesteader, a man, waiting for his woman.
Logan Wade, waiting for his Amber.

"Logan!"

Logan straightened and greeted Benny with
a smile. Moses was following the running
Benny at a slower pace.

"Having a good time?" Logan said to the
boy.

"Yes. Guess what, Logan? There's a wagon
at the edge of town that has people who sing,
and dance, and play a banjo. Me and Moses
heard tell of it, and we're goin' down there to
see them. Want to come?"

"Sounds fine," Logan said. "Hello, Moses,"
he said, as the big man came to where they
stood. "Benny wear you out yet?"

"Twice over," Moses said, laughing. "Keepin'
up with this boy is harder work than plowin'
a rock-filled field."

"Come on, come on," Benny said, grabbing
Moses's hand. "I want to see the dancin' people."

"Tell you what," Logan said. "You go in this
store and tell Amber to come on out, so we
can go with you."

Benny cupped his hands against the window
and peered through the glass. "Not me," he
said, shaking his head. "That's a womenfolks'
store. You go get her, Logan."

"If I wanted to be in there, I'd be in there. Moses?"

"No. Nope. No, no," Moses said, raising his hands and shaking his head.

"Well, hell," Logan said, tugging his Stetson roughly forward on his head.

At that moment, Amber came out of the door and was greeted by three of the biggest smiles she had ever seen.

"Gentlemen," she said, eyeing the trio warily.

"Want to go see a traveling minstrel show?" Logan asked.

"Oh, yes," Amber said. "Where? When?"

"Come on," Benny said, taking Amber's hand.

Benny dragged Amber along the sidewalk, and Logan and Moses followed, making certain they had a clear view of the excited pair ahead of them.

"Things better?" Moses inquired.

"Not really," Logan said, frowning. "Amber's pushing it aside for now, I guess, allowing herself to have a good time. Reminds me of the time I was sitting on a wagon filled with dynamite. Don't know if I was more scared then, or now. If Amber doesn't get this thing straightened around in her head, I could lose her, Moses. I swear to God I could."

"Is that a fact?" Moses said, his eyes widening.

"That my friend, is a bone-chilling fact," Logan said, a muscle twitching in his jaw.

A crowd had gathered by the wagon housing the performers and the mood was light, happy, as laughter, music, and spurts of applause danced through the air.

Logan found himself scanning the faces of the people, then realized he had no reason to be determining who was there. The men he had sought for the five long years were dead. It was over, all behind him, buried.

He had a new purpose, direction to his life now; Amber Prescott Wade, his wife. He watched her instead of the performers, saw the excitement in her eyes, heard her lilting laughter. His heart nearly burst with love for her, and he longed to pull her to him, hold her, kiss her, never let her go. She was standing right next to him, yet seemed so far away.

As the afternoon hours went by, Logan became very aware that Amber was directing her full attention to Benny. She held her brother's hand, talked, laughed with him, pointed out interesting sights as the foursome wandered in and out of the multitude of stores.

Moses gave Logan a comforting pat on the back, but Logan only shook his head and frowned. While he could partially understand Amber's desire to keep distance between them, a section of his mind resented it, and his anger smoldered within him.

Memories of another night of anger and frustration slammed against Logan's brain. While held in the grip of those emotions, he had flung Amber onto her bed and taken her so roughly the thought of it still brought a knot of pain to his gut. Yes, Amber had responded to him, given herself to him, but he had been out of control at the onset. He was responsible for his own strength, and he would never, ever, take her so harshly again.

What if Amber refused him tonight? he thought suddenly. What if she turned her back to him in their bed when he reached for her? Damn it, he was her husband. He had the right to . . . No, he'd never demand his husbandly rights. She would come to him willingly, or he wouldn't have her. How in the hell would he react if she refused him? He could feel the anger building within him as she ignored him through the hours of the afternoon. He had to keep himself under control. He had to.

It was getting dark when the group ate dinner at Rosie's Cafe, then Moses said he and Benny would relieve Sean so the Irishman could eat.

"Be at the livery at dawn," Logan said. "We've got a long trip ahead of us. Don't be wasting any time getting that surprise of yours in the morning, Benny."

"Oh, I won't," Benny said, smiling brightly. "Everythin' is all set."

"I don't suppose . . ." Amber started.

"Nope, I'm not tellin'," Benny said.

Again, the group parted company at the door of the hotel, and Amber and Logan walked up the stairs in silence, then entered their room. Logan lit the lamp, then pushed his Stetson to the back of his head with his thumb as he turned to look at Amber. She stood by the door, her hands clutched tightly together in the folds of her skirt, her face suddenly pale.

"Damn it," he said, "don't look at me as though you're scared to death of me. I'm not a stupid man, Amber. You spent the afternoon delivering your message loud and clear. I spent those hours trailing behind you like a damn stranger. Now, here you stand, acting like you're afraid I'll rip your clothes off and slam myself into you right against that door."

"Logan," Amber gasped. "That was crude."

"Well, excuse me all to hell, Miss High and Mighty."

"This doesn't call for nasty talk."

"No, it doesn't. It calls for us getting into that bed, reaching for each other, making love, together. It calls for you to believe me when I say that I love you more than life itself. Damn it, Amber, what more can I say to you except what I already have? Every word was true. I did not declare my love for you and ask you to marry me to ease my guilt. The guilt was gone before I said those things to you."

"No! I don't believe you."

"Damn you," he said, staring at the ceiling to control his raging temper.

Amber lifted her chin. "You have the choice

of claiming your husbandly rights, if you so choose."

"No, thank you," he said, striding toward the door. Amber scurried out of his way. "I like my woman hot and willing. I'm not interested in having sex with someone who's lying there like a cold fish."

"It's not sex, it's making love," Amber shrieked.

Logan stopped, his hand on the doorknob as he turned to look at her. "Oh?" he said, sarcasm ringing in his voice. "Is that a fact? Well, you're not making much sense there, Amber. To *make* love, people have to *be* in love, and to hear you tell it, that ingredient is missing between us."

"I . . ."

"Go to bed," he said, then yanked open the door. "Alone."

"Where are you going?"

"My dear wife, I am going out to get riproarin' drunk." He left the room and slammed the door with a resounding thud.

Amber marched to the door and gave it a swift kick, accomplishing nothing more than sending a shooting pain up her leg. She hobbled back to the bed and sank onto the edge.

"Drunk, is it?" she mumbled. "Well, fine, I don't care. He just better not touch one of those sleazy saloon whores. Logan Wade is a married man, my husband, and the only bed he belongs in is mine. And . . ."

Logan was right, she thought dismally. She wasn't making sense. There she sat babbling on as to how he should be in that bed with her, and she'd just refused to go into that bed with him. She'd known he wouldn't execute his husbandly rights when she'd said it. To quote Mr. Wade, 'he liked his woman hot and willing.' Mercy, what a mouth on that man.

"Oh, dear," Amber said, flopping back onto the bed, "I'm so muddled up."

She loved her Logan so much, so very much. If only she could forget what he had told her, pretend she'd never heard it, but she couldn't. Logan's and Nathan's betrayal was not going to disappear by wishing it away. It was real and it hurt. Dear heaven above, how it hurt.

Amber prepared for bed, then lay staring up into the darkness, straining her ears for the sound of Logan's return.

But hours later when she finally drifted off to sleep, the expanse of bed next to her was empty.

Sixteen

"Sweet Jesus," Logan said. He moaned and pressed his hands to his head. He was stretched out on the bed fully clothed, his boots still on his feet. "Quit banging around, Amber."

"Just packing to go," she said pleasantly. "You said we had to be at the livery stable by dawn, and it's nearly that. Best be getting up and shave."

"Oh-h-h, my head. Shaving is too noisy."

"Suit yourself."

"Were you sick this morning?" he said, not opening his eyes.

"Yes."

"Shoulda helped you," he said, his voice trailing off as he began to doze.

"Logan!"

"What?" he yelled, shooting bolt upward. "Oh, my God, my head is falling off."

"We have to be leaving now."

"Yeah, yeah," he muttered, moving his feet cautiously to the floor. "Why did I get drunk? Why? Amber, I want you to know I didn't touch one of those saloon whores. I swear I didn't."

"I believe you."

"You do?" he said, surprise evident on his face. "Why?"

"Well, because you said so, I guess," she said, shrugging.

"Then why in the hell . . . Oh-h-h, my head. Why . . ." he began again in a quieter voice, "don't you believe me when I say I love you? And when I say I was freed of my guilt before I told you that I loved you?"

Amber stopped her packing to stare into space. "I don't know."

"Think about it," he said, pushing himself to his feet. A knock sounded at the door and he went to answer it, squeezing the bridge of his nose as he went. "Moses," he said, after opening the door. "Come in."

"You're lookin' fit," Moses said, chuckling.

"Where's Benny?" Amber asked.

"I let him go get his surprise. There's no one out there to do him harm this early. He'll meet us at the wagon." He grinned at Logan where he had wandered back to stand by the dresser. Logan had planted his arms on the top, then rested his forehead on stacked fists. "Feelin' poorly are you, Logan?"

"Shut up, Moses," came the muffled reply. "I'm a dying man."

Amber rolled her eyes to the heavens, picked

up the parcels of clothing, and marched from the room.

At the livery stable, Sean shook hands all around, collected his wages from Logan, then ambled away, wishing them a safe journey home. There was no sign of Benny.

"He'll be along," Moses said, seeing Amber's worried expression.

Logan leaned against the building and closed his eyes. The pig and cow were mercifully quiet.

"I'm comin', I'm comin'," Benny called. He appeared around the side of the building. Logan opened one eye to peer at him. "Here I am with my surprise."

"Dear heaven," Amber said, "what is that?"

"I think . . . it's a dog," Moses said. "I'm not sure, but I think so."

Whatever it was it was big, a definite armload for a staggering Benny. It was a nondescript mixture of strange colors, had fur of varying lengths, a tail that was thumping against Benny's leg, and a very busy, slathering tongue that was doing a thorough job of washing Benny's face. Benny was beaming.

"This is my dog," the little boy said proudly. "I paid for him with my milk pennies, and he's all mine. Isn't he somethin'?"

"He's wonderful," Amber said, her eyes wide. "I've . . . never seen a dog quite like that before."

Logan ran his hand down his beard-roughened face and laughed. "You Prescotts sure do pick up some strange strays," he said, looking directly at Amber. She averted her eyes from his.

"Don't you like my dog, Logan?" Benny asked, frowning.

"Oh, yeah, I like him fine, just fine," Logan said, hunkering down in front of Benny. "Looks like someone gave him a haircut. Well, no matter. His fur will even up as it grows. You did very well with your pennies. I'm proud of you, son. Every homestead should have a dog, and you got yourself a beauty. What's his name?"

"Henry."

"Henry?" Logan asked. "Why?"

"Because I like the name Henry."

"Good enough reason. Well, let's get a length of rope on him so he won't jump out of the wagon, then make some room back there for him next to you. Yes, sir, that is one fine animal."

"Thanks," Benny said, smiling. "You like him, Moses?"

"Oh, you bet," Moses said nodding.

Logan pushed himself up and reached into the wagon for a piece of rope. Amber placed her hand on his arm.

"Thank you," she whispered. "You handled that so well. It was so important to Benny."

"I love him, Amber," he said, looking directly at her. "I love that boy as if he were my own. Even," he whispered, grinning at her, "if he does have lousy taste in dogs."

Amber matched his smile and their gaze held in a long moment. Then the sadness settled into Amber's dark eyes, and Logan frowned. The spell was broken, and they each turned away.

And they began the journey toward home.

Henry spent the first full hour barking at high volume at the pig. The pig squealed for all it was worth. The cow bellowed in dismay, and Logan Wade swore in a steady stream, his head pounding with the cadence of a thousand drummers.

At noon they stopped to eat, Amber already yearning for her soft bed in the cabin and hours of soothing sleep. She was exhausted, physically and emotionally drained. She didn't speak as the wagon made its slow, steady progress through the afternoon. Benny chattered on about everything he had seen and done in Waverly, and seemed oblivious to the fact that Moses was the only one commenting on what he said.

That night it rained. A cold drizzle fell in a steady rhythm, causing Amber to huddle close to Benny and Henry under the tarp in the wagon bed. Logan and Moses sought shelter under the wagon. It was a mud-caked Logan Wade that hurried to Amber's side the next morning as she ran from the wagon and became sick.

"Oh, Lord. Oh, damn, damn, damn," Amber said, shivering against the cold.

"It's all right," Logan said soothingly. "I put some kindling under the tarp last night. I'll get a fire going and some coffee made. Oh, Amber, I'm so sorry you're sick like this every day," he said, pulling her to his chest. "I'd change it if I could, make me the one who's feeling so poorly."

Amber rested her head against Logan's chest, not caring that he was muddy and cold, not caring at that moment that he had lied to her, had come to her to declare his love for reasons she considered deceitful. Not caring, because Logan's strong arms were wrapped around her, holding her, protecting her. He was there. And she loved him. She sighed. It was a weary sigh, a sad sigh, and his hold on her tightened.

"We'll be home by late afternoon," he said. "I'll bring the tub in from the barn, and you can have a hot bath right in front of the fire. Would you like that?"

"Yes," she said, then sniffled.

"Then, if you treat me right, I'll make some more of my great stew."

Amber's eyes widened and she tilted her head back to look up at him. "Oh, no, don't do that. What I mean is, I'll fix supper because you have all those provisions to unload and . . ." Her voice trailed off as he smiled at her. "You know you make terrible stew," she said, bursting into laughter. "You were just trying to trick me into . . ."

"Smiling," he said, serious again. "It's your smile that's going to get me through the rest of these miles. Here I stand, wet, cold, muddy, starving to death, and it doesn't even matter. Your smile warms me, Amber, inside and out. I love you."

"I . . ."

Before Amber could reply, Logan's mouth came down hard onto hers, and she clung to him for support as her knees began to tremble. The dreary campsite faded into a hazy mist as she responded to the kiss, gave way to the desire that swirled within her.

A soft purr escaped from her throat, the sound igniting Logan's passion as he increased the intensity of the kiss, plummeting his tongue deep into her mouth. She leaned further into him, annoyed at the bulky layers of coats and clothes that separated her from his naked body, his heat, his manhood that held the promise of the fulfillment her femininity ached for.

"Jesus," Logan said, tearing his mouth from hers. "I want you so damn much. I've got to stop kissing you, Amber. This is hardly the time or the place to make love with you."

"What?" she said, gazing up at him with smoky brown eyes. "Oh, goodness. Land's sake."

"Tonight," he said, his voice gritty. "We'll make love tonight in our own home, in our bed. And I won't have this scratchy beard to mar your pretty skin. Ah, Amber, I do love you. Think about tonight while we're traveling these miles. We're going to make love, together, the two of us. I'll start the fire and get some hot coffee in you."

Logan kissed her once more, a hard, fast kiss, that caused Amber to stagger slightly when he released her and walked away. She absently brushed at the mud he'd left clinging to her coat, her mind whirling.

Tonight, her mind repeated over and over. Tonight they would make love. In their home, in their bed, they'd come together as husband and wife, man and woman, two people in love. In love? When Logan said he loved her, he looked directly into her eyes as though he were giving her access to the path to his soul to see the truth of his words.

Dear heaven, how desperately she wanted, needed, to believe him.

But she couldn't.

"Mornin', missy," Moses said, stretching his stiff muscles.

"Hello, Moses," she said quietly. "We sure are a sorry-looking group."

"That's a fact," he said, chuckling. "But we'll be home 'fore night fall, then everythin' will be fine."

"Will it?" she asked, not looking at him.

"If you let it."

"Me?" she said, her head snapping up. "I'm

not the one who lied. I'm not the one who used me to ease inner burdens of guilt. Those honors belong to my pa and Logan Wade. I was nothing more than a tool for them, Moses, for each to do what they needed done for themselves."

"That's how you see it?"

"That's what I know the truth to be."

"You wouldn't recognize the truth if it hit you in the nose," Moses said. "You're so busy feelin' sorry for yourself, you're stompin' on the love of a good, decent man, and tarnishin' the memory of another. You're turnin' into a hateful woman, missy, and it's breakin' my heart to watch it happen. How you gonna nurture that babe within you with love, when you're so full of hate and cruel thoughts?"

"Don't you dare speak to me that way," Amber said, her eyes flashing with anger. "I'll have you know . . ." She blinked once slowly. "Babe?" she whispered. "How did . . ."

"I'm no fool," he said, smiling. "I been prayin' for a babe since that night Logan went to the cove to fetch you."

"You know about that, too? I don't believe this. Everyone knew the plans for my life, except me. But can't you understand why I feel betrayed and used?"

"Missy," Moses said quietly, "what I understand and know to be the truth, is that your pa loved you and Benny more than any father I've ever come across. What Nathan did, he did *for* you, not against you. And Logan? Missy, that man struggled back from hell itself, so he could come to you free of the devils within him. Now *you* hold the power to destroy him, and you're goin' to do it, sure as I'm born, if you don't start thinkin' with your heart instead of your muddled up womanly mind."

"Well," Amber said indignantly. "Are you quite finished insulting me, sir?"

"Guess so," Moses said, stroking his chin. "Yep, that's all I got to say. I smell coffee. That's just what I need to take the chill off."

Moses ambled away, and Amber pressed her fingertips to her aching temples as she watched him walk to the campfire and greet Logan. The two men looked at the others' muddied clothes and laughed, the masculine sound beating against Amber's throbbing head.

Men, she thought fiercely. She was surrounded by them. Logan, Benny, Moses. Even Henry and the stupid pig were male. Men made up their mind to do something, then up and did it, pure and simple. They didn't think it through, mull it over, like women did. Not men. Want to do it? Do it. Want to say it? Just open their big mouth and say it. They just spoke from their heart and . . . Spoke from their heart? Acted on the message from their heart's song?

"Amber," Logan called. "Come get some coffee and food. I don't want you catching a chill."

"Yes, I'm coming. I'll wake Benny."

"And Henry," Logan said, chuckling. "Don't forget ole Henry. He's one of the family now."

Amber's heart thudded beneath her breast. The family, her mind echoed. Their family. Hers and Logan's. A family made up of men, with only one woman to add the gentle, soothing feminine word and touch. One woman to smile and sing softly, to tend to the men who loved and needed her. Logan had struggled back from hell for her, Moses had said. Had fought his ghosts and demons to come to her free, whole.

And then, because he knew no other way than that of a good and decent man, Logan had spoken from his heart.

He loved her.

"Oh, dear heaven," Amber whispered, a sob catching in her throat, "what have I done? Logan, Pa, forgive me. Please, please, forgive me."

"Amber," Logan yelled. "Are you coming?"

"Yes," she said, hurrying to the wagon. "Benny, wake up. You, too, silly Henry. We're going home."

Tonight, Amber's heart sang. Tonight she would tell Logan how sorry she was for distrusting him, not believing his declaration of love, his desire to marry her, and his joy that there was a babe within her.

How clear it all was now. She'd lost the innocence of her childhood, but not fully understood the emergence of the woman newly born. She'd hovered between the two worlds; confused, doubting, making judgments unfairly.

She'd misused her womanly wisdom by expecting the men in her life to possess the same complexities of thought. And they didn't. They lived their lives the only way they knew how, with hard labor and straight spoken words. Oh, how far she'd come, how much she'd grown, but not without making mistakes. Mistakes she would set to rights. Tonight.

The group set off again, welcoming the warming sun as it appeared, and counting the miles that moved slowly by. They stopped only briefly at noon to consume a hurried meal, everyone eager to reach the homestead.

Amber said little. Wrapped in the cocoon of her own peaceful thoughts, she sat silently next to Moses on the wagon seat, only occasionally commenting on something Benny said. There was a serene expression on her face, a soft smile on her lips as the hours ticked by.

Logan grew more tense with every creak of the wagon wheels. He glanced often at Amber, his deep frown never lessening. What was she thinking? he asked himself. She had that funny little smile on her face, the one that made him nervous because he never knew what it meant.

When he'd kissed her that morning, the blood had pounded through his veins with the want of her. She'd responded to that kiss. Hell, he was clinging to the memory of that kiss like a thirsty man savoring his last swallow of water.

But, he knew, Amber had not said one thing to indicate she believed he truly loved her. He'd spoken of the lovemaking they would share that night, poured out the words with the irrational hope that saying them aloud would bring it about.

No, he realized, there'd be no lovemaking in that bed that night, because Amber didn't trust in his love. Damn it to hell. She was ripping him to shreds. He loved her. Jesus, how he loved that woman. And he was losing her. As she took her love from him, she took his soul, his reason for being. Little by little, he was dying.

" 'Bout a mile to go," Moses suddenly boomed.

"Yipee!" Benny shouted. "We're nearly home, Henry."

"I'll ride on ahead and get a fire going in the cabin," Logan said. "Air out the place a bit. Could start a stew simmering, I guess."

"No!" came a chorus of voices.

Logan tugged his Stetson firmly forward and spurred Thunder into a gallop. The sleek horse charged ahead, anxious to run, and Logan allowed him the freedom. Amber watched until they disappeared from view, marveling at the beauty of the man and beast moving nearly as one; power and strength. Magnificent.

"Did you come home, missy?" Moses said quietly.

"I've come home, Moses," she said, placing her hand on his arm. "With my heart filled with love, I've come home."

"Then git up, horse," Moses yelled, flicking the reins. "We're bringin' sunshine to this homestead."

Darkness had long since fallen by the time the last of the supplies had been put away and the animals tended to. The weary travelers ate a quiet meal, Benny nearly nodding off at the table. After Moses had bidden everyone good night and gone to the barn, and Benny and Henry were sound asleep in the bedroom, Logan filled the tub with hot water.

"There's the bath I promised you, Amber," he said.

"Thank you. It looks heavenly."

"Well, I guess I'll go for a walk, and leave you some privacy."

"That's not necessary."

"Yeah, I think it is. But before I go, there's something I want to give you."

"Oh?" she said, looking up at him in surprise.

Logan walked to the side cupboard and took out his saddlebags, withdrawing a package wrapped in brown paper. He placed a chair in front of the rocker where Amber sat and held the parcel in both hands, his elbows resting on his knees.

"Amber," he said, his voice sounding slightly unsteady, "this was to be your birthday present, but I'm giving it to you now. Your pa gave the storekeeper a dollar to hold this back, then planned to surprise you by letting you trade the quilt for it. The quilt went for the beans, so I paid the rest. So, you see, this birthday present is from both Nathan and me. I know you don't believe this, but the two men giving you this gift never intended to cause you any pain. Nathan loved you, Amber, and so do I."

"Logan, I . . ."

"Let me finish," he said, gazing directly into her eyes. "I've run out of ways to convince you that I love you, I truly have. I'm staying on this homestead. I'll watch over you and our family, I'll labor hard on this land, but I won't touch you. I'll be your husband in name only, because I know you won't make love with someone you don't believe loves you."

"Logan, please, I . . ."

He placed the package on her lap. "There's just one other thing I think you should know. To get the money for that present, I sold my gun."

"Oh, God, Logan," she gasped, tears filling her eyes.

"Open it."

With trembling hands, Amber brushed back the paper to reveal a delicate china box.

"Lift the lid," Logan said quietly.

As the tinkling music filled the air, tears

spilled onto Amber's cheeks. "A music box. You sold your gun to . . . And Pa . . . Oh, Logan, it's beautiful. I've never had anything so pretty. Thank you."

"Maybe you could think of some words and sing softly along with that tune or . . . Well," he said, clearing his throat roughly and getting to his feet, "I'll leave you to take your bath now. Happy birthday, Amber."

As Logan walked slowly toward the door, Amber placed the still-playing music box on the hearth and got up from the rocker.

"Logan?"

"Yeah?" he said, his back to her, his hand on the doorknob.

Amber unbuttoned her dress and allowed it to fall in a heap at her feet. "I've made terrible mistakes because I didn't understand my newly found womanly wisdom. I have so much to learn about being a woman. I'm asking, I'm begging you, to forgive me for doubting you. I love you," she said, nearly choking on a sob. "Oh, Logan, please. I love you so much, and I'm so very sorry."

Logan turned slowly to face her, sucking in his breath as he saw her silhouetted against the firelight clad only in her chemise. "Say it again," he said, his voice gritty. "Sweet Jesus, Amber, I need to hear you say that you love me."

"I do. I do love you, Logan Wade, and I believe in your love for me. I want to be your wife, I want this babe within me. Oh, God, Logan, I want *you*."

They moved at the same time, meeting in the center of the room, and holding tightly to the other. Hardly breathing, they held fast to the one they loved, drinking in the warmth, the feel, the aroma of the other. Then Amber tilted her head back to gaze up at Logan, her heart nearly bursting with love as she saw the tears glistening in his blue eyes.

"I thought I'd lost you," he said, in a hoarse whisper. "I thought I'd lost your love, and with it, my very soul. You are my life. And I love you."

"And I," she said, tears streaming down her face, "love you."

Logan cradled her face in his trembling hands and kissed her; softly, reverently, with infinite gentleness. Then the kiss intensified, and passions flared with licking flames like those in the hearth.

"Your bath," Logan murmured, trailing a ribbon of kisses down Amber's throat.

"Yes, I need to wash away the travel dust. You're all clean shaven and smell so good. I . . . Oh!" she said, as his lips continued their foray across the top of her breasts pushing above the chemise.

"Quick bath," he said, his breathing labored. "Very quick."

"Yes," she said, moving reluctantly out of his embrace.

Amber hurried into the bedroom for her nighty, towel, and lavender soap, then returned to the tub. Logan was standing by the hearth, his shoulder propped against the mantel, arms crossed loosely over his chest. She met his gaze steadily as she slowly removed her remaining clothes, and smiled as she saw his hands curl into tight fists. Her heart sang with joy with the knowledge that she was woman, and her man, her Logan, wanted her.

Amber stepped into the tub and sat down, sighing in pleasure at the soothing warmth of the water. She lathered the fragrant soap down her arms, then across her breasts, lifting her lashes to meet Logan's smoldering gaze.

"Logan," she said, raising one leg to soap it, "could people make love in a bathtub?"

Without speaking, Logan pulled his shirt free of his pants and unbuttoned it, dropping it to the floor, and hunkering down next to the tub. He scooped the water over her breasts with his hand, watching the droplets glisten on her dewy skin.

"Make love in a bathtub," he said. "Well, yes, it could be done."

"That a fact?" she said, leaning over and kissing his moist chest, her lips resting for a moment on the small puckered scar on his shoulder.

"Be a bit crowded, though," he added. Amber's lips skimmed lower to find his nipple.

"Amber! This water is getting too cool. Time to get out. Now."

"But how do people make love in a bathtub?"

Logan chuckled deep in his chest, then scooped her out of the water, holding her tightly in his arms. "Amber Prescott Wade," he said, striding toward the bedroom, "you ask the damnest questions."

Amber's lilting laughter mingled with the tinkling of the music box, that slowed its tempo, then stopped. But beyond the closed bedroom door, the whispered endearments of love went on and on through the hours of the night.

Epilogue

"Logan," Moses said, "you just watered that same corn seedlin' three times. I think you drowned it."

"What?" Logan said.

Moses laughed and shook his head. "Do me a favor and go for a walk or somethin'. You're worthless today."

"Well, damn it," Logan said. "How long does it take to have a babe? I'm telling you, Moses, there's something wrong."

"Hasn't been more than five hours since you fetched Mrs. James from Hunter's old homestead. Fine folks, those Jameses. Mighty glad they came west. Good to have neighbors again and . . ."

"Moses, Amber's in there having my baby, and I'm losing my mind. I can't stand this. I'm going in that cabin."

"Can't let you do that, Logan. Mrs. James said I was to sit on your chest if you tried bargin' in there. Havin' babes is woman's work, so leave Amber be to do it."

"Damn it to hell. Took me to get that babe

started, didn't it? Don't tell me it's all woman's work."

"You got a point there," Moses said, nodding. "Still not lettin' you in that cabin, though."

"Jesus."

"Mmm," Moses said, pouring water on the corn seedlings.

Logan took off his Stetson, raked a restless hand through his hair, then tugged the Stetson firmly back into place. He strode to the end of the long row of corn, his glance falling on Nathan's grave. Walking to the mound of dirt that boasted a layer of spring flowers, Logan pictured Nathan Prescott in his mind.

"She's having my baby today, Nathan," Logan said quietly. "Amber's giving birth to our child. I love her. More than life, I love her, and she loves me. Thank you, Nathan, for everything."

Logan turned to look at the trees of the cove, memories flooding over him. He saw himself; bleeding of body, broken in spirit, lying by the stream waiting to die, and not caring if he did. Then the angel had come, his Amber. And in that cove they'd made love for the first time, joining their bodies, uniting their hearts and souls. Amber.

Through the past months, with a sense of awe, Logan had watched Amber grow big with his child, seen her glow with serenity, heard her sing softly as she went through the days.

His love for her was beyond description in its intensity and depth. She was his life, his love, his reason for being. She was Amber.

"Logan! Logan!" Benny yelled.

"What?" Logan answered, spinning around.

"Mrs. James says you're to come to the cabin right quick," Benny said, gasping for breath as he reached Logan with Henry right beside him.

"Why? What's wrong?" Logan said, gripping Benny's shoulders.

"Don't know. She just said to hurry."

Logan took off at a dead run for the cabin, voices screaming in his mind. Amber! What had gone wrong? Dear God, what had happened to his Amber? It was his fault. He'd planted the seed in her and . . . Amber.

As Logan came flying to the front door of the cabin, his path was blocked by an enormous woman standing on the threshold, her hands planted on her ample hips.

"Hold it, young man," she said sternly, "you're not barreling in here like a bull loose from his pen."

"What's wrong with Amber?" Logan yelled. "Damn it, woman, tell me what's wrong?"

"Land's sake," Mrs. James clucked, "you're a noisy buck. A lusty young buck, too, I'd say. There is nothing wrong, Logan Wade. You have yourself a fine, strappin' son."

"A who?" he said, his eyes widening.

"Mercy," Mrs. James said, throwing up her

hands. "I might as well be talkin' to the bull. Go see for yourself. Go on with you."

Logan inched past the big woman and strode to the open bedroom door. Amber was propped up against the pillows, her hair brushed free, shining in the sunlight that filled the room. She held a tiny bundle wrapped in a blanket in her arms.

"Amber?" Logan said.

She turned her head to smile at him. "Logan, come see our son. Come say hello to Nathan Logan Wade."

Logan walked slowly forward, then sat down heavily on the chair next to the bed, acutely aware of the weakness in his knees. "Are you all right, Amber?" he said, studying her face. "You look beautiful, wonderful. Are you sure you're all right?"

"I'm fine, I swear I am. Logan, don't you want to look at your son?"

"Oh, of course," he said. "My son." He shifted his gaze to the infant in Amber's arms. The baby was asleep, one tiny fist curled next to his cheek. He had a head full of dark, silky hair like his father's. "His face is awfully red," Logan said, frowning. "Is he supposed to be like that?"

Amber laughed. "He's beautiful. Trust me."

"My son," Logan repeated. "I'm not sure I believe this."

"You will when he cries."

"You've got a lot of men to tend to, Amber. Are you sorry he wasn't a girl?"

"No, oh, no. I have enough womanly wisdom now for all of you," she said, smiling warmly at Logan. "Maybe the next one will be a girl."

"I'm not certain I can go through this again," he said, shaking his head. "I was scared to death. Ah, Amber," he said, taking her hand, "I love you so much. Thank you for my son. Thank you for loving me as much as you do."

"I do love you, Logan, and I will forever. Will you wind my music box for me? I want our son to hear music when he wakes."

"Then, Amber, sing softly for our baby, because that is the most beautiful music of all," Logan said, his blue eyes radiating a warm message of eternal love.

Dear Reader:

Wildflowers grow in abundance in the West, the seeds carried by the wind acting as nature's delivery service. One year the flowers seemed to be everywhere, causing people to take endless pictures, and newspapers to print articles about the phenomenon.

On a sunny afternoon, I was walking through a field of the wildflowers while humming the melody played by a lovely music box I'd received on my birthday.

Slowly but steadily a story began to take shape in my mind. The wildflowers around me were opening their petals to the warming sunshine, reaching out for what would nurture them. So it would be for a young girl coming of age, embracing her newly discovered womanhood. She would blossom like a beautiful flower, if nurtured and cared for. Amber.

Her story haunted me, demanding to be written, shared with those who would, hopefully, come to know and love her as I did. Somewhere in Amber's legacy, I knew, would be a music box, which would be a cherished gift to her, just as mine was to me.

Many, many months have passed since my quiet walk in the field of flowers, and to my joy I am now able to introduce you to Amber, Logan, Benny, Nathan, Moses, and all the others you will meet within the pages of this book. I hope you enjoy this journey into the past.

Warmest regards,

Joan Elliott Pickart